Stories
of the
Far North

EDITED BY

JON TUSKA

*University of
Nebraska Press
Lincoln
and
London*

Copyright © 1998 by Golden West Literary Agency
All rights reserved
Manufactured in the United States of America
⊗ The paper in this book meets the minimum
requirements of American National Standard
for Information Sciences—Permanence of Paper
for Printed Library Materials,
ANSI Z39.48-1984.
Library of Congress Cataloging-in-
Publication Data
Stories of the far North / edited by Jon Tuska.
    p.   cm.
ISBN 0-8032-9434-4 (pa: alk. paper)
1. Frontier and pioneer life—Yukon Territory—
Klondike River Valley—Fiction. 2. Frontier and
pioneer life—Northwest, Canadian—Fiction.
3. Frontier and pioneer life—Alaska—Fiction.
4. American fiction—20th century.
5. Adventure stories, American.
6. Western stories. I. Tuska, Jon.
PS648.F74S75 1998
813'.08708327191—dc21   98-3735
CIP

Contents

*Stories
of the
Far North*

JON TUSKA

Introduction

The last great gold rush the world was to know began in the Klondike, and in 1897 at twenty-one years of age Jack London, who had been living in San Francisco, joined the stampede. He spent the winter of 1897–1898 in the Yukon. When he returned to San Francisco, he began writing a series of imaginative stories based on his experiences.

A generation before Bret Harte had won an international reputation for his Western stories set during the California gold rush of 1849. "It *was* a very special world, that gold-rush world," Walter Van Tilburg Clark wrote in his foreword to *Bret Harte: Stories of the Early West* (Platt & Munk, 1964), "with ways of living, thinking, feeling, and acting so particularly its own that there has never been anything quite like it anywhere, before or since. Which is what the literary histories mean when they call Bret Harte a local-color writer." In *San Francisco's Literary Frontier* (Knopf, 1939), Franklin Walker gave credit where credit was due when he observed that "with situations in which what was said was only less forceful than what was implied, Harte created the land of a million Westerns, a land in which gun play was chronic, vigilante committees met before breakfast, and death was as common as a rich strike in the diggings." Walker felt Harte's stories "succeeded in turning the gold-rush days into what he called 'an era replete with a certain heroic Greek poetry.' Roaring Camp, Poker Flat, Sandy Bar, Wingdam, and Red Gulch were mythical towns inhabited by a society grown in two decades almost as romantic as Camelot or Bagdad." What Walker did not point out, but well could have, is that the geography was nearly as mythical as the place names themselves.

Jack London in his own way did with his stories of the Far North what

Bret Harte earlier had done with his stories of the Far West, and the first of them appeared in the same magazine that had carried Bret Harte's early stories, *The Overland Monthly*. It seemed that Jack London created a new and mythical world filled with characters and events no one ever had read before. Also like Harte, London populated this new world with characters that would recur in story after story. The Malemute Kid is a character with a major role in London's "To the Man on the Trail" in *The Overland Monthly* (Jan. 1899), in "The White Silence" in *The Overland Monthly* (Feb. 1899), in "An Odyssey of the North" in *The Atlantic Monthly* (Jan. 1900), and he is mentioned in passing in "The Son of the Wolf" in *The Overland Monthly* (Apr. 1899). In "The Son of the Wolf" Scuff Mackenzie seeks to take as his wife Zarinska, the comely daughter of Chief Thling-Tinneh of the Upper Tanana Sticks. The chief tells Mackenzie of his other daughter who has already married a white man named Mason. Mason's death is narrated in "The White Silence," and Mackenzie relates to Chief Thling-Tinneh how Mason's wife, called Ruth by the white men, and her son with Mason took Mason's gold and went south to live where there is "'no biting frost, no snow, no summer's midnight sun, no winter's noonday night!'"

Stanley Price in "To the Man on the Trail" is described as "a young mining expert who had been in two years"—where being "in" means having lived in the Far North. In "An Odyssey of the North" Price is living with Malemute Kid and is present with the Kid when the Indian Naass tells the story of how his bride was taken from him on his wedding night and how, many years later, he found her again, how he killed her second husband, only to learn to his eternal anguish how profoundly she had come to love the man who once had stolen her. She stabs Naass twice before she withdraws from him to remain next to her dead husband until she, too, is dead. "'But, Kid,'" Price objects at the end of Naass's narrative, "'this is murder!' 'Hush!' commanded Malemute Kid. 'There be things greater than our wisdom, beyond our justice. The right and wrong of this we cannot say, and it is not for us to judge.'"

Father Robeau is the Jesuit mentioned in "To the Man on the Trail" as having married Mason and Ruth after they had fled the Tananas. In "The Men of Forty-Mile" in *The Overland Monthly* (May 1899) Father Robeau and Malemute Kid are among the *dramatis personae*, as is Scuff Mackenzie, and the reader learns that Mackenzie's marriage to Zariska has prospered.

On the other hand, some of London's most familiar Far North stories have characters who, of necessity, are seen but once. Perhaps his most famous short story is "To Build a Fire," which first appeared in *The Youth's Companion* (May 29, 1902). London himself later expanded and polished this story, and it appeared under the same title in *The Century Magazine* (Aug. 1908). "In a Far County" in *The Overland Monthly* (June 1899) is probably the London short story that has been most anthologized after "To Build a Fire." It is a tale of two shirkers in the Far North for the first time who find themselves isolated in an Arctic cabin for an entire winter with dire results.

Five of London's novels are set in the Klondike region of Yukon Territory during the 1896–1898 gold rush. The most celebrated of these is *The Call of the Wild* (Macmillan, 1903), a 32,000-word short novel originally serialized in *The Saturday Evening Post*. It sold 10,000 copies on its first day of issue in book form. London, desperate for money, made one of the few mistakes in his professional writing life by acceding to Macmillan's "best" offer for what they considered a dog story: $2,000 for an outright purchase of the copyright without royalties. He had received $700 from the *Post* for the magazine serialization, and, while $2,700 was a sizable sum in 1903, London would have earned a small fortune in royalties from this book alone for the next forty-two years, the maximum period of protection provided by the Copyright Act in effect at that time. London said he wrote the short novel as a sort of species-redeeming sequel to his "Bâtard," first published as "Diable—A Dog" in *Cosmopolitan* (June 1902), a grim Yukon tale of a dog who finds sweet revenge after being brutalized by his master. Ostensibly, *The Call of the Wild* is the story of Buck, a domestic dog who is stolen, taken into the Yukon wilderness, starved and beaten into submission until he becomes later, in turn, a great sled animal, a vicious killer, the property of a kindly gold hunter and, after the murder of this man by Indians, a ghostly legend as leader of a wolf pack. For all of its apparent simplicity, *The Call of the Wild* portrays vividly a naturalistic view of the brutality of life controlled by biological and environmental impulses. Yet the eerily lyrical, romantic prose of this novel also suggests a significant ambiguity on the author's part, the terror of surrender to a wholly naturalistic universe. This, for me, is the theological quandary Jack London sought to confront, even if the confrontation is oblique, and it is easily mistaken. So much theology depends on the notion of a benevolent Deity who can, and will upon occasion, intervene and suspend the laws of His own creation. In the Far North, it occurred to Jack London, I believe, that it is very possible, indeed, that even if He is all-powerful, God has chosen from the beginning of time which He created to act only within the laws of His own creation. This does provide a great latitude, however, for quite possibly the laws of the universe at base may very well be merely a matter of hazard, and the probability of such a common occurrence even as the sun rising tomorrow, no matter how many days in the past it may have arisen, still remains only one out of two. It could simply be that God has infinitely more imagination than any of His creatures. It could also be that the truly mortal sin for which Prometheus was pinioned for all eternity and Adam and Eve banished from the Garden of Paradise may actually have been the illusion prompting an all-too-human belief that knowledge is power, rather than imagination—which is the essence of all creation.

A year after *The Call of the Wild* was published, London announced to his publisher that he had decided to write a "complete antithesis" and "companion book" to his best-seller. *White Fang* (Macmillan, 1906), an even more naturalistic story than its predecessor, takes a sort of reverse twist on *The Call of the Wild*. Fang is a wolf dog, born in the Yukon wilderness, brutalized by his masters but eventually domesticated. A remarkable feature of this novel is London's depiction of the white silence of the Arctic wilderness in even more forbidding terms than he had described it previously: "Life is an offense to it, for life is movement, and the Wild aims always to destroy movement. It freezes the water to prevent it running to the sea; it drives the sap out of the trees till they are frozen to their mighty hearts; and most ferociously and terribly of all does the Wild harry and crush into submission man—man, who is the most restless of life. . . ."

Burning Daylight (Macmillan, 1910) is London's most important Northwestern story in terms of his development as a writer and social thinker, and has rightly been termed "an unjustly forgotten book" by Dale L. Walker, co-author with James E. Sisson III of *The Fiction of Jack London: A Chronological Bibliography* (Texas Western Press, 1972). It is a sprawling narrative of a legendary Klondike Eldorado king named Elam Harnish who has spent thirteen years searching for gold in the Yukon before the great rush and who now takes his hard-won millions outside to face a far different world than the one of trusting, faithful, work-hardened men to which he is accustomed. London's other extended works set in the Northland include *A Daughter of the Snows* (Lippincott, 1902) and a series of interconnected stories titled *Smoke Bellew* (Century, 1912) about an effete litterateur who finds manhood among the rough-and-tumble miners of the Klondike.

Robert Service in his ballads about life in the Far North and the one novel he wrote about the Klondike added further imaginative dimensions to this new literary world. In the spirit of Vergil before him who had opened his epic paean of Rome in *The Æneid* with the words—*Arma virumque cano*—Robert Service sang of "The Law of the Yukon":

> Send me the best of your breeding,
> lend me your chosen ones;
> Them will I take to my bosom,
> them will I call my sons;

Them will I gild with my treasure,
them will I glut with my meat;
But the others—the misfits, the failures—
I trample under my feet.

Service was born two years before Jack London and spent his boyhood in Glasgow. He became apprenticed as a bank clerk but was restless and sailed to Canada to seek his fortune. In 1904 he took the position of a bank clerk in Whitehorse, and later the Canadian Bank of Commerce transferred him to its branch in the former roaring camp of Dawson where he lived in a little bungalow. The days of the gold rush were over by then, but he retold and embellished tales he had heard, transforming them into legends. His first collection of poetry, *Songs of a Sourdough* (Stern and Company, 1907), contained "The Shooting of Dan McGrew" and "The Cremation of Sam McGee," ballads that soon became two of the most-often memorized poems in the English language. The lines I have quoted above come from this first book of ballads.

Service was able with the money he earned from this volume to quit his bank job and pursue the career of an author. *Ballads of a Cheechako* (Stern and Company, 1909) followed. In Jack London's stories this Siwash word for a greenhorn (literally a person from Chicago, i.e., Chicagoan) was rendered *che-cha-qua*. By the time Robert Service used it, his rendering of it had become a part of the English language.

In *Jack London and the Klondike: The Genesis of an American Writer* (Huntington Library, 1966) Franklin Walker provided an invaluable commentary on Jack London's life in the Far North compared with the stirring evocation of the Far North in his Northwest fiction. Such a study has never been made with regard to the images of the Far North in Robert Service's poetry and fiction. Yet in his case there is an equally indispensable book titled *The Best of Robert Service* (Running Press, 1990) with a brief preface by Tam Mossman, who edited the book. It consists of most of Service's finest ballads illustrated with photographs taken around the time and in the places that Service used as settings or background for his narratives. Just as motion pictures can capture beyond a person's lifetime the movements, facial expressions, gestures, and spoken words of actors and actresses, giving them in this sense a practical, albeit incorporeal, immortality which they might never have imagined, so photographs can capture forever images and impressions. It is even possible for us by this means to journey to a remote valley in the Canadian Northwest Territories and capture forever the brief blooming of lush moss campion and flowers amid the granite spires of the Logan Mountains that surround these treeless and usually barren meadows.

In *The Spoilers* (Universal, 1942) Marlene Dietrich, playing saloon-owner Cherry Malotte, passes the second-floor tables in her Nome saloon and pauses briefly at one of them to have a word with a poet sitting there writing. His name is Robert Service. The author, of course, of the novel *The Spoilers* (Harper, 1905) on which this and several other film versions were based was Rex Beach. He came to be called the "Victor Hugo of the North" for his Northwestern novels which were avidly read by many of the same readers who loved Jack London's Northland stories. Beach went to Rampart City in Alaska at the turn of the century, and for three years he worked in various mines before returning to the States. Seeing there was an avid market for fiction set in the North, he sold his first story, "The Thaw at Slisco," to *McClure's Magazine* (Nov. 1904) for fifty dollars and followed it with numerous other stories and novels. He was a master at capturing accents, that of the Yukon natives as well as French-Canadians and Russians. In his autobiography, *Personal Exposures* (Harper, 1940), Beach wrote of his own work and a writer's responsibilities that "however fertile may be his inevitable genius, it seems to me that he owes it to his readers to respect the realities of his environment and, if he proposes to make use of facts, he should see that they are accurate. All of which is perhaps another way of saying that I'm a sort of longhand cameraman."

In terms of the era of the great gold rush, James Oliver Curwood came upon the scene after London, Service, and Beach, but I rather suspect he had more first-hand experience of the terrain than any of them. For two years he was employed by the Canadian government as an explorer and a descriptive writer. It was in this capacity that he lived among the Eskimos as well as traveled thousands of miles by canoe, snowshoes, and pack train through the Hudson's Bay country. His love for the wild Northland and his intimate knowledge of its ways were reflected in the backgrounds and settings for his many novels, the first of which to appear was *The Courage of Captain Plum* (Bobbs-Merrill, 1908). Frequently Curwood's protagonists were red coats in the Royal Canadian Mounted Police, heroes who are strong, handsome, and morally above reproach and his heroines beautiful, innocent, and intelligent. His plots seem today to be too often contrived and even sentimental. But it would be wrong to dismiss all of what he wrote as flat or two-dimensional, because amid these romantic and flamboyant characterizations there remains his exuberant descriptions of the land and the elements that still are capable of mesmerizing a reader.

Given such a powerful and provocative impetus, by the 1920s the Northwestern story had become a legitimate variety of the Western story, and it was commonplace to find Northwestern stories appearing regularly in such magazines as Street & Smith's *Western Story Magazine*, some of the best of them written by Frank Richardson Pierce and Robert Ormond Case. Fiction House, replacing an unsuccessful pulp magazine called *Illustrated Novelets* (there were no illustrations!) but continuing the volume and issue numbers, launched *North-West Stories* with the issue dated May 1925. About half of the stories in each issue are set in the Northland. Unlike its predecessor, this new magazine proved so popular with readers that by the end of the year it began being issued bi-weekly. Walt Coburn, the cowboy author from Montana who was the headliner in other Fiction House magazines like *Action Stories* and *Lariat Story Magazine*, at the request of Jack Kelly, editor of all the company's magazines, tried his hand at a Northwestern story in the third issue, "Superstition House" (July 1925). Coburn, however, writing a story about a mounted policeman in the Northland was out of his element, and most of his stories in later issues were set in either Montana or the Southwest. More successful, however, were stories by Frederick L. Nebel, A. De Herries Smith, Jack Bechdolt, Dex Volney, and Victor Rousseau.

With Jack Kelly's death in 1932, Fiction House closed down all of its magazines, and publication was resumed very slowly after 1934, one magazine at a time. Shortly after *North-West Stories* came back, beginning with the Fall 1938 issue it had a new editor, Malcolm Reiss, and was given a new name, *North-West Romances*. This magazine differed from the former one in more than title, however. All of the stories in it were set in the Northland. *North-West Romances* was continuously published as a quarterly magazine until the issue dated Winter 1953, coming near the end of the era of all pulp magazines. Many of the same authors were back as well, Frederick L. Nebel who wrote his best Northland fiction in the late 1930s for *North-West Romances*, Jack Bechdolt, Victor Rousseau, as well as a newcomer, John Starr. When Starr retired from writing fiction to pursue a career as a book editor, Fiction House, which had done so much to showcase his name, bought the rights to use John Starr as a house name. That is how years later, when Dan Cushman would have two stories in one issue, his own name was used as the byline for one of them, John Starr his byline for the other. "The White Hunger," which I have included in this collection, was a Dan Cushman story that first saw the light of day under the house name John Starr. Les Savage Jr., who headlined many Fiction House magazines in the 1940s, as did Dan Cushman, also wrote extensively for *North-West Romances* in that decade, along with Tom W. Blackburn, William Heuman, Jim Kjelgaard, and Curtis Bishop. Many of their stories can still be read with pleasure. Only limitations due to space have confined me to select exemplary stories from this period by just Dan Cushman and Les Savage Jr. By the late 1940s *North-West*

Romances began including reprints of stories by Jack London and ballads by Robert Service in many issues. "The League of the Old Men" by Jack London was reprinted in the issue dated Fall 1948. In that same issue is also found "The Law of the Yukon" by Robert Service.

The late 1930s may be regarded as a halcyon period for stories of the Northwest in magazines. *Complete Northwest Novel Magazine* was launched in 1935 by the Double-Action pulp group as a bi-monthly. In addition to reprints of short stories by James Oliver Curwood, new novel-length stories were regularly published in its pages by authors like William Byron Mowery, some of which were later published in book form, and reprints of Northwestern fiction that had previously appeared only in book form, such as *Royce of The Royal Mounted* (Macaulay, 1932) by Amos Moore, pseudonym for George Hubbard, which appeared in the February 1937 issue under the title "The Mountie from Texas." Double-Action also launched *Real Northwest Adventures* in late 1935 with reprints of James Oliver Curwood's stories and new Northwest fiction by William Byron Mowery and Frank Richardson Pierce.

James B. Hendryx, although he did travel to the Klondike, did not actually write Northwestern fiction until *The Promise: A Tale of the Great Northwest* (Putnam, 1915). For nearly four decades he continued to write Northland stories, many featuring his series characters, Corporal Downey of the Royal Canadian Mounted Police, and Black John, a miner and trapper in the frontier town of Halfaday Creek. Hendryx's short novels and short stories appeared in magazines like *Short Stories* and were later welded into picaresque novels published by Doubleday, Doran.

However, beyond this necessarily sketchy survey of Northwestern fiction published in the hundred years since the last great gold rush, I should not wish to leave my subject without at least a word about the direction we take in all of the stories in this collection. From the dawn of civilization, human beings have watched the heavens at night and tried to understand the meaning of the universe in terms of the celestial motion of the planets and stars visible to the naked eye. Johannes Kepler, the sixteenth-century German astronomer who first formulated laws according to mathematics for the motions of the planets, created a trigon diagram he called *Schema magnarum Coniunctionum Saturni et Jovis* concerned with the conjunctions of Saturn with Jupiter. His trigonic series illustrated how every 794⅓ years, or after forty such conjunctions, the triangle had turned through one-third of the ecliptic and thus will appear to be in the same position as at the beginning. However, to move through the entire zodiac, one of the angles of the trigon requires 2,383 years.

Before this alliance of mathematics and astronomy gave mankind the means to chart and predict celestial motion and precession of the equinoxes, human beings had to resort to other ways, of which perhaps the most captivating remains the technical language encoded in mythology. The Greek name for Saturn was Kronos and for Jupiter, Zeus. Greek legend tells us that there was once a great battle between Kronos and Zeus and that Zeus emerged the victor. By looking into the heavens over a sufficient period of time we can see how in the conjunction of Jupiter with Saturn—Jupiter being larger than Saturn and closer to the Earth—it would appear to the naked eye that Jupiter had engulfed Saturn because, truly, for a time from the Earth's perspective Saturn disappears behind the greater planet.

In the ancient Near East, the Persian Magi saw, in the return of the conjunction of Jupiter with Saturn to Pisces, the dawn of a new age—as the defeat of Kronos by Zeus had once meant the dawn of a new age for the Greeks—and so they set forth, following the "star in the east" to find the new king of the new age. In Christendom that event is still observed annually in what in the northern hemisphere is the cold time following the winter solstice. In Andean myth the god Viracocha "left the earth" in the northwest, and so a new age was ushered in. In fact, all mythologies, no matter their geographical origin, seem to agree that northwest is the direction in which one must travel to have access to the land of the gods. In this collection of stories of the Far North it is no coincidence that northwest is, indeed, the direction in which these authors take us. Yet the land of the midnight sun can be more than a locus. It can be a metaphor for an odyssey of the human soul.

JACK LONDON

The League of the Old Men

Jack London (1876–1916) was born John Griffith Chaney in San Francisco, California. The surname he later adopted was that of his stepfather, John London, a farmer from Pennsylvania, who married Jack's mother, Flora Wellman, the year Jack was born. His stories of the Northwest, beginning with "To the Man on the Trail" in *The Overland Monthly* (Jan. 1899), won him immediate popularity with readers, and created a wholly different kind of story. By this I do not mean merely the physical setting of his Far North fiction, but rather the added dimension to be found in London's finest stories. Earle Labor, one of London's ablest critics, put it well in his Introduction to *The Great Short Works of Jack London* (Harper, 1965): "When London writes that 'like giants they toiled, days flashing on the heels of days like dreams as they heaped the treasure up,' he is obviously modulating his imagery in terms of a farther and deeper music than that of the ordinary phenomenal world . . . a world of the *un*conscious (Jung called it the 'collective unconscious'), the primordial world against which modern man has erected inhibiting barriers of rationality and the social ethic but nonetheless a real world to which he would return, in dreams, to find his soul." In London's best stories this deeper music is to be heard as a subtext co-existing with the action embodied in surface events—what it all means to the human soul is a tale he tells simultaneously with what happens to the characters in a story. At the same time, like so many of the world's great storytellers, London knew in his heart that perhaps all we can ever know is part of a tale and, quite possibly, not the most important part. Yet, withal, we do continue to read in order to hear, perhaps, just a little more of that farther and deeper music.

London's original title for the narrative that follows was "The Perplexity of Imber," and it was turned down by three magazines before it was accepted for publication in *Brandur Magazine* (Oct. 4, 1902) under the title "The League of the Old Men." It was collected by London in book form in *Children of the Frost* (Macmillan, 1902). "Though 'The League of the Old Men' has no love motif, that is not my reason for thinking it my best story," London commented in a letter published in *Grand Magazine* (Aug. 1906). "In ways, the motif of this story is greater than any love-motif; in fact, its wide sweep includes the conditions and situations for ten-thousand love-motifs. The voices of millions are in the voice of Old Imber, the tears and sorrows of millions in his throat as he tells his story; and his story epitomizes the whole vast tragedy of the contact of the Indian with the white man. In conclusion, I may say that nobody else agrees with me in the selection which I have made and which has been my selection for years." I do; and so I have included it here.

At the Barracks a man was being tried for his life. He was an old man, a native from the Whitefish River, which empties into the Yukon below Lake Le Barge. All Dawson was wrought up over the affair, and likewise the Yukon-dwellers for a thousand miles up and down. It has been the custom of the land-robbing and sea-robbing Anglo-Saxon to give the law to conquered peoples, and ofttimes this law is harsh. But in the case of Imber the law for once seemed inadequate and weak. In the mathematical nature of things, equity did not reside in the punishment to be accorded him. The punishment was a foregone conclusion, there could be no doubt of that; and though it was capital, Imber had but one life, while the tale against him was one of scores.

In fact, the blood of so many was upon his hands that the killings attributed to him did not permit of precise enumeration. Smoking a pipe by the trailside or lounging around the stove, men made rough estimates of the number that had perished at his hand. They had been whites, all of them, these poor murdered people, and they had been slain singly, in pairs, and in parties. And so purposeless and wanton had been these killings, that they had long been a mystery to the mounted police, even in the time of the captains, and later, when the creeks realized, and a governor came from the Dominion to make the land pay for its prosperity.

But more mysterious still was the coming of Imber to Dawson to give himself up. It was in the late spring, when the Yukon was growling and writhing under its ice, that the old Indian climbed painfully up the bank from the river trail and stood blinking on the main street. Men who had witnessed his advent, noted that he was weak and tottery, and that he staggered over to a heap of cabin-logs and sat down. He sat there a full day, staring straight before him at the unceasing tide of white men that flooded past. Many a head jerked curiously to the side to meet his stare, and more than one remark was dropped anent the old Siwash with so strange a look upon his face. No end of men remembered afterward that they had been struck by his extraordinary figure, and forever afterward prided themselves upon their swift discernment of the unusual.

But it remained for Dickensen, Little Dickensen, to be the hero of the occasion. Little Dickensen had come into the land with great dreams and a pocketful of cash; but with the cash the dreams vanished, and to earn his passage back to the States he had accepted a clerical position with the brokerage firm of Holbrook and Mason. Across the street from the office of Holbrook and Mason was the heap of cabin-logs upon which Imber sat. Dickensen looked out of the window at him before he went to lunch; and when he came back from lunch he looked out of the window, and the old Siwash was still there.

Dickensen continued to look out of the window, and he, too, forever afterward prided himself upon his swiftness of discernment. He was a romantic little chap, and he likened the immobile old heathen to the genius of the Siwash race, gazing calm-eyed upon the hosts of the invading Saxon. The hours swept along, but Imber did not vary his posture, did not by a hair's-breadth move a muscle; and Dickensen remembered the man who once sat upright on a sled in the main street where men passed to and fro. They thought the man was resting, but later, when they touched him, they found him stiff and cold, frozen to death in the midst of the busy street. To undouble him, that he might fit into a coffin, they had been forced to lug him to a fire and thaw him out a bit. Dickensen shivered at the recollection.

Later on, Dickensen went out on the sidewalk to smoke a cigar and cool off; and a little later Emily Travis happened along. Emily Travis was dainty and delicate and rare, and whether in London or Klondike she gowned herself as befitted a daughter of a millionaire mining engineer. Little Dickensen deposited his cigar on an outside window ledge where he could find it again, and lifted his hat.

They chatted for ten minutes or so, when Emily Travis, glancing past Dickensen's shoulder, gave a startled little scream. Dickensen turned about to see, and was startled, too. Imber had crossed the street and was standing there, a gaunt and hungry-looking shadow, his gaze riveted upon the girl.

"What do you want?" Little Dickensen demanded, tremulously plucky.

Imber grunted and stalked up to Emily Travis. He looked her over, keenly and carefully, every square inch of her. Especially did he appear interested in her silky brown hair, and in the color of her cheek, faintly sprayed and soft, like the downy bloom of a butterfly wing. He walked around her, surveying her with the calculating eye of a man who studies the lines upon which a horse or a boat is builded. In the course of his circuit the pink shell of her ear came between his eye and the westering sun, and he stopped to contemplate its rosy transparency. Then he returned to her face and looked long and intently into her blue eyes. He grunted and laid a hand on her arm midway between the shoulder and elbow. With his other hand he lifted her forearm and doubled it back. Disgust and wonder showed in his face, and he dropped her arm with a contemptuous grunt. Then he muttered a few guttural syllables, turned his back upon her, and addressed himself to Dickensen.

Dickensen could not understand his speech, and Emily Travis laughed. Imber turned from one to the other, frowning, but both shook their heads. He was about to go away, when she called out: "Oh, Jimmy! Come here!"

Jimmy came from the other side of the street. He was a big, hulking Indian clad in approved white-man style, with an Eldorado king's sombrero on his head. He talked with Imber, haltingly, with throaty spasms. Jimmy was a Sitkan, possessed of no more than a passing knowledge of the interior dialects.

"Him Whitefish man," he said to Emily Travis. "Me savve um talk no very much. Him want to look see chief white man."

"The Governor," suggested Dickensen.

Jimmy talked some more with the Whitefish man, and his face went grave and puzzled.

"I t'ink um want Cap'n Alexander," he explained. "Him say um kill white man, white woman, white boy, plenty kill um white people. Him want to die."

"Insane, I guess," said Dickensen.

"What you call dat?" queried Jimmy.

Dickensen thrust a finger figuratively inside his head and imparted a rotary motion thereto.

"Mebbe so, mebbe so," said Jimmy, returning to Imber, who still demanded the chief man of the white men.

A mounted policeman (unmounted for Klondike service) joined the group and heard Imber's wish repeated. He was a stalwart young fellow, broad-shouldered, deep-chested, legs cleanly built and stretched wide apart, and tall though Imber was, he towered above him by half a head. His eyes were cool, and gray, and steady, and he carried himself with the peculiar confidence of power that is bred of blood and tradition. His splendid masculinity was emphasized by his excessive boyishness,—he was a mere lad,—and his smooth cheek promised a blush as willingly as the cheek of a maid.

Imber was drawn to him at once. The fire leaped into his eyes at sight of a saber slash that scarred his cheek. He ran a withered hand down the young fellow's leg and caressed the swelling thew. He smote the broad chest with his knuckles, and pressed and prodded the thick muscle-pads that covered the shoulders like a cuirass. The group had been added to by curious passers—by husky miners, mountaineers, and frontiersmen, sons of the long-legged and broad-shouldered generations. Imber glanced from one to another, then he spoke aloud in the Whitefish tongue.

"What did he say?" asked Dickensen.

"Him say um all the same one man, dat p'liceman," Jimmy interpreted.

Little Dickensen was little, and what of Miss Travis, he felt sorry for having asked the question.

The policeman was sorry for him and stepped into the breach. "I fancy there may be something in his story. I'll take him up to the captain for examination. Tell him to come along with me, Jimmy."

Jimmy indulged in more throaty spasms, and Imber grunted and looked satisfied.

"But ask him what he said, Jimmy, and what he meant when he took hold of my arm."

So spoke Emily Travis, and Jimmy put the question and received the answer.

"Him say you no afraid," said Jimmy.

Emily Travis looked pleased.

"Him say you no *skookum*, no strong, all the same very soft like little baby. Him break you, in um two hands, to little pieces. Him t'ink much funny, very strange, how you can be mother of men so big, so strong, like dat p'liceman."

Emily Travers kept her eyes up and unfaltering, but her cheeks were sprayed with scarlet. Little Dickensen blushed and was quite embarrassed. The policeman's face blazed with his boy's blood.

"Come along, you," he said gruffly, setting his shoulder to the crowd and forcing a way.

Thus it was that Imber found his way to the Barracks, where he made full and voluntary confession, and from the precincts of which he never emerged.

Imber looked very tired. The fatigue of hopelessness and age was in his face. His shoulders drooped depressingly, and his eyes were lack-lustre. His mop of hair should have been white, but sun and weatherbeat had burned and bitten it so that it hung limp and lifeless and colorless. He took no interest in what went on around him. The courtroom was jammed with the men of the creeks and trails, and there was an ominous note in the rumble and grumble of their low-pitched voices, which came to his ears like the growl of the sea from deep caverns.

He sat close by a window, and his apathetic eyes rested now and again on the dreary scene without. The sky was overcast, and a gray drizzle was falling. It was flood-time on the Yukon. The ice was gone, and the river was up in the town. Back and forth on the main street, in canoes and poling-boats, passed the people that never rested. Often he saw these boats turn aside from the street and enter the flooded square that marked the Barracks' parade-ground. Sometimes they disappeared beneath him, and he heard them jar against the house-logs and their occupants scramble in through the window. After that came the slush of water against men's legs as they waded across the lower room and mounted the stairs. Then they appeared in the doorway, with doffed hats and dripping sea-boots, and added themselves to the waiting crowd.

And while they centered their looks on him, and in grim anticipation enjoyed the penalty he was to pay, Imber looked at them, and mused on their ways, and on their Law that never slept, but went on unceasing, in good times and bad, in flood and famine, through trouble and terror and death, and which would go on unceasing, it seemed to him, to the end of time.

A man rapped sharply on a table, and the conversation droned away into silence. Imber looked at the man. He seemed one in authority, yet Imber divined the square-browed man who sat by a desk farther back to be the one chief over them all and over the man who had rapped. Another man by the same table uprose and began to read aloud from many fine sheets of paper. At the top of each sheet he cleared his throat, at the bottom moistened his fingers. Imber did not understand his speech, but the others did, and he knew that it made them angry. Sometimes it made them very angry, and once a man cursed him, in single syllables, stinging and tense, till a man at the table rapped him to silence.

For an interminable period the man read. His monotonous, sing-song utterance lured Imber to dreaming, and he was dreaming deeply when the man ceased. A voice spoke to him in his own Whitefish tongue, and he roused up, without surprise, to look upon the face of his sister's son, a young man who had wandered away years agone to make his dwelling with the whites.

"Thou dost not remember me," he said by way of greeting.

"Nay," Imber answered. "Thou art Howkan who went away. Thy mother be dead."

"She was an old woman," said Howkan.

But Imber did not hear, and Howkan, with hand upon his shoulder, roused him again.

"I shall speak to thee what the man has spoken, which is the tale of the troubles thou hast done and which thou hast told, O fool, to the Captain Alexander. And thou shalt understand and say if it be true talk or talk not true. It is so commanded."

Howkan had fallen among the mission folk and been taught by them to read and write. In his hands he held the many fine sheets from which the man had read aloud, and which had been taken down by a clerk when Imber first made confession, through the mouth of Jimmy, to Captain Alexander. Howkan began to read. Imber listened for a space, when a wonderment rose up in his face and he broke in abruptly.

"That be my talk, Howkan. Yet from thy lips it comes when thy ears have not heard."

Howkan smirked with self-appreciation. His hair was parted in the middle. "Nay, from the paper it comes, O Imber. Never have my ears heard. From the paper it comes, through my eyes, into my head, and out of my mouth to thee. Thus it comes."

"Thus it come? It be there in the paper?" Imber's voice sank in whisperful awe as he crackled the sheets 'twixt thumb and finger and stared at the charactery scrawled thereon. "It be a great medicine, Howkan, and thou art a worker of wonders."

"It be nothing, it be nothing," the young man responded carelessly and pridefully. He read at hazard from the document: "*In that year, before the break of the ice, came an old man, and a boy who was lame of one foot. These also did I kill, and the old man made much noise. . . .*"

"It be true," Imber interrupted breathlessly. "He made much noise and would not die for a long time. But how dost thou know, Howkan? The chief man of the white men told thee, mayhap? No one beheld me, and him alone have I told."

Howkan shook his head with impatience. "Have I not told thee it be there in the paper, O fool?"

Imber stared hard at the ink-scrawled surface. "As the hunter looks upon the snow and says, Here but yesterday there passed a rabbit; and here by the willow scrub it stood and listened, and heard, and was afraid; and here it turned upon its trail; and here it went with great swiftness, leaping wide; and here, with greater swiftness and wider leapings, came a lynx; and here, where the claws cut deep into the snow, the lynx made a very great leap; and here it struck, with the rabbit under and rolling belly up; and here leads off the trail of the lynx alone, and there is no more rabbit, . . . as the hunter looks upon the markings of the snow and says thus and so and here, dost thou, too, look upon the paper and say thus and so and here be the things old Imber hath done?"

"Even so," said Howkan. "And now do thou listen, and keep thy woman's tongue between thy teeth till thou art called upon for speech."

Thereafter, and for a long time, Howkan read to him the confession, and Imber remained musing and silent. At the end, he said:

"It be my talk, and true talk, but I am grown old, Howkan, and forgotten things come back to me which were well for the head man there to know. First, there was the man who came over the Ice Mountains, with cunning traps made of iron, who sought the beaver of the Whitefish. Him I slew. And there were three men seeking gold on the Whitefish long ago. Them I also slew, and left them to the wolverines. And at the Five Fingers there was a man with a raft and much meat."

At the moments when Imber paused to remember, Howkan translated and a clerk reduced to writing. The courtroom listened stolidly to each unadorned little tragedy, till Imber told of a red-haired man whose eyes were crossed and whom he had killed with a remarkably long shot.

"Hell," said a man in the forefront of the onlookers. He said it soulfully and sorrowfully. He was red-haired. "Hell," he repeated. "That was my brother Bill." And at regular intervals throughout the session, his solemn "Hell" was heard in the courtroom; nor did his comrades check him, nor did the man at the table rap him to order.

Imber's head drooped once more, and his eyes went dull, as though a film rose up and covered them from the world. And he dreamed as only age can dream upon the colossal futility of youth.

Later, Howkan roused him again, saying: "Stand up, O Imber. It be commanded that thou tellest why you did these troubles, and slew these people, and at the end journeyed here seeking the Law."

Imber rose feebly to his feet and swayed back and forth. He began to speak in a low and faintly rumbling voice, but Howkan interrupted him.

"This old man, he is damn crazy," he said in English to the square-browed man. "His talk is foolish and like that of a child."

"We will hear his talk which is like that of a child," said the square-browed man. "And we will hear it, word for word, as he speaks. Do you understand?"

Howkan understood, and Imber's eyes flashed, for he had witnessed the play between his sister's son and the man in authority. And then began the story, the epic of a bronze patriot which might well itself be wrought into bronze for the generations unborn. The crowd fell strangely silent, and the square-browed judge leaned head on hand and pondered his soul and the soul of his race. Only was heard the deep tones of Imber, rhythmically alternating with the shrill voice of the interpreter, and now and again, like the bell of the Lord, the wondering and meditative "Hell" of the red-haired man.

"I am Imber of the Whitefish people." So ran the interpretation of Howkan, whose inherent barbarism gripped hold of him, and who lost his mission culture and veneered civilization as he caught the savage ring and rhythm of old Imber's tale. "My father was Otsbaok, a strong man. The land was warm with sunshine and gladness when I was a boy. The people did not hunger after strange things, nor hearken to new voices, and the ways of their fathers were their ways. The women found favor in the eyes of the young men, and the young men looked upon them with content. Babes hung at the breasts of the women, and they were heavy-hipped with increase of the tribe. Men were men in those days. In peace and plenty, and in war and famine, they were men.

"At that time there was more fish in the water than now, and more meat in the forest. Our dogs were wolves, warm with thick hides and hard to the frost and storm. And as with our dogs so with us, for we were likewise hard to the frost and storm. And when the Pellys came into our land we slew them and were slain. For we were men, we Whitefish, and our fathers and our fathers' fathers had fought against the Pellys and determined the bounds of the land.

"As I say, with our dogs, so with us. And one day came the first white man. He dragged himself, so, on hand and knee, in the snow. And his skin was stretched tight, and his bones were sharp beneath. Never was such a man, we thought, and we wondered of what strange tribe he was, and of its land. And he was weak, most weak, like a little child, so that we gave him a place by the fire, and warm furs to lie upon, and we gave him food as little children are given food.

"And with him was a dog, large as three of our dogs, and very weak. The hair of this dog was short, and not warm, and the tail was frozen so that the end fell off. And this strange dog we fed, and bedded by the fire, and fought from it our dogs, which else would have killed him. And what of the moose meat and the sun-dried salmon, the man and dog took strength to themselves; and what of the strength they became big and unafraid. And the man spoke loud words and laughed at the old men and young men, and looked boldly upon the maidens. And the dog fought with our dogs, and for all of his short hair and softness slew three of them in one day.

"When we asked the man concerning his people, he said, 'I have many brothers,' and laughed in a way that was not good. And when he was in his full strength he went away, and with him went Noda, daughter to the chief. First, after that, was one of our bitches brought to pup. And never was there such a breed of dogs, . . . big-headed, thick-jawed, and short-haired, and helpless. Well do I remember my father, Otsbaok, a strong man. His face was black with anger at such helplessness, and he took a stone, so, and so, and there was no more helplessness. And two summers after that came Noda back to us with a man-child in the hollow of her arm.

"And that was the beginning. Came a second white man, with short-haired dogs, which he left behind him when he went. And with him went six of our strongest dogs, for which, in trade, he had given Koo-So-Tee, my mother's brother, a wonderful pistol that fired with great swiftness six times. And Koo-So-Tee was very big, what of the pistol, and laughed at our bows and arrows. 'Woman's things,' he called them, and went forth against the bald-face grizzly, with the pistol in his hand. Now it be known that it is not good to hunt the bald-face with a pistol, but how were we to know? and how was Koo-So-Tee to know? So he went against the bald-face, very brave, and fired the pistol with great swiftness six times; and the bald-face but grunted and broke in his breast like it were an egg, and like honey from a bee's nest dripped the brains of Koo-So-Tee upon the ground. He was a good hunter, and there was no one to bring meat to his squaw and children. And we were bitter, and we said, 'That which for the white men is well, is for us not well.' And this be true. There be many white men and fat, but their ways have made us few and lean.

"Came the third white man, with great wealth of all manner of wonderful foods and things. And twenty of our strongest dogs he took from us in trade. Also, what of presents and great promises, ten of our young hunters did he take with him on a journey which fared no man knew where. It is said they died in the snow of the Ice Mountains where man has never been, or in the Hills of Silence which are beyond the edge of the earth. Be that as it may, dogs and young hunters were seen never again by the Whitefish people.

"And more white men came with the years, and ever, with pay and presents, they led the young men away with them. And sometimes the young men came back with strange tales of dangers and toils in the lands beyond the Pellys, and sometimes they did not come back. And we said, 'If they be unafraid of life, these white men, it is because they have many lives; but we be few by the Whitefish, and the young men shall go away no more.' But the young men did go away; and the young women went also; and we were very wroth.

"It be true, we ate flour, and salt pork, and drank tea which was a great delight; only, when we could not get tea, it was very bad and we became short of speech and quick of anger. So we grew to hunger for the things the white men brought in trade. Trade! trade! all the time was it trade! One winter we sold our meat for clocks that would not go, and watches with broken guts, and files worn smooth, and pistols without cartridges and worthless. And then came famine, and we were without meat, and two score died ere the break of spring.

"'Now are we grown weak,' we said; 'and the Pellys will fall upon us, and our bounds be overthrown.' But as it fared with us, so had it fared with the Pellys, and they were too weak to come against us.

"My father, Otsbaok, a strong man, was now old and very wise. And he spoke to the chief, saying, 'Behold, our dogs be worthless. No longer are they thick-furred and strong, and they die in the frost and harness. Let us go into the village and kill them, saving only the wolf ones, and these let us tie out in the night that they may mate with the wild wolves of the forest. Thus shall we have dogs warm and strong again.'

"And his word was harkened to, and we Whitefish became known for our dogs, which were the best in the land. But known we were not for ourselves. The best of our young men and women had gone away with the white men to wander on trail and river to far places. And the young women came back old and broken, as Noda had come, or they came not at all. And the young men came back to sit by our fires for a time, full of ill speech and rough ways, drinking evil drinks and gambling through long nights and days, with a great unrest always in their hearts, till the call of the white men came to them and they went away again to the unknown places. And they were without honor and respect, jeering the old-time customs and laughing in the faces of chief and shamans.

"As I say, we were become a weak breed, we Whitefish. We sold our warm skins and furs for tobacco and whiskey and thin cotton things that left us shivering in the cold. And the coughing sickness came upon us, and men and women coughed and sweated through the long nights, and the hunters on trail spat blood upon the snow. And now one, and now another, bled swiftly from the mouth and died. And the women bore few children, and those they bore were weak and given to sickness. And other sicknesses came to us from the white men, the like of which we had never known and could not understand. Smallpox, likewise measles, have I heard these sicknesses named, and we died of them as die the salmon in the still eddies when in the fall their eggs are spawned and there is no longer need for them to live.

"And yet, and here be the strangeness of it, the white men come as the breath of death; all their ways lead to death, their nostrils are filled with it; and yet they do not die. Theirs the whiskey, and tobacco, and short-haired dogs; theirs the many sicknesses, the smallpox and measles, the coughing and mouth-bleeding; theirs the white skin, and softness to the frost and storm; and theirs the pistols that shoot six times very swift and are worthless. And yet they grow fat on their many ills, and prosper, and lay a heavy hand over all the world and tread mightily upon its peoples. And their women, too, are soft as little babes, most breakable and never broken, the mothers of men. And out of all this softness, and sickness, and weakness, come strength, and power, and authority. They be gods, or devils, as the case may be. I do not know. What do I know, I, old Imber of the Whitefish? Only do I know that they are past understanding, these white men, far-wanderers and fighters over the earth that they be.

"As I say, the meat in the forest became less and less. It be true, the white man's gun is most excellent and kills a long way off; but of what worth the gun, when there is no meat to kill? When I was a boy on the Whitefish there was moose on every hill, and each year came the caribou uncountable. But now the hunter may take the trail ten days and not one moose gladden his eyes, while the caribou uncountable come no more at all. Small worth the gun, I say, killing a long way off, when there be nothing to kill.

"And I, Imber, pondered upon these things, watching the while the Whitefish, and the Pellys, and all the tribes of the land, perishing as perished the meat of the forest. Long I pondered. I talked with the shamans and the old men who were wise. I went apart that the sounds of the village might not disturb me, and I ate no meat so that my belly should not press upon me and make me slow of eye and ear. I sat long and sleepless in the forest, wide-eyed for the sign, my ears patient and keen for the word that was to come. And I wandered alone in the blackness of night to the river bank, where was wind-moaning and sobbing of water, and where I sought wisdom from the ghosts of old shamans in the trees and dead and gone.

"And in the end, as in a vision, came to me the short-haired and detestable dogs, and the way seemed plain. By the wisdom of Otsbaok, my father and a strong man, had the blood of our own wolf-dogs been kept clean, wherefore had they remained warm of hide and strong in the harness. So I returned to my village and made oration to the men. 'This be a tribe, these white men,' I said. 'A very large tribe, and doubtless there is no longer meat in their land, and they are come among us to make a new land for themselves. But they weaken us, and we die. They are a very hungry folk. Already has our meat gone from us, and it were well, if we would live, that we deal by them as we have dealt by their dogs.'

"And further oration I made, counseling fight. And the men of the Whitefish listened, and some said one thing, and some spoke of other and worthless things, and no man made brave talk of deeds and war. But while the young men were weak as water and afraid, I watched that the old men sat silent, and that in their eyes fires came and went. And later, when the village slept and no one knew, I drew the old men away into the forest and made more talk. And now we were agreed, and we remembered the good young days, and the free land, and the times of plenty, and the gladness and sunshine; and we called ourselves brothers, and swore great secrecy, and a mighty oath to cleanse the land of the evil breed that had come upon it. It be plain we were fools, but how were we to know, we old men of the Whitefish?

"And to hearten the others, I did the first deed. I kept guard upon the Yukon till the first canoe came down. In it were two white men, and when I stood upright upon the bank and raised my hand they changed their course and drove in to me. And as the man in the bow lifted his head, so, that he might know wherefore I wanted him, my arrow sang through the air straight to his throat, and he knew. The second man, who held paddle in the stern, had his rifle half to his shoulder when the first of my three spear-casts smote him.

"'These be the first,' I said, when the old men had gathered to me. 'Later we will bind together all the old men of all the tribes, and after that the young men who remain strong, and the work will become easy.'

"And then the two dead white men we cast into the river. And of the canoe, which was a very good canoe, we made a fire, and a fire, also, of the things within the canoe. But first we looked at the things, and they were pouches of leather which we cut open with our knives. And inside these pouches were many papers, like that from which thou hast read, O How-kan, with markings on them which we marveled at and could not understand. Now, I am become wise, and I know them for the speech of men as thou hast told me."

A whisper and buzz went around the courtroom when Howkan finished interpreting the affair of the canoe, and one man's voice spoke up: "That was the lost 'Ninety-One mail, Peter James and Delaney bringing it in and last spoken at Le Barge by Matthews going out." The clerk scratched steadily away, and another paragraph was added to the history of the North.

"There be a little more," Imber went on slowly. "It be there on the paper, the things we did. We were old men, and we did not understand. Even I, Imber, do not understand. Secretly we slew, and continued to slay, for with our years we were crafty and we had learned the swiftness of going without haste. When white men came among us with black looks and rough words, and took away six of the young men with irons binding them helpless, we knew we must slay wider and farther. And one by one we old men departed up river and down to the unknown lands. It was a brave thing. Old we were, and unafraid, but the fear of far places is a terrible fear to men who are old.

"So we slew, without haste and craftily. On the Chilcoot and in the Delta we slew, from the passes to the sea, wherever the white men camped or broke their trails. It be true, they died, but it was without worth. Ever did they come over the mountains, ever did they grow and grow, while we, being old, became less and less. I remember, by the Caribou Crossing, the camp of a white man. He was a very little white man, and three of the old men came upon him in his sleep. And the next day I came upon the four of them. The white man alone still breathed, and there was breath in him to curse me once and well before he died.

"And so it went, now one old man, and now another. Sometimes the word reached us long after of how they died, and sometimes it did not reach us. And the old men of the other tribes were weak and afraid, and would not join with us. As I say, one by one, till I alone was left. I am Imber, of the Whitefish people. My father was Otsbaok, a strong man. There are no Whitefish now. Of the old men I am the last. The young men and young women are gone away, some to live with the Pellys, some with the Salmons, and more with the white men. I am very old, and very tired, and it being vain fighting the Law, as thou sayest, Howkan, I am come seeking the Law."

"O Imber, thou art indeed a fool," said Howkan.

But Imber was dreaming. The square-browed judge likewise dreamed, and all his race rose up before him in a mighty phantasmagoria his steel-shod, mail-clad race, the lawgiver and world-maker among the families of men. He saw it dawn red-flickering across the dark forests and sullen seas; he saw it blaze, bloody and red, to full and triumphant noon; and down the shaded slope he saw the blood-red sands dropping into night. And through it all he observed the Law, pitiless and potent, ever unswerving and ever ordaining, greater than the motes of men who fulfilled it or were crushed by it, even as it was greater than he, his heart speaking for softness.

ROBERT SERVICE

The Trail of 'Ninety-Eight

Robert (William) Service was born January 14, 1874, in Preston, a city about twenty-five miles from Liverpool, but like his narrator in the novel, *The Trail of '98* (Dodd, Mead, 1910), he spent his boyhood in Glasgow. He emigrated to the Pacific Northwest and eventually came to work as a bank teller in Dawson. Only in two collections of ballads and *The Trail of '98* did Service attempt to capture the Klondike and the Yukon in the days of the great gold rush. During the Great War, he became a foreign correspondent for the *Toronto Star* and was sent to the Balkans. Later, in part because he had long been an admirer of the life and fiction of Robert Louis Stevenson, he wandered to the South Seas, and finally he came to reside in France where he lived until his death in 1958. There is a Gothic romance at the center of *The Trail of '98* that might not appeal to a modern reader, but its images of the gold rush, of the people and places, remain imperishable. Much of his poetry has never been out of print. Like Coleridge, Service in his ballads favored internal rhymes, and, since meter is essential to meaning in his poetry, the verses that follow break only according to their meter, as the poet intended—a concern not always shown by his various publishers.

I

Gold! We leapt from our benches.
Gold! We sprang from our stools.
Gold! We wheeled in the furrow,
fired with the faith of fools.
Fearless, unfound, unfitted,
far from the night and the cold.
Heard we the clarion summons,
followed the master-lure—Gold!

Men from the sands of the Sunland;
men from the woods of the West;
Men from the farms and the cities,
into the Northland we pressed.

Graybeards and striplings and women,
good men and bad men and bold,
Leaving our homes and our loved ones,
crying exultantly, "Gold!"

Never was seen such an army,
pitiful, futile, unfit;
Never was seen such a spirit,
manifold courage and grit.
Never has been such a cohort
under one banner unrolled
As surged to the ragged-edged Arctic,
urged by the arch-tempter—Gold.

"Farewell!" we cried to our dearests;
little we cared for their tears.
"Farewell!" we cried to the humdrum
and the yoke of the hireling years;
Just like a pack of schoolboys,
and the big crowd cheered us good bye.
Never were hearts so uplifted,
never were hopes so high.

The spectral shores flitted past us,
and every whirl of the screw
Hurled us nearer to fortune,
and ever we planned what we'd do—

Do with the gold when we got it—
big, shiny nuggets like plums,
There in the sand of the river,
gouging it out with our thumbs.

And one man wanted a castle,
another a racing stud;
A third would cruise in a palace yacht
like a red-necked prince of blood.
And so we dreamed and we vaunted,
millionaires to a man,
Leaping to wealth in our visions
long ere the trail began.

II

We landed in wind-swept Skagway.
We joined the weltering mass,
Clamoring over their outfits,
waiting to climb the Pass.
We tightened our girths and our pack-straps;
we linked on the Human Chain,
Struggling up to the summit,
where every step was a pain.

Gone was the joy of our faces,
grim and haggard and pale;
The heedless mirth of the shipboard
was changed to the care of the trail.
We flung ourselves in the struggle,
packing our grub in relays,
Step by step to the summit
in the bale of the winter days.

Floundering deep in the sump-holes,
stumbling out again;
Crying with cold and weakness,
crazy with fear and pain.
Then from the depths of our travail,
ere our spirits were broke,
Grim, tenacious and savage,
the lust of the trail awoke.

For grub meant gold to our thinking,
and all that could walk must pack;
The sheep for the shambles stumbled,
each with a load on its back;
And even the swine were burdened,
and grunted and squealed and rolled,
And men went mad in the moment,
huskily clamoring, "Gold!"

"Klondike or bust!" rang the slogan;
every man for his own.
Oh, how we flogged the horses,
staggering skin and bone!

Oh, how we cursed their weakness,
anguish they could not tell,
Breaking their hearts in our passion,
lashing them on till they fell!

Oh, we were brutes and devils,
goaded by lust and fear!
Our eyes were strained to the summit;
the weaklings dropped to the rear,
Falling in heaps by the trail-side,
heart-broken, limp, and wan;
But the gaps closed up in an instant,
and heedless the chain went on.

Never will I forget it,
there on the mountain face,
Ant-like, men with their burdens,
clinging in icy space;
Dogged, determined and dauntless,
cruel and callous and cold,
Cursing, blaspheming, reviling,
and ever that battle-cry—"Gold!"

Thus toiled we, the army of fortune,
in hunger and hope and despair,
Till glacier, mountain and forest
vanished, and, radiantly fair,
There at our feet lay Lake Bennett,
and down to its welcome we ran:
The trail of the land was over,
the trail of the water began.

III

We built our boats and we launched them.
Never has been such a fleet;
A packing-case for a bottom,
a mackinaw for a sheet.
Shapeless, grotesque, lopsided,
flimsy, makeshift and crude,
Each man after his fashion

builded as best he could.

Each man worked like a demon,
as prow to rudder we raced;
The winds of the Wild cried "Hurry!"
the voice of the waters, "Haste!"
We hated those driving before us;
we dreaded those pressing behind;
We cursed the slow current that bore us;
we prayed to the God of the wind.

Spring! and the hillsides flourished,
vivid in jeweled green;
Spring! and our hearts' blood nourished
envy and hatred and spleen.
Little cared we for the Spring-birth;
much cared we to get on—
Stake in the Great White Channel,
stake ere the best be gone.

The greed of the gold possessed us;
pity and love were forgot;
Covetous visions obsessed us;
brother with brother fought.
Partner with partner wrangled,
each one claiming his due;
Wrangled and halved their outfits,
sawing their boats in two.

Thuswise we voyaged Lake Bennett,
Tagish, then Windy Arm,
Sinister, savage and baleful,
boding us hate and harm.
Many a scow was shattered
there on that iron shore;
Many a heart was broken
straining at sweep and oar.

We roused Lake Marsh with a chorus,
we drifted many a mile.
There was the canyon before us—
cave-like its dark defile;
The shores swept faster and faster;

the river narrowed to wrath;
Waters that hissed disaster
reared upright in our path.

Beneath us the green tumult churning,
above us the cavernous gloom;
Around us, swift twisting and turning,
the black, sullen walls of a tomb.
We spun like a chip in a mill-race;
our hearts hammered under the test;
Then—oh, the relief on each chill face!—
we soared into sunlight and rest.

Hand sought for hand on the instant.
Cried we, "Our troubles are o'er!"
Then, like a rumble of thunder,
heard we a canorous roar.
Leaping and boiling and seething,
saw we a cauldron afume;
There was the rage of the rapids,
there was the menace of doom.

The river springs like a racer,
sweeps through a gash in the rock;
Butts at the boulder-ribbed bottom,
staggers and rears at the shock;
Leaps like a terrified monster,
writhes in its fury and pain;
Then with the crash of a demon
springs to the onset again.

Dared we that ravening terror;
heard we its din in our ears;
Called on the Gods of our fathers,
juggled forlorn with our fears;
Sank to our waists in its fury,
tossed to the sky like a fleece;
Then, when our dread was the greatest,
crashed into safety and peace.

But what of the others that followed,
losing their boats by the score?
Well could we see them and hear them,

strung down that desolate shore.
What of the poor souls that perished?
Little of them shall be said—
On to the Golden Valley!
Pause not to bury the dead.

Then there were days of drifting,
breezes soft as a sigh;
Night trailed her robe of jewels
over the floor of the sky.
The moonlit stream was a python,
silver, sinuous, vast,
That writhed on a shroud of velvet—
well, it was done at last.

There were the tents of Dawson,
there the scar of the slide;
Swiftly we poled o'er the shallows,
swiftly leapt o'er the side.
Fires fringed the mouth of Bonanza;
sunset gilded the dome;
The test of the trail was over—
thank God, thank God, we were Home!

REX BEACH

The Test

Rex Beach (1877–1949) was born in Atwood, Michigan, but at an early age was taken to Florida by his parents where they became "squatters" under the Homestead Act on a deserted military base near Tampa. Before venturing to Alaska, Beach attended the Kent College of Law in Chicago. *The Spoilers* was published in 1905 and became a best-seller. This novel, *The Barrier* (Harper, 1908), and *The Silver Horde* (Harper, 1909)—all set in Alaska—comprise his best work and may still be read with enjoyment to this day. He was the first American author to include a clause in all his book contracts reserving film rights, and his aptitude for business was in turn reflected by the success he later enjoyed as a film producer. The last two years of his life were fraught with suffering from inoperable cancer of the throat and increasing blindness. He shot himself on December 7, 1949. "The Test" was Rex Beach's second published story, appearing in *McClure's Magazine* (Dec. 1904). It was subsequently collected in book form by the author in *Pardners* (McClure, 1905).

This is a story of a burden, the tale of a load that irked a strong man's shoulders. To those who do not know the North it may seem strange, but to those who understand the humors of men in solitude, and the extravagant vagaries that steal in upon their minds, as fog drifts with the night, it will not appear unusual. There are spirits in the wilderness, eerie forces which play pranks—some droll or whimsical, others grim.

Johnny Cantwell and Mortimer Grant were partners, trailmates, brothers in soul if not in blood. The ebb and flow of frontier life had brought them together; its hardships had united them until they were as one. They were something of a mystery to each other, neither having surrendered all his confidence, and because of this they retained their mutual attraction. Had they known each other fully, had they thoroughly sounded each other's depths, they would have lost interest, just like husbands and wives who give themselves too freely and reserve nothing.

They had met by accident, but they remained together by desire, and so satisfactory was the union that not even the jealousy of women had come between them. There had been women, of course, just as there had been adventures of other sorts, but the love of the partners was larger and finer than anything else they had experienced. It was so true and fine and unselfish, in fact, that either would have willingly relinquished the woman of his desires had the other wished to possess her. They were young, strong men, and the world was full of sweethearts, but where was there a partnership like theirs? they asked themselves.

The spirit of adventure bubbled merrily within them, too, and it led them into curious byways. It was this which sent them northward from the States in the dead of winter, on the heels of the Stony River strike; it was this which induced them to land at Katmai instead of Illiamna, whither their land journey should have commenced.

"There are two routes over the coast range," the captain of the *Dora* told them, "and only two. Illiamna Pass is low and easy, but the distance is longer than by way of Katmai. I can land you at either place."

"Katmai is pretty tough, isn't it?" Grant inquired.

"We've understood it's the worst pass in Alaska." Cantwell's eyes were eager.

"It's a heller! Nobody travels it except natives, and they don't like it. Now, Illiamna. . . ."

"We'll try Katmai. Eh, Mort?"

"Sure! They don't come hard enough for us, Cap. We'll see if it's as bad as it's painted."

So, one gray January morning they were landed on a frozen beach; their outfit was flung ashore through the surf, the lifeboat pulled away, and the *Dora* disappeared after a farewell toot of her whistle. Their last glimpse of her showed the captain waving good bye and the purser flapping a red tablecloth at them from the after-deck.

"Cheerful place, this," Grant remarked, as he noted the desolate surroundings of dune and hillside.

The beach itself was black and raw where the surf washed it, but elsewhere all was white, save for the thickets of alder and willow which protruded nakedly. The bay was little more than a hollow scooped out of the Alaskan range; along the foothills behind there was a belt of spruce and cottonwood and birch. It was a lonely and apparently unpeopled wilderness in which they had been set down.

"Seems good to be back in the North again, doesn't it?" said Cantwell cheerily. "I'm tired of the booze, and the streetcars, and the dames, and all that civilized stuff. I'd rather be broke in Alaska . . . with you . . . than a banker's son, back home."

Soon a globular Russian half-breed, the Katmai trader, appeared among the dunes, and with him were some native villagers. That night the partners slept in a snug log cabin, the roof of which was chained down with old ships' cables. Petellin, the fat little trader, explained that roofs in Katmai had a way of sailing off to seaward when the wind blew. He listened to their plan of crossing the divide and nodded.

It could be done, of course, he agreed, but they were foolish to try it, when the Illiamna route was open. Still, now that they were here, he would find dogs for them, and a guide. The village hunters were out after meat, however, and, until they returned, the white men would need to wait in patience.

There followed several days of idleness, during which Cantwell and Grant amused themselves around the village, teasing the squaws, playing games with the boys, and flirting harmlessly with the girls, one of whom, in particular, was not unattractive. She was perhaps three-quarters Aleut, the other quarter being plain coquette, and, having been educated at the town of Kodiak, she knew the ways and the wiles of the white man.

Cantwell approached her, and she met his extravagant advances more than halfway. They were getting along nicely together when Grant, in a spirit of fun, entered the game and won her fickle smiles for himself. He joked his partner unmercifully, and Johnny accepted defeat gracefully, never giving the matter a second thought.

When the hunters returned, dogs were bought, a guide was hired, and, a week after landing, the friends were camped at timberline awaiting a favorable moment for their dash across the range. Above them white hillsides rose in irregular leaps to the gash in the saw-toothed barrier which formed the pass; below them a short valley led down to Katmai and the sea. The day was bright, the air clear; nevertheless, after the guide had stared up at the peaks for a time, he shook his head, then reentered the tent and lay down. The mountains were "smoking"—from their tops streamed a gossamer veil which the travelers knew to be drifting snow clouds carried by the wind. It meant delay, but they were patient.

They were up and going on the following morning, however, with the Indian in the lead. There was no trail; the hills were steep; in places they were forced to unload the sled and hoist their outfit by means of ropes; and, as they mounted higher, the snow deepened. It lay like loose sand, only lighter; it shoved ahead of the sled in a feathery mass; the dogs wallowed in it and were unable to pull, hence the greater part of the work devolved upon the men. Once above the foothills and into the range proper, the going became more level, but the snow remained knee-deep.

The Indian broke trail stolidly; the partners strained at the sled, which hung back like a leaden thing. By afternoon the dogs had become disheartened and refused to heed the whip. There was neither fuel nor running water, and therefore the party did not pause for luncheon. The men were sweating profusely from their exertions and had long since become parched with thirst, but the dry snow was like chalk and scoured their throats.

Cantwell was the first to show the effects of his unusual exertions, for not only had he assumed a lion's share of the work, but the last few months of easy living had softened his muscles, and in consequence his vitality was quickly spent. His undergarments were drenched; he was fearfully dry inside; a terrible thirst seemed to penetrate his whole body; he was forced to rest frequently.

Grant eyed him with some concern, finally inquiring: "Feel bad, Johnny?"

Cantwell nodded. Their fatigue made both men economical of language. "What's the matter?"

"Thirsty!" The former could barely speak.

"There won't be any water till we get across. You'll have to stand it."

They resumed their duties; the Indian *swish-swished* ahead, as if wading through a sea of swan's-down; the dogs followed listlessly; the partners leaned against the stubborn load.

A faint breath finally came out of the north, causing Grant and the guide to study the sky anxiously. Cantwell was too weary to heed the increasing cold. The snow on the slopes above began to move; here and there, on exposed ridges, it rose in clouds and puffs; the clean-cut outlines of the hills became obscured as by a fog; the languid wind bit cruelly.

After a time Johnny fell back upon the sled and exclaimed: "I'm . . . all in, Mort. Don't seem to have the . . . guts." He was pale; his eyes were tortured. He scooped a mitten full of snow and raised it to his lips, then spat it out, still dry.

"Here! Brace up!" In a panic of apprehension at this collapse Grant shook him; he had never known Johnny to fail like this. "Take a drink of booze . . . it'll do you good." He drew a bottle of brandy from one of the dunnage bags, and Cantwell seized it avidly. It was wet; it would quench his thirst, he thought. Before Mort could check him, he had drunk a third of the contents.

The effect was almost instantaneous, for Cantwell's stomach was empty and his tissues seemed to absorb the liquor like a dry sponge; his fatigue fell away; he became suddenly strong and vigorous again. But before he had gone a hundred yards the reaction followed. First his mind grew thick, then his limbs became unmanageable and his muscles flabby. He was drunk. Yet it was a strange and dangerous intoxication, against which he struggled desperately. He fought it for perhaps a quarter of a mile before it mastered him; then he gave up.

Both men knew that stimulants are never taken on the trail, but they had never stopped to reason why, and even now they did not attribute Johnny's breakdown to the brandy. After a while he stumbled and fell; then, the cool snow being grateful to his face, he sprawled there motionless until Mort dragged him to the sled. He stared at his partner in perplexity and laughed foolishly. The wind was increasing; darkness was near; they had not yet reached the Bering slope.

Something in the drunken man's face frightened Grant and, extracting a ship's biscuit from the grub box, he said, hurriedly: "Here, Johnny. Get something under your belt, quick."

Cantwell obediently munched the hard cracker, but there was no moisture on his tongue; his throat was paralyzed; the crumbs crowded themselves from the corners of his lips. He tried with limber fingers to stuff them down, or to assist the muscular action of swallowing, but finally expelled them in a cloud. Mort drew the parka hood over his partner's head, for the wind cut like a scythe and the dogs were turning tail to it, digging holes in the snow for protection. The air about them was like yeast; the light was fading.

The Indian snow-shoed his way back, advising a quick camp until the storm abated, but to this suggestion Grant refused to listen, knowing only too well the peril of such a course. Nor did he dare take Johnny on the sled, since the fellow was half asleep already, but instead whipped up the dogs and urged his companion to follow as best he could.

When Cantwell fell, for a second time, he returned, dragged him forward, and tied his wrists firmly, yet loosely, to the load.

The storm was pouring over them now, like water out of a spout; it seared and blinded them; its touch was like that of a flame. Nevertheless they struggled on into the smother, making what headway they could. The Indian led, pulling at the end of a rope; Grant strained at the sled and hoarsely encouraged the dogs; Cantwell stumbled and lurched in the rear like an unwilling prisoner. When he fell, his companion lifted him, then beat him, cursed him, tried in every way to rouse him from his lethargy.

After an interminable time they found they were descending and this gave them heart to plunge ahead more rapidly. The dogs began to trot as the sled overran them; they rushed blindly into gullies, fetching up at the bottom in a tangle, and Johnny followed in a nerveless, stupefied condition. He was dragged like a sack of flour, for his legs were limp and he lacked muscular control, but every dash, every fall, every quick descent drove the sluggish blood through his veins and cleared his brain momentarily. Such moments were fleeting, however; much of the time his mind was a blank, and it was only by a mechanical effort that he fought off unconsciousness.

He had vague memories of many beatings at Mort's hands, of the slippery clean-swept ice of a stream over which he limply skidded, of being carried into a tent where a candle flickered and a stove roared. Grant was holding something hot to his lips, and then. . . .

It was morning. He was weak and sick; he felt as if he had awakened from a hideous dream. "I played out, didn't I?" he queried wonderingly.

"You sure did," Grant laughed. "It was a tight squeak, old boy. I never thought I'd get you through."

"Played out! I . . . can't understand it." Cantwell prided himself on his strength and stamina, therefore the truth was unbelievable. He and Mort had long been partners; they had given and taken much at each other's hands, but this was something altogether different. Grant had saved his life, at risk of his own; the older man's endurance had been the greater, and he had used it to good advantage. It embarrassed Johnny tremendously to realize that he had proven unequal to his share of the work, for he had never before experienced such an obligation. He apologized repeatedly during the few days he lay sick, and meanwhile Mort waited upon him like a mother.

Cantwell was relieved when at last they had abandoned camp, changed guides at the next village, and were on their way along the coast, for somehow he felt very sensitive about his collapse. He was, in fact, extremely ashamed of himself.

Once he had fully recovered, he had no further trouble, but soon rounded into fit condition and showed no effects of his ordeal. Day after day he and Mort traveled through the solitudes, their isolation broken only by occasional glimpses of native villages, where they rested briefly and renewed their supply of dog feed.

But although the younger man was now as well and strong as ever, he was uncomfortably conscious that his trailmate regarded him as the weaker of the two and shielded him in many ways. Grant performed most of the unpleasant tasks, and occasionally cautioned Johnny about overdoing. This protective attitude at first amused, then offended, Cantwell; it galled him until he was upon the point of voicing his resentment, but reflected that he had no right to object, for, judging by past performance, he had proven his inferiority. This uncomfortable realization forever arose to prevent open rebellion, but he asserted himself secretly by robbing Grant of his self-appointed tasks. He rose first in the mornings; he did the cooking; he lengthened his turns ahead of the dogs; he mended harness after the day's hike had ended. Of course, the older man objected, and for a time they had a good-natured rivalry as to who should work and who should rest—only it was not quite so good-natured on Cantwell's part as he made it appear.

Mort broke out in friendly irritation one day: "Don't try to do everything, Johnny. Remember I'm no cripple."

"Humph! You proved that. I guess it's up to me to do your work."

"Oh, forget that day on the pass, can't you?"

Johnny grunted a second time, and from his tone it was evident that he would never forget, unpleasant though the memory remained. Sensing his sullen resentment, the other tried to rally him, but made a bad job of it. The humor of men in the open is not delicate; their wit and their words become coarsened in direct proportion as they revert to the primitive; it is one effect of the solitudes.

Grant spoke extravagantly, mockingly, of his own superiority in a way which ordinarily would have brought a smile to Cantwell's lips, but the latter did not smile. He taunted Johnny humorously on his lack of physical prowess, his lack of good looks and manly qualities—something which had never failed to result in a friendly exchange of badinage; he even teased him about his defeat with the Katmai girl.

Cantwell did respond finally, but afterward he found himself wondering if Mort could have been in earnest. He dismissed the thought with some impatience. But men on the trail have too much time for their thoughts; there is nothing in the monotonous routine of the day's work to distract them, so the partner who had played out dwelt more and more upon his debt and upon his friend's easy assumption of preeminence. The weight of obligation began to chafe him, lightly at first, but with ever-increasing discomfort. He began to think that Grant honestly considered himself the better man, merely because chance had played into his hands.

It was silly, even childish, to dwell on the subject, he reflected, and yet he could not banish it from his mind. It was always before him, in one form or another. He felt the strength in his lean muscles, and sneered at the thought that Mort should be deceived. If it came to a physical test, he felt sure he could break his slighter partner with his bare hands, and as for endurance—well, he was hungry for a chance to demonstrate it.

They talked little; men seldom converse in the wastes, for there is something about the silence of the wilderness which discourages speech. And no land is so grimly silent, so hushed and soundless, as the frozen North. For days they marched through desolation, without glimpse of human habitation, without sight of track or trail, without sound of a human voice to break the monotony. There was no game in the country, with the exception of an occasional bird or rabbit, nothing but the white hills, the fringe of aldertops along the watercourses, and the thickets of gnarled, unhealthy spruce in the smothered valleys.

Their destination was a mysterious stream at the headwaters of the un-mapped Kuskokwim, where rumor said there was gold, and whither they feared other men were hastening from the mining country far to the north.

Now it is a penalty of the White Country that men shall think of women. The open life brings health and vigor, strength and animal vitality, and these clamor for play. The cold of the still, clear days is no more biting than the fierce memories and appetites which charge through the brain at night. Passions intensify with imprisonment; recollections come to life; longings grow vivid and wild. Thoughts change to realities, the past creeps close, and dream figures are filled with blood and fire. One remembers pleasures and excesses, women's smiles, women's kisses, the invitation of outstretched arms. Wasted opportunities mock at one.

Cantwell began to brood upon the Katmai girl, for she was the last; her eyes were haunting, and distance had worked its usual enchantment. He reflected that Mort had shouldered him aside and won her favor, then boasted of it. Johnny awoke one night with a dream of her, and lay quivering.

"Hell! She was only a squaw," he said, half aloud. "If I'd really tried. . . ."

Grant lay beside him, snoring; the heat of their bodies intermingled. The waking man tried to compose himself, but his partner's stertorous breathing irritated him beyond measure; for a long time he remained motionless, staring into the gray blur of the tent-top. He had played out. He owed his life to the man who had cheated him of the Katmai girl, and that man knew it. He had become a weak, helpless thing, dependent upon another's strength, and that other now accepted his superiority as a matter of course. The obligation was insufferable, and—it was unjust. The North had played him a devilish trick; it had betrayed him; it had bound him to his benefactor with chains of gratitude which were irksome. Had they been real chains they could have galled him no more than at this moment.

As time passed, the men spoke less frequently to each other. Grant joshed his mate roughly, once or twice, masking beneath an assumption of jocularity his own vague irritation at the change that had come over them. It was as if he had probed at an open wound with clumsy fingers.

Cantwell had by this time assumed most of those petty camp tasks which provoke tired trailers, those humdrum duties which are so trying to exhausted nerves, and, of course, they wore upon him as they wear upon every man. But, once he had taken them over, he began to resent Grant's easy relinquishment; it rankled him to realize how willingly the other allowed him to do the cooking, the dishwashing, the fire-building, the bed-making. Little monotonies of this kind form the hardest part of winter travel; they are the rocks upon which friendships founder and partnerships are wrecked.

Out on the trail, nature equalizes the work to a great extent, and no man can shirk unduly, but in camp, inside the cramped confines of a tent pitched on boughs laid over the snow, it is very different. There one must busy himself while the other rests and keeps his legs out of the way if possible. One man sits on the bedding at the rear of the shelter, and shivers, while the other squats over a tantalizing fire of green wood, blistering to his face and parboiling his limbs inside his sweaty clothing. Dishes must be passed, food divided, and it is poor food, poorly prepared at best. Sometimes men criticize and voice longings for better grub and better cooking. Remarks of this kind have been known to result in tragedies, bitter words and flaming curses—then, perhaps, wild actions, memories of which the later years can never erase. It is but one prank of the wilderness, one grim manifestation of its silent forces.

Had Grant been unable to do his part, Cantwell would have willingly accepted the added burden, but Mort was able; he was nimble and "handy"; he was the better cook of the two; in fact, he was the better man in every way—or so he believed. Cantwell sneered at the last thought, and the memory of his debt was like bitter medicine.

His resentment—in reality nothing more than a phase of insanity begot of isolation and silence—could not help but communicate itself to his companion, and there resulted a mutual antagonism, which grew into a dislike, then festered into something more, something strange, reasonless, yet terribly vivid and amazingly potent for evil. Neither man ever mentioned it—their tongues were clenched between their teeth, and they held themselves in check with harsh hands—but it was constantly in their minds, nevertheless. No man who has not suffered the manifold irritations of such an intimate association can appreciate the gnawing canker of animosity like this. It was dangerous because there was no relief from it: the two were bound together as by gyves; they shared each other's every action and every plan; they trod in each other's tracks, slept in the same bed, ate from the same plate. They were like prisoners ironed to the same staple.

Each fought the obsession in his own way, but it is hard to fight the impalpable, hence their sick fancies grew in spite of themselves. Their minds needed food to prey upon, but found none. Each began to criticize the other silently, to sneer at his weaknesses, to meditate derisively upon his peculiarities. After a time they no longer resisted the advance of these poisonous thoughts, but welcomed it.

On more than one occasion the embers of their wrath were upon the point of bursting into flame, but each realized that the first ill-considered word would serve to slip the leash from those demons that were straining to go free, and so managed to restrain himself.

The crisis came one crisp morning when a dog team whirled around a bend in the river and a white man hailed them. He was the mail carrier, on his way out from Nome, and he brought news of the "inside."

"Where are you boys bound for?" he inquired when greetings were over and gossip of the trail had passed.

"We're going to the Stony River strike," Grant told him.

"Stony River? Up the Kuskokwim?"

"Yes!"

The mailman laughed. "Can you beat that? Ain't you heard about Stony River?"

"No!"

"Why, it's a fake . . . no such place."

There was a silence; the partners avoided each other's eyes.

"MacDonald, the fellow that started it, is on his way to Dawson. There's a gang after him, too, and, if he's caught, it'll go hard with him. He wrote the letters . . . to himself . . . and spread the news just to raise a grubstake. He cleaned up big before they got onto him. He peddled the tips for real money."

"Yes," Grant spoke quietly. "Johnny bought one. That's what brought us from Seattle. We went out on the last boat and figured we'd come in from this side before the breakup. So . . . fake. By God!"

"Gee! You fellers bit good." The mail carrier shook his head. "Well, you'd better keep going now. You'll get to Nome before the season opens. Better take dog fish from Bethel . . . it's four bits a pound on the Yukon. Sorry I didn't hit your camp last night. We'd 'a' had a visit. Tell the gang that you saw me." He shook hands ceremoniously, yelled at his panting dogs, and went swiftly on his way, waving a mitten on high as he vanished around the next bend.

The partners watched him go, then Grant turned to Johnny, and repeated: "Fake! By God! MacDonald stung you."

Cantwell's face went as white as the snow behind him; his eyes blazed. "Why did you tell him I bit?" he demanded harshly.

"Hunh! *Didn't* you bite? Two thousand miles afoot . . . three months of hell, for nothing. That's biting some."

"*Well!*" The speaker's face was convulsed, and Grant's flamed with an answering anger. They glared at each other for a moment. "Don't blame me. You fell for it, too."

"I. . . ," Mort checked his rushing words.

"Yes, *you!* Now, what are you going to do about it? Welch?"

"I'm going through to Nome." The sight of his partner's rage had set Mort to shaking with a furious desire to fly at his throat, but, fortunately, he retained a spark of sanity.

"Then shut up, and quit chewing the rag. You . . . talk too damned much."

Mort's eyes were bloodshot; they fell upon the carbine under the sled lashings, and lingered there, then wavered. He opened his lips, reconsidered, spoke softly to the team, then lifted the heavy dog whip and smote the malamutes with all his strength.

The men resumed their journey without further words, but each was cursing inwardly.

So! I talk too much, Grant thought. The accusation stuck in his mind, and he determined to speak no more.

He blames me, Cantwell reflected bitterly. *I'm in wrong again, and he couldn't keep his mouth shut. A hell of a partner, he is!*

All day they plodded on, neither trusting himself to speak. They ate their evening meal like mutes; they avoided each other's eyes. Even the guide noticed the change and looked on curiously.

There were two robes and these the partners shared nightly, but their hatred had grown so during the past few hours that the thought of lying side by side, limb to limb, was distasteful. Yet neither dared suggest a division of the bedding, for that would have brought further words and resulted in the crash which they longed for, but feared. They stripped off their furs, and lay down beside each other with the same repugnance they would have felt had there been a serpent in the bedding.

This unending malevolent silence became terrible. The strain of it increased, for each man now had something definite to cherish in the words and the looks that had passed. They divided the camp work with scrupulous nicety; each man waited upon himself and asked no favors. The knowledge of his debt forever chafed Cantwell; Grant resented his companion's lack of gratitude.

Of course, they spoke occasionally—it was beyond human endurance to remain entirely dumb—but they conversed in monosyllables, about trivial things, and their voices were throaty, as if the effort choked them. Meanwhile they continued to glow inwardly at a white heat.

Cantwell no longer felt the desire merely to match his strength against Grant's; the estrangement had become too wide for that; a physical victory would have been flat and tasteless; he craved some deeper satisfaction. He began to think of the axe—just how or when or why he never knew. It was a thin-bladed, polished thing of frosty steel, and the more he thought of it the stronger grew his impulse to rid himself once and for all of that presence which exasperated him. It would be very easy, he reasoned; a sudden blow, with the weight of his shoulders behind it—he fancied he could feel the bit sink into Grant's flesh, cleaving bone and cartilage in its course—a slanting downward stroke, aimed at the neck where it joined the body, and he would be forever satisfied. It would be ridiculously simple. He practiced in the gloom of evening as he felled spruce trees for firewood; he guarded the axe religiously; it became a living thing which urged him on to violence. He saw it standing by the tent fly when he closed his eyes to sleep; he dreamed of it; he sought it out with his eyes when he first awoke. He slid it loosely under the sled lashings every morning, thinking that its use could not long be delayed.

As for Grant, the carbine dwelt forever in his mind, and his fingers itched for it. He secretly slipped a cartridge into the chamber, and, when an occasional ptarmigan offered itself for a target, he saw the white spot on the breast of Johnny's reindeer parka, dancing ahead of the Lyman bead.

The solitude had done its work; the North had played its grim comedy to the final curtain, making sport of men's affections and turning love to rankling hate. But into the mind of each man crept a certain craftiness. Each longed to strike, but feared to face the consequences. It was lonesome, here among the white hills and the deathly silences, yet they reflected that it would be still more lonesome if they were left to keep step with nothing more substantial than a memory. They determined, therefore, to wait until civilization was nearer, meanwhile rehearsing the moment they knew was inevitable. Over and over in their thoughts each of them enacted the scene, ending it always with the picture of a prostrate man in a patch of trampled snow which grew crimson as the other gloated.

They paused at Bethel Mission long enough to load with dried salmon, then made the ninety-mile portage over the lake and tundra to the Yukon. There they got their first touch of the "inside" world. They camped in a *barabara* where white men had slept a few nights before, and heard their own language spoken by native tongues. The time was growing short now, and they purposely dismissed their guide, knowing that the trail was plain from there on. When they hitched up on the next morning, Cantwell placed the axe, bit down, between the tarpaulin and the sled rail, leaving the helve projecting where his hand could reach it. Grant thrust the barrel of the rifle beneath a lashing, with the butt close by the handlebars, and it was loaded.

A mile from the village they were overtaken by an Indian and his squaw, traveling light behind hungry dogs. The natives attached themselves to the white men and hung stubbornly to their heels, taking advantage of their tracks. When night came, they camped alongside, in the hope of food. They announced that they were bound for St. Michael's, and in spite of every effort to shake them off they remained close behind the partners until that point was reached.

At St. Michael's there were white men, practically the first Johnny and Mort had encountered since landing at Katmai, and for a day at least they were sane. But there were still three hundred miles to be traveled, three hundred miles of solitude and haunting thoughts. Just as they were about to start, Cantwell came upon Grant and the A. C. agent, and heard his name pronounced, also the word "Katmai." He noted that Mort fell silent at his approach, and instantly his anger blazed afresh. He decided that the latter had been telling the story of their experience on the pass and boasting of his service. So much the better, he thought, in a blind rage; that which he planned doing would appear all the more like an accident, for who would dream that a man could kill the person to whom he owed his life?

That night he waited for a chance.

They were camped in a dismal hut on a windswept shore; they were alone. But Grant was waiting also, it seemed. They lay down beside each other, ostensibly to sleep; their limbs touched; the warmth from their bodies intermingled, but they did not close their eyes.

They were up and away early, with Nome drawing rapidly nearer. They had skirted an ocean, foot by foot; Bering Sea lay behind them, now, and its northern shore swung westward to their goal. For two months they had lived in silent animosity, feeding on bitter food while their elbows rubbed.

Noon found them floundering through one of those unheralded storms which make coast travel so hazardous. The morning had turned off gray; the sky was of a leaden hue which blended perfectly with the snow underfoot; there was no horizon; it was impossible to see more than a few yards in any direction. The trail soon became obliterated, and their eyes began to play tricks. For all they could distinguish, they might have been suspended in space; they seemed to be treading the measures of an endless dance in the center of a whirling cloud. Of course it was cold, for the wind off the open sea was damp, but they were not men to turn back.

They soon discovered that their difficulty lay not in facing the storm, but in holding to the trail. That narrow, two-foot causeway, packed by a winter's travel and frozen into a ribbon of ice by a winter's frosts, afforded their only avenue of progress, for the moment they left it the sled plowed into the loose snow, well-nigh disappearing and bringing the dogs to a standstill. It was the duty of the driver, in such case, to wallow forward, right the load if necessary, and lift it back into place. These mishaps were forever occurring, for it was impossible to distinguish the trail beneath its soft covering. However, if the driver's task was hard, it was no more trying than that of the man ahead, who was compelled to feel out and explore the ridge of hardened snow and ice with his feet, after the fashion of a man walking a plank in the dark. Frequently he lunged into the drifts with one foot, or both; his glazed mukluk soles slid about, causing him to bestride the invisible hogback, or again his legs crossed awkwardly, throwing him off his balance. At times he wandered away from the path entirely and had to search it out again. These exertions were very wearing, and they were dangerous, also, for joints are easily dislocated, muscles twisted, and tendons strained.

Hour after hour the march continued, unrelieved by any change, unbroken by any speck or spot of color. The nerves of their eyes, wearied by constant nearsighted peering at the snow, began to jump so that vision became untrustworthy. Both travelers appreciated the necessity of clinging to the trail, for, once they lost it, they knew they might wander about indefinitely until they chanced to regain it or found their way to the shore, while always to seaward was the menace of open water, of air holes, or cracks which might gape beneath their feet like jaws. Immersion in this temperature, no matter how brief, meant death.

The monotony of progress through this unreal, leaden world became almost unbearable. The repeated strainings and twistings they suffered in walking the slippery ridge reduced the men to weariness; their legs grew clumsy and their feet uncertain. Had they found a camping place, they would have stopped, but they dared not forsake the thin thread that linked them with safety to go and look for one, not knowing where the shore lay. In storms of this kind men have lain in their sleeping bags for days within a stone's throw of a road house or village. Bodies have been found within a hundred yards of shelter after blizzards have abated. Cantwell and Grant had no choice, therefore, except to bore into the welter of drifting flakes.

It was late in the afternoon when the latter met with an accident. Johnny, who had taken a spell at the rear, heard him cry out, saw him stagger, struggle to hold his footing, then sink into the snow. The dogs paused instantly, lay down, and began to strip the ice pellets from between their toes.

Cantwell spoke harshly, leaning upon the handlebars: "Well! What's the idea?"

It was the longest silence of the day.

"I've . . . hurt myself." Mort's voice was thin and strange; he raised himself to a sitting posture, and reached beneath his parka, then lay back weakly.

He writhed; his face was twisted with pain. He continued to lie there, doubled into a knot of suffering. A groan was wrenched from between his teeth.

"Hurt? How?" Johnny inquired dully.

It seemed very ridiculous to see that strong man kicking around in the snow.

"I've ripped something loose . . . here." Mort's palms were pressed in upon his groin; his fingers were clutching something. "Ruptured . . . I guess." He tried again to rise, but sank back. His cap had fallen off, and his forehead glistened with sweat.

Cantwell went forward and lifted him. It was the first time in many days that their hands had touched, and the sensation affected him strangely. He struggled to repress a devilish mirth at the thought that Grant had played out—it amounted to that and nothing less; the trail had delivered him into his enemy's hands; his hour had struck. Johnny determined to square the debt now, once for all, and wipe his own mind clean of that poison which corroded it. His muscles were strong; his brain clear; he had never felt his strength so irresistible as at this moment, while Mort, for all his boasted superiority, was nothing but a nerveless thing hanging limp against his breast. Providence had arranged it all. The younger man was impelled to give raucous voice to his glee, and yet—his helpless burden exerted an odd effect on him.

He deposited his foe upon the sled and stared at the face he had not met for many days. He saw how white it was, how wet and cold, how weak and dazed; then, as he looked, he cursed inwardly, for the triumph of his moment was spoiled.

The axe was there; its polished bit showed like a piece of ice; its helve protruded handily, but there was no need of it now; his fingers were all the weapons Johnny needed; they were more sufficient, in fact, for Mort was like a child.

Cantwell was a strong man, and, although the North had coarsened him, yet underneath the surface was a chivalrous regard for all things weak, and this the trail madness had not affected. He had longed for this instant, but now that it had come he felt no enjoyment, since he could not harm a sick man and waged no war on cripples. Perhaps, when Mort had rested, they could settle their quarrel; this was as good a place as any. The storm hid them; they would leave no traces; there could be no interruption.

But Mort did not rest. He could not walk; movement brought excruciating pain.

Finally Cantwell heard himself saying: "Better wrap up and lie still for a while. I'll get the dogs under way." His words amazed him dully. They were not at all what he had intended to say.

The injured man demurred, but the other insisted gruffly, then brought him his mittens and cap, slapping the snow out of them before rousing the team to motion. The load was very heavy now; the dogs had no footprints to guide them, and it required all of Cantwell's efforts to prevent capsizing. Night approached swiftly; the whirling snow particles continued to flow past upon the wind, shrouding the earth in an impenetrable pall.

The journey soon became a terrible ordeal, a slow, halting progress that led nowhere and was accomplished at the cost of tremendous exertion. Time after time Johnny broke trail, then returned and urged the Huskies forward to the end of his tracks. When he lost the path, he sought it out, laboriously hoisted the sledge back into place, and coaxed his four-footed helpers to renewed effort. He was drenched with perspiration; his inner garments were steaming; his outer ones were frozen into a coat of armor; when he paused, he chilled rapidly. His vision was untrustworthy, also, and he felt snow-blindness coming on. Grant begged him more than once to unroll the bedding and prepare to sleep out the storm; he even urged Johnny to leave him and make a dash for his own safety, but at this the younger man cursed and bade him hold his tongue.

Night found the lone driver slipping, plunging, lurching ahead of the dogs, or shoving at the handlebars and shouting at the dogs. Finally during a pause for rest he heard a sound which roused him. Out of the gloom to the right came the faint, complaining howl of a malamute; it was answered by his own dogs, and the next moment they had caught a scent which swerved them shoreward and led them scrambling through the drifts. Two hundred yards, and a steep bank loomed above, up and over which they rushed, with Cantwell yelling encouragement; then a light showed, and they were in the lee of a low-roofed hut.

A sick native, huddled over a Yukon stove, made them welcome to his mean abode, explaining that his wife and son had gone to Unalaklik for supplies.

Johnny carried his partner to the one unoccupied bunk and stripped his clothes from him. With his two hands he rubbed the warmth back into Mortimer's limbs, then swiftly prepared hot food, and, holding him in the hollow of his aching arm, fed him, a little at a time. He was like to drop from exhaustion, but he made no complaint. With one folded robe he made the hard boards comfortable, then spread the other as a covering. For himself he sat beside the fire and fought his weariness. When he dozed off and the cold awakened him, he renewed the fire; he heated beef tea, and, rousing Mort, fed it to him with a teaspoon. All night long at intervals, he tended the sick man, and Grant's eyes followed him with an expression that brought a fierce pain to Cantwell's throat.

"You're mighty good . . . after the rotten way I acted," the former whispered once.

And Johnny's big hand trembled so that he spilled the broth.

His voice was low and tender as he inquired: "Are you resting easier now?"

The other nodded.

"Maybe you're not hurt badly, after . . . all. God! That would be awful . . . ," Cantwell choked, turned away, and, raising his arms against the log wall, buried his face in them.

The morning broke clear; Grant was sleeping. As Johnny stiffly mounted the creek bank with a bucket of water, he heard a jingle of sleigh-bells and saw a sled with two white men swing in toward the cabin.

"Hello!" he called, then heard his own name pronounced.

"Johnny Cantwell, by all that's holy!"

The next moment he was shaking hands vigorously with two old friends from Nome.

"Martin and me are bound for Saint Mike's," one of them explained. "Where the deuce did you come from, Johnny?"

"The outside . . . started for Stony River, but. . . ."

"Stony River!" The newcomers began to laugh loudly and Cantwell joined them. It was the first time he had laughed for weeks. He realized the fact with a start, then recollected also his sleeping partner, and said: "Sh-h! Mort's inside, asleep!"

During the night everything had changed for Johnny Cantwell; his mental attitude, his hatred, his whole reasonless insanity. Everything was different now, even his debt was canceled, the weight of obligation was removed, and his diseased fancies were completely cured.

"Yes! Stony River," he repeated, grinning broadly. "I bit!"

Martin burst forth gleefully: "They caught MacDonald at Holy Cross and ran him out on a limb. He'll never start another stampede. Old Man Baker gun-branded him."

"What's the matter with Mort?" inquired the second traveler.

"He's resting up. Yesterday, during the storm, he. . . ." Johnny was on the point of saying "played out," but changed it to "had an accident. We thought it was serious, but a few days' rest'll bring him around all right. He saved me at Katmai, coming in. I petered out and threw up my tail, but he got me through. Come inside and tell him the news."

"Sure thing."

"Well, well!" Martin said. "So you and Mort are still partners, eh?"

"*Still* partners!" Johnny took up the pail of water. "Well, rather! We'll always be partners." His voice was young and full and hearty as he continued: "Why, Mort's the best damned fellow in the world. I'd lay down my life for him!"

JAMES OLIVER CURWOOD

The Strength of Men

James Oliver Curwood (1879–1927) was born in Owosso, Michigan. He was expelled from school at sixteen, although later he would attend the University of Michigan 1898–1900. He was first employed as a reporter for the *Detroit News-Tribune*
and, before he resigned to work for the Canadian government, he became the man-
aging editor. His novel, *Kazan* (Cosmopolitan Book Corporation, 1914), would be
his best-known work because of the number of motion pictures based on this canine
character. In fact, even more than for Rex Beach, it was motion-picture adaptations
that brought Curwood his greatest success and, in time, they exceeded even the
number of books he published in his lifetime. In all justice to Curwood, although he
was credited and paid for the stories, the screen adaptations often have nothing more
to do with his fiction than that they are set in the Canadian Northwest and have
Royal Mounted Policemen as protagonists. Curwood died at a relatively early age,
and his popularity with readers did not extend far beyond the 1930s when stories reprinted in pulp magazines and in economy hard-cover editions kept his name alive.
Judith A. Eldridge has provided a truly fine biography of the man and his work in
God's Country and the Man (Bowling Green Popular Press, 1993).

Jack London was the author Curwood most sought to emulate—sometimes he
would labor all day to write twelve lines that were acceptable to himself. Yet, there is
an inherent virtue in being first. If "The Test" by Rex Beach may be regarded as a
variation on a theme based on Jack London's "In a Far Country," this story by James
Oliver Curwood I would view as another.

There was the scent of battle in the air. The whole of Porcupine City knew
that it was coming, and every man and woman in its two hundred popula-
tion held their breath in anticipation of the struggle between two men for a
fortune—and a girl. For in some mysterious manner rumor of the girl had
got abroad, passing from lip to lip, until even the children knew that there
was some other thing than gold that would play a part in the fight between
Clarry O'Grady and Jan Larose. On the surface it was not scheduled to be a
fight with fists or guns. But in Porcupine City there were a few who knew
the "inner story"—the story of the girl, as well as the gold, and those among
them who feared the law would have arbitrated in a different manner for the
two men if it had been in their power.

But law is law, and the code was the code. There was no alternative. It was an unusual situation, and yet apparently simple of solution. Eighty miles north, as the canoe was driven, young Jan Larose had one day staked out a rich "find" at the headquarters of Pelican Creek. The same day, but later, Clarry O'Grady had driven his stakes beside Jan's. It had been a race to the mining recorder's office, and they had come in neck and neck. Popular sentiment favored Larose, the slim, quiet, dark-eyed half Frenchman. But there was the law, which had no sentiment. The recorder had sent an agent north to investigate. If there were two sets of stakes, there could be but one verdict. Both claims would be thrown out, and then. . . .

All knew what would happen, or thought that they knew. It would be a magnificent race to see who could set out fresh stakes and return to the recorder's office ahead of the other. It would be a fight of brawn and brain, unless—and those few who knew the "inner story" spoke softly among themselves.

An ox in strength, gigantic in build, with a face that for days had worn a sneering smile of triumph, O'Grady was already picked as a ten to one winner. He was a magnificent canoeman; no man in Porcupine City could equal him for endurance; and for his bow paddle he had the best Indian in the whole Reindeer Lake country. He stalked up and down the one street of Porcupine City, treating to drinks, cracking rough jokes, and offering wagers, while Jan Larose and his long-armed Cree sat quietly in the shade of the recorder's office waiting for the final moment to come.

There were a few of those who knew the "inner story" who saw something besides resignation and despair in Jan's quiet aloofness, and in the disconsolate droop of his head. His face turned a shade whiter when O'Grady passed near, dropping insult, and taunt, and looking sidewise at him in a way that only *he* could understand. But he made no retort, though his dark eyes glowed with a fire that never quite died—unless it was when, alone and unobserved, he took from his pocket a bit of buckskin in which was a silken tress of curling brown hair. Then his eyes shone with a light that was soft and luminous, and one seeing him then would have known that it was not a dream of gold that filled his heart but of a brown-haired girl who had broken it.

On this day, the forenoon of the sixth since the agent had departed into the north, the end of the tense period of waiting was expected. Porcupine City had almost ceased to carry on the daily monotony of business. A score were lounging about the recorder's office. Women looked forth at frequent intervals through the open doors of the city's cabins, or gathered in twos and threes to discuss this biggest sporting event ever known in the history of the town. Not a minute but scores of anxious eyes were turned searchingly up the river, down which the returning agent's canoe would first appear. With the dawn of this day O'Grady had refused to drink. He was stripped to the waist. His laugh was louder. Hatred as well as triumph glittered in his eyes, for today Jan Larose looked him coolly and squarely in the face, and nodded whenever he passed. It was almost noon when Jan spoke a few low words to his watchful Indian and walked to the top of the cedar-capped ridge that sheltered Porcupine City from the north winds.

From this ridge he could look straight into the north—the north where he was born. Only the Cree knew that for five nights he had slept, or sat awake, on the top of this ridge, with his face turned toward the polar star, and his heart breaking with loneliness and grief. Up there, far beyond where the green-topped forests and the sky seemed to meet, he could see a little cabin nestling under the stars—and Marie.

Always his mind traveled back to the beginning of things, no matter how hard he tried to forget—even to the old days of years and years ago when he had toted the little Marie around on his back, and had crumpled her brown curls, and had revealed to her one by one the marvelous mysteries of the wilderness, with never a thought of the wonderful love that was to come. A half-frozen little outcast brought in from the deep snows one day by Marie's father, he became first her playmate and brother—and after that lived in a few swift years of paradise and dreams. For Marie he had made of himself what he was. He had gone to Montreal. He had learned to read and write; he had worked for the Hudson's Bay Company; he had come to know the outside world, and at last the government had employed him. This was a triumph.

He could still see the glow of pride and love in Marie's beautiful eyes when he came home after those two years in the great city. The government sent for him each autumn after that. Deep into the wilderness he led the men who made the red-and-black-lined maps. It was he who blazed out the northern limit of Banksian pine, and his name was in government reports—down in black and white—so that Marie and all the world could read.

One day he came back—and he found Clarry O'Grady at the Cummins' cabin. He had been there for a month with a broken leg. Perhaps it was the dangerous knowledge of the power of her beauty—the woman's instinct in her to tease with her prettiness, that led to Marie's flirtation with O'Grady. But Jan could not understand, and she played with fire—the fire of two hearts instead of one. The world went to pieces under Jan after that. There came the day when, in fair fight, he choked the taunting sneer from O'Grady's face back in the woods. He fought like a tiger, a mad demon. No one ever knew of that fight. And with the demon still raging in his breast he faced the girl. He could never quite remember what he had said. But it was terrible—and came straight from his soul. Then he went out, leaving Marie standing there white and silent. He did not go back. He had sworn never to do that, and during the weeks that followed it spread about that Marie Cummins had turned down Jan Larose, and that Clarry O'Grady was now the lucky man. It was one of the unexplained tricks of fate that had brought them together, and had set their discovery stakes side by side on Pelican Creek.

Today, in spite of his smiling coolness, Jan's heart rankled with a bitterness that seemed to be concentrated of all the dregs that had ever entered into his life. It poisoned him, heart and soul. He was not a coward. He was not afraid of O'Grady. And yet he knew that fate had already played the cards against him. He would lose. He was almost confident of that, even while he nerved himself to fight.

O'Grady had gone into the home that was almost his own and had robbed him of Marie. In that fight in the forest he should have killed him. That would have been justice, as he knew it. But he had relented, half for Marie's sake, and half because he hated to take a human life, even though it were O'Grady's. But this time there would be no relenting. He had come alone to the top of the ridge to settle the last doubts with himself. Whoever won out, there would be a fight. It would be a magnificent fight, like that which his grandfather had fought and won for the honor of a woman years and years ago. He was even glad that O'Grady was trying to rob him of what he had searched for and found. There would be twice the justice in killing him now. And it would be done fairly, as his grandfather had done it.

Suddenly there came a piercing shout from the direction of the river, followed by a wild call for him through Jackpine's moose-horn. He answered the Cree's signal with a yell and tore down through the bush. When he reached the foot of the ridge at the edge of the clearing, he saw the men, women, and children of Porcupine City running to the river. In front of the recorder's office stood Jackpine, bellowing through his horn. O'Grady and his Indian were already shoving their canoe out into the stream, and even as he looked there came a break in the line of excited spectators, and through it hurried the agent toward the recorder's cabin.

Side by side, Jan and his Indian ran to their canoe. Jackpine was stripped to the waist, like O'Grady and his Chippewayan. Jan threw off only his caribou-skin coat. His dark woolen shirt was sleeveless, and his long slim arms, as hard as ribbed steel, were free. Half the crowd followed him. He smiled, and waved his hand, the dark pupils of his eyes shining big and black. Their canoe shot out until it was within a dozen yards of the other, and those ashore saw him laugh into O'Grady's sullen, set face. He was cool. Between smiling lips his white teeth gleamed, and the women stared with brighter eyes and flushed cheeks, wondering how Marie Cummins could have given up this man for the giant hulk and drink-reddened face of his rival. Those among the men who had wagered heavily against him felt a misgiving. There was something in Jan's smile that was more than coolness, and it was not bravado. Even as he smiled ashore, and spoke in low Cree to Jackpine, he felt at the belt that he had hidden under the caribou-skin coat. There were two sheaths there, and two knives, exactly alike. It was thus that his grandfather had set forth one summer day to avenge a wrong, nearly seventy years ago.

The agent had entered the cabin, and now he reappeared, wiping his sweating face with a big red handkerchief. The recorder followed. He paused at the edge of the stream and made a megaphone of his hands.

"Gentlemen," he cried raucously, "both claims have been thrown out!"

A wild yell came from O'Grady. In a single flash four paddles struck the water, and the two canoes shot bow and bow up the stream toward the lake above the bend. The crowd ran even with them until the low swamp at the lake's edge stopped them. In that distance neither had gained a yard advantage. But there was a curious change of sentiment among those who returned to Porcupine City. That night betting was no longer two and three to one on O'Grady. It was even money.

For the last thing that the men of Porcupine City had seen was that cold, quiet smile of Jan Larose, the gleam of his teeth, the something in his eyes that is more to be feared among men than bluster and brute strength. They laid it to confidence. None guessed that this race held for Jan no thought of the gold at the end. None guessed that he was following out the working of a code as old as the name of his race in the north.

As the canoes entered the lake, the smile left Jan's face. His lips tightened until they were almost a straight line. His eyes grew darker; his breath came more quickly. For a while O'Grady's canoe drew steadily ahead of them, and, when Jackpine's strokes went deeper and more powerful, Jan spoke to him in Cree, and guided the canoe so that it cut straight as an arrow in O'Grady's wake. There was an advantage in that. It was small, but Jan counted on the cumulative results of good generalship.

His eyes never for an instant left O'Grady's huge, naked back. Between his knees lay his .303 rifle. He had figured on the fraction of time it would take him to drop his paddle, pick up the gun, and fire. This was his second point in generalship—getting the drop on O'Grady.

Once or twice in the first half hour O'Grady glanced back over his shoulder, and it was Jan who now laughed tauntingly at the other. There was something in that laugh that sent a chill through O'Grady. It was as hard as steel, a sort of madman's laugh.

It was seven miles to the first portage, and there were nine in the eighty-mile stretch. O'Grady and his Chippewayan were a hundred yards ahead when the prow of their canoe touched shore. They were a hundred and fifty ahead when both canoes were once more in the water on the other side of the portage, and O'Grady sent back a hoarse shout of triumph. Jan hunched himself a little lower. He spoke to Jackpine—and the race began. Swifter and swifter the canoes cut through the water. From five miles an hour to six, from six to six and a half—seven—seven and a quarter, and then the strain told. A paddle snapped in O'Grady's hands with a sound like a pistol shot. A dozen seconds were allowed him. He shouted to Jan, and pointed down at the canoe. The next instant, with a powerful shove, he sent the empty birchbark speeding far out into the open water.

Jan caught his breath. He heard Jackpine's cry of amazement behind him. Then he saw the two men start on a swift run over the portage trail, and with a fierce, terrible cry he sprang toward his rifle. In that moment he would have fired, but O'Grady and the Indian had disappeared into the timber. He understood—O'Grady had tricked him, as he had tricked him in other ways. He had a second canoe waiting for him at the end of the portage, and perhaps others farther on. It was unfair. He could still hear O'Grady's taunting laughter as it had rung out in Porcupine City, and the mystery of it was solved. His blood grew hot—so hot that his eyes burned, and his breath seemed to parch his lips. In that short space in which he was paralyzed and unable to act, his brain blazed like a volcano. Who was helping O'Grady by having a canoe ready for him at the other side of the portage? He knew that no man had gone north from Porcupine City during those tense days of waiting. The code which all understood had prohibited that. Who, then, could it be?—who but Marie herself? In some way O'Grady had got word to her, and it was the Cummins' canoe that was waiting for him!

With a strange cry Jan now lifted the bow of their canoe to his shoulder and led Jackpine in a run. His strength had returned. He did not feel the whip-like sting of boughs that struck him across the face. He scarcely looked at the little cabin of logs when they passed it. Deep down in his heart he called upon the Virgin to curse those two—Marie Cummins and Clarry O'Grady, the man and the girl who had cheated him out of love, out of home, out of everything he had possessed, and who were beating him now through perfidy and trickery.

His face and his hands were scratched and bleeding when they came to the narrow waterway, half lake and half river, which let into the Blind Loon. Another minute and they were racing again through the water. From the mouth of the channel he saw O'Grady and the Chippewayan a quarter of a mile ahead. Five miles beyond them was the fourth portage. It was hidden now by a thick pall of smoke rising slowly into a clear sky. Neither Jan nor the Indian had caught the pungent odors of burning forests in the air, and they knew that it was a fresh fire.

Never in the years that Jan could remember had that portage been afire, and he wondered if this was another trick of O'Grady's. The fire spread rapidly as they advanced. It burst forth in a dozen places along the shore of the lake, sending up huge volumes of black smoke riven by lurid tongues of flame. O'Grady and his canoe became less and less distinct. Finally they disappeared entirely in the lowering clouds of the conflagration. Jan's eyes searched the water as they approached the shore, and at last he saw what he had expected to find—O'Grady's empty canoe drifting slowly away from the beach. O'Grady and the Chippewayan were gone.

Over that half-mile portage Jan staggered with his eyes half closed and his breath coming in gasps. The smoke blinded him, and at times the heat of the fire scorched his face. In several places it had crossed the trail, and the hot embers burned through their moccasins. Once Jackpine uttered a cry of pain. But Jan's lips were set. Then, above the roar of the flames sweeping down upon the right of them, he caught the low thunder of Dead Man's Whirlpool and the cataract that had made the portage necessary. From the heated earth their feet came to a narrow ledge of rock, worn smooth by the furred and moccasined tread of centuries with the chasm on one side of them and a wall of rock on the other. Along the crest of that wall, a hundred feet above them, the fire swept in a tornado of flame and smoke. A tree crashed behind them, a dozen seconds too late. Then the trail widened and sloped down into the dip that ended the portage. For an instant Jan paused to get his bearing, and behind him Jackpine shouted a warning.

Up out of the smoldering oven where O'Grady should have found his canoe two men were rushing toward them. They were O'Grady and the Chippewayan. He caught the gleam of a knife in the Indian's hand. In O'Grady's there was something larger and darker—a club, and Jan dropped his end of the canoe with a glad cry, and drew one of the knives from his belt. Jackpine came to his side, with his hunting knife in his hand, measuring with glittering eyes the oncoming foe of his race—the Chippewayan.

And Jan laughed softly to himself, and his teeth gleamed again, for at least fate was playing his game. The fire had burned O'Grady's canoe, and it was to rob him of his own canoe that O'Grady was coming to fight. A canoe! He laughed again, while the fire roared over his head and the whirlpool thundered at his feet. O'Grady would fight for a canoe—for gold—while he—*he* would fight for something else, for the vengeance of a man whose soul and honor had been sold. He cared nothing for the outcome. He cared nothing for the gold. He told himself, in this one tense moment of waiting, that he cared no longer for Marie. It was the fulfillment of the code.

He was still smiling when O'Grady was so near that he could see the red glare in his eyes. There was no word, no shout, no sound of fury or defiance as the two men stood for an instant just out of striking distance. Jan heard the coming together of Jackpine and the Chippewayan. He heard them struggling, but not for the flicker of an eyelash did his gaze leave O'Grady's face. Both men understood. This time had to come. Both had expected it, even from that day of the fight in the woods when fortune had favored Jan. The burned canoe had only hastened the hour a little. Suddenly Jan's free hand reached behind him to his belt. He drew forth the second knife and tossed it at O'Grady's feet.

O'Grady made a movement to pick it up, and then, while Jan was partly off his guard, came at him with a powerful swing of the club. It was his cat-like quickness, the quickness almost of the great northern loon that evades a rifle ball, that had won for Jan in the forest fight. It saved him now. The club cut through the air over his head, and, carried by the momentum of his blow, O'Grady lurched against him with the full force of his two hundred pounds of muscle and bone. Jan's knife swept in an upward flash and plunged to the hilt through the flesh of his enemy's forearm. With a cry of pain O'Grady dropped his club, and the two crashed to the stone floor of the trail. This was the attack that Jan had feared and tried to foil, and with a lightning-like squirming movement he swung himself half free and on his back. With O'Grady's huge hands linking his throat, he drew back his knife arm for the fatal plunge.

In this instant, so quick that he could scarcely have taken a breath in the time, his eyes took in the other struggle between Jackpine and the Chippewayan. The two Indians had locked themselves in a deadly embrace. All thought of masters, of life, or death were forgotten in the roused-up hatred that fired them now in their desire to kill. They had drawn close to the edge of the chasm. Under them the thundering roar of the whirlpool was unheard; their ears caught no sound of the moaning surge of the flames far over their heads. Even as Jan stared horror-stricken in that one moment, they rocked at the edge of the chasm. Over the tumult of the flood below and the fire above there rose a wild yell, and the two plunged down into the abyss, locked and fighting even as they fell in a twisting, formless shape to the death below.

It happened in an instant—like the flash of a quick picture on a screen—and even as Jan caught the last of Jackpine's terrible face, his hand drove eight inches of steel toward O'Grady's body. The blade struck something hard—something that was neither bone nor flesh, and he drew back again to strike. He had struck the steel buckle of O'Grady's belt. This time. . . .

A sudden hissing roar filled the air. Jan knew that he did not strike—but he scarcely knew more than that in the first shock of the fiery avalanche that had dropped upon them from the rock wall of the mountain. He was conscious of fighting desperately to drag himself from under a weight that was not O'Grady's—a weight that stifled the breath in his lungs, that crackled in his ears, that scorched his face and hands, and was burning out his eyes. A shriek rang in his ears unlike any other cry of man he had ever heard, and he knew that it was O'Grady's. He pulled himself out, foot by foot, until fresher air struck his nostrils, and dragged himself nearer and nearer to the edge of the chasm. He could not rise. His limbs were paralyzed. His knife arm dragged at his side. He opened his eyes and found that he could see. Where they had fought was the smoldering ruin of a great tree, and standing out of the ruin of that tree, half naked, his hands tearing wildly at his face, was O'Grady. Jan's fingers clutched at a small rock. He called out, but there was no meaning to the sound he made. Clarry O'Grady threw out his great arms.

"Jan . . . Jan Larose . . . !" he cried. "My God, don't strike now! I'm blind . . . blind . . . !"

He backed to the wall, his huge form crouched, his hands reaching out as if to ward off the death blow.

Jan tried to move, and the effort brought a groan of agony to his lips. A second crash filled his ears as a second avalanche of fiery débris plunged down upon the trail farther back. He stared straight up through the stifling smoke. Lurid tongues of flame were leaping over the wall of the mountain where the edge of the forest was enveloped in a sea of twisting and seething fire. It was only a matter of minutes—perhaps seconds. Death had them both in its grip.

He looked again at O'Grady, and there was no longer the desire for the other's life in his heart. He could see that the giant was unharmed, except for his eyes.

"Listen, O'Grady," he cried. "My legs are broken, I guess, and I can't move. It's sure death to stay here another minute. You can get away. Follow the wall . . . to your right. The slope is still free of fire, and . . . and. . . ."

O'Grady began to move, guiding himself slowly along the wall. Then, suddenly, he stopped.

"Jan Larose . . . you say you can't move?" he shouted.

"Yes."

Slowly O'Grady turned and came gropingly toward the sound of Jan's voice. Jan held tight to the rock that he had gripped in his left hand. Was it possible that O'Grady would kill him now, stricken as he was? He tried to drag himself to a new position, but his effort was futile.

"Jan . . . Jan Larose!" called O'Grady, stopping to listen.

Jan held his breath. Then the truth seemed to dawn upon O'Grady. He laughed, differently than he had laughed before, and stretched out his arms.

"My God, Jan," he cried, "you don't think I'm clean *beast* do you? The fight's over, man, an' I guess God A'mighty brought this on us to show what fools we was. Where are y', Jan Larose? I'm goin' t'carry you out!"

"I'm here," called Jan.

He could see truth and fearlessness in O'Grady's sightless face, and he guided him without fear. Their hands met. Then O'Grady lowered himself and hoisted Jan to his shoulders as easily as he would have lifted a boy. He straightened himself and drew a deep breath, broken by a sobbing throb of pain.

"I'm blind, an' I won't see any more," he said, "an' mebbe you won't ever walk any more. But if we ever git to that gold, I kin do the work, and you kin show me how. Now . . . p'int the way, Jan Larose!"

With his arms clasped about O'Grady's naked shoulders, Jan's smarting eyes searched through the thickening smother of fire and smoke for a road that the other's feet might tread. He shouted—"Left" . . . "right" . . . "right" . . . "left"—into this blind companion's ears until they touched the wall.

As the heat smote them more fiercely, O'Grady bowed his great head upon his chest and obeyed mutely the signals that rang in his ears. The bottoms of his moccasins were burned from his feet; live embers ate at his flesh; his broad chest was a fiery blister; and yet he strode on straight into the face of still greater heat and greater torture, uttering no sound that could be heard above the steady roar of the flames. And Jan, limp and helpless on his back, felt then the throb and pulse of a giant life under him, the straining of thick neck, of massive shoulders, and the grip of powerful arms whose strength told him that at last he had found the comrade and the man in Clarry O'Grady. "Right" . . . "left" . . . "left" . . . "right," he shouted, and then he called for O'Grady to stop in a voice that was shrill with warning.

"There's fire ahead," he yelled. "We can't follow the wall any longer.

There's an open space close to the chasm. We can make that, but there's only about a yard to spare. Take short steps . . . one step each time I tell you. Now . . . left . . . left . . . left . . . left. . . ."

Like a soldier on drill, O'Grady kept time with his scorched feet until Jan turned him again to face the storm of fire, while one of his broken legs dangled over the abyss into which Jackpine and the Chippewayan had plunged to their deaths. Behind them, almost where they had fought, there crashed down another avalanche from the edge of the mountain. Not a shiver ran through O'Grady's great body. Steadily, and unflinchingly—step—step—step—he went ahead, while the last threads of his moccasins smoked and burned. Jan could no longer see half a dozen yards in advance. A wall of black smoke rose in their faces, and he pulled O'Grady's ear: "We've got just one chance, Clarry. I can't see any more. Keep straight ahead . . . and run for it, and may the good God help us now!"

And Clarry O'Grady, drawing one great breath that was half fire into his lungs, ran straight into the face of what looked like death to Jan Larose. In that one moment Jan closed his eyes and waited for the plunge over the cliff. But in place of death a sweep of air that seemed almost cold struck his face, and he opened his eyes to find the clear and uncharred slope leading before them down to the edge of the lake. He shouted the news into O'Grady's ear, and then there arose from O'Grady's chest a great sobbing cry, partly of joy, partly of pain, and more than all else of that terrible grief which came of the knowledge that back in the pit of death from which he had escaped he had left forever the vision of life itself. He dropped Jan in the edge of the water, and, plunging in to his waist, he threw handful after handful of water in his own swollen face, and then stared upward, as though his last experiment was also his last hope.

"My God, I'm blind . . . stone blind!"

Jan was staring hard into O'Grady's face. He called him nearer, the swollen and blackened face between his two hands, and his voice was trembling with joy when he spoke.

"You're not blind . . . not for good . . . O'Grady," he said. "I've seen men like you before . . . twice. You . . . you'll get well. O'Grady . . . Clarry O'Grady . . . let's shake! I'm a brother to you from this day on. And I'm glad . . . glad that Marie loves a man like you!"

O'Grady had gripped his hand, but he dropped it now as though it had been one of the live brands that had hurtled down upon them from the top of the mountain.

"Marie . . . man . . . why . . . she *hates* me!" he cried. "It's you . . . *you* . . . Jan Larose, that she loves! I went there with a broken leg, an' I fell in love with her. But she wouldn't so much as let me touch her hand, an' she talked of you . . . always . . . until I had learned to hate you before you came. I dunno why she did it . . . that other thing . . . unless it was to make you jealous. I guess it was all f'r fun, Jan. She didn't know. The day you went away she sent me after you. But I hated you . . . hated you worse'n she hated me. It's you . . . you. . . ."

He clutched his hands at his sightless face again, and suddenly Jan gave a wild shout. Creeping around the edge of a smoking headland, he had caught sight of something.

"There's a man in a canoe!" he cried. "He sees us! O'Grady . . . !"

He tried to lift himself, but fell back with a groan. Then he laughed, and, in spite of his agony, there was a quivering happiness in his voice.

"He's coming, O'Grady. And it looks . . . it looks like a canoe we both know. We'll go back to her cabin together, O'Grady. And when we're on our legs again . . . well, I never wanted the gold. That's yours . . . all of it."

A determined look had settled in O'Grady's face. He groped his way to Jan's side, and their hands met in a clasp that told more then either could have expressed of the brotherhood and strength of men.

"You can't throw me off like that, Jan Larose," he said. "We're pardners!"

MAX BRAND

The Man Who Goes Alone

Frederick Faust (1892–1944) was born in Seattle, Washington, but grew up in California. He was a most creative and fecund author who wrote in his lifetime the equivalent of 500 books under various pen names, of which at least 300 were Western stories. The name by which he is best known is Max Brand, and much about his life and work, including a comprehensive bibliography, can be found in *The Max Brand Companion* (Greenwood Press, 1996), edited by Jon Tuska and Vicki Piekarski. Among his finest Western stories are those set in the Northwest. The earliest of these to be published in book form was *The White Wolf* (Putnam, 1926). Four decades later it was followed by the equally fine *Mighty Lobo* (Dodd, Mead, 1962) and *Torture Trail* (Dodd, Mead, 1965). More recently in Five Star Westerns there have appeared *Sixteen in Nome* (1995), the prologue to *Sixteen in Nome*, "Alec the Great," in *Outlaws All: A Western Trio* (1996), *The Lightning Warrior* (1996), *Chinook* (1998), and forthcoming in this series will be *The Masterman* (2000).

The story that follows first appeared as "Devil Dog" by Max Brand in *Maclean's Magazine* (June 15, 1938), a Canadian periodical. Because of the *ad interim* provision of the Copyright Act of 1909, if a work by an American author was published first in a foreign country, it was incumbent upon that author to publish the same work with an American publisher within the next five years or lose the copyright in it. Accordingly, this story was subsequently published in the American market as "The Man Who Goes Alone" in *Argosy* (Feb. 15, 1941). This marks the first time it has been collected in book form.

Samuel Cornwall Gresham was one of those fellows who have the blunt, square jaw of a fighter and the will power to hold on. As a matter of fact, he had a lot of fighting to do because his habit was not to take advice but to figure out everything for himself.

For instance, when he wanted to go through a medical school he decided to make the money for it by digging gold; the place he chose to dig gold in was Alaska; the particular spot he selected was one of those dreary little forests scattered through a bog frozen over in winter; and the methods he chose were what he found written up in books about '96.

No one but a convinced old sourdough or a Samuel Cornwall Gresham would have faced the loneliness of that existence single-handed, but it never occurred to Gresham to look for a partner. He wanted to dig his own money and save it by himself. He never had asked another human being into his life.

His purpose now was to save sixteen hundred dollars. A four-year medical course, eight months a year, fifty dollars a month, would cost sixteen hundred dollars. In his first Alaskan year he traveled as a stowaway and work-a-way; eventually he got together some dogs, discovered that the biggest of the lot was only a six-month-old puppy that he therefore sold, and then he followed a foolish barroom story to the district where he pegged out his claim.

Through the dark of the winter he cut frozen trees to make fires to thaw the frozen ground of the bog, and labored and mucked and washed until he had five hundred dollars out of the soil. The second winter found him at the same toil, a brutal, grinding, blind life.

When he roused from sleep on this day of the second winter, his body begged pitifully for more repose. But as usual he took two or three deep breaths while he summoned that resolution which used his body as a wretched slave, then he got up, started the fire in the stove, and put on the pan of beans.

His two dogs sat down and watched him with starving eyes. He put two small frozen fish into a pot with some snow. When they were thawed, he gave a fish to each dog.

That was when the door opened, and Jarvis stood on the threshold with a rifle. Gresham knew Jarvis because it was to him that he had sold the overgrown puppy a year and a half before. Jarvis was as big as a mountain, and he was a beast, not a man. Instead of a beard he had fur on his face, and his breath had sheathed the hair on his chin with ice.

Gresham's two dogs, Midge and Charley, came out of their corner with the devil in their eyes and their teeth bared, snarling.

Jarvis said: "Chris . . . take 'em!"

The biggest thing that Gresham ever had seen in the way of a dog or a wolf slid in past his master. He was covered with a soft gray fluff against the Arctic weather. He had a white vest and a white mark of wisdom between his eyes.

Then he took those two big Huskies as a timber wolf would take a pair of lap dogs. Two or three slashes, like sword strokes, laid Charley dead; Midge, horribly wounded, screamed like a woman and died in turn.

Jarvis kicked the door shut. He kept his rifle pointing at Gresham all the time.

"What d'you want?" asked Gresham.

"Chuck," said Jarvis. "Where's it kept?"

"In the shed," said Gresham. He was about to say that he had just enough to last him through the winter, but then he realized that it was useless to speak.

Jarvis pointed Gresham out to the great dog and said: "Maybe you know him well enough to understand that he's gotta be watched. So . . . watch!"

Then he turned his back, kicked open the door of the shed, and carried the lantern into the dark of it. There was only a vague light left behind. It came from the red of the stove sides and from the cracks of the stove door.

The Husky, or overgrown wolf, or whatever he was, seemed to be reaching slowly for the kill as he stuck out his blood-stained muzzle by degrees, with his mane ruffed up and his lip curled back from his fangs. The light dripped down on them, as long as the teeth of a grizzly.

Gresham had no way at all with women, but God had given him a way with dogs. He said very quietly: "Well, boy, do you think you've ever smelled this chunk of beef on the hoof before? Steady does it. Be easy, old son."

He went on talking like that, and it seemed to Gresham that the green went out of those eyes and the mane fell and the teeth were no longer bared. He made sure, a moment later, that the big brute—only a Mackenzie River Husky ever could grow to that poundage, surely—was actually sniffing at his bare hand.

That was when it came over him that he might have a chance to pacify the dog long enough to get to his revolver which hung in a belted holster against the wall.

He took a chance of losing his hand at the wrist by reaching out a bit and touching the muzzle of that big killer. Chris ducked his head back with a snaky fencing movement; but an instant later the dog's nose was sniffing at that same hand, and this time Gresham managed to touch the fur between the eyes.

He felt the brute shudder under his fingertips. Yet what came out of the throat of the Husky was not a growl but a whine—very soft. Gresham was so surprised that he spent an instant reaching for an explanation. Then he remembered that overgrown fluff of a puppy which he had sold to Jarvis. He remembered also the bad case of distemper through which he had nursed that youngster, and it was reasonably clear that Chris had not forgotten.

By that time his hand was petting the head of the dog, and a whine was keeping that massive skull always in a slight tremor. Another moment and Gresham would have been up and reaching for his gun, but just then Jarvis came back. He carried a tarpaulin like a handkerchief with a hundred pounds of stuff inside it. This he dumped on the table and fetched out something which he tossed aside.

"There's three days' rations," he said. "You can fetch to the cabins up on Willow Creek with that chuck. The reason I gotta eat on you is my dogs got at my stuff and ate a week's grub in ten minutes. And besides, Alaska owes me something when I'm goin' out. Alaska oughta pay to get rid of me, eh?"

He began to laugh as he said this. His voice had a greasy bubbling in it; it sounded like a seal barking. Then he was holding the lantern up head high and staring with immense eyes.

"Chris!" he shouted.

The Husky bombed clear across the room to the door.

Jarvis came striding to the stool on which Gresham sat.

He roared at him: "What you done to that dog of mine?"

"I've talked to him," said Gresham. He studied the face of Jarvis. The man was in a sweat that could not be accounted for by the heat of the room.

"You lie," said Jarvis. "You lie . . . you got something in your hand! Leave me see what's in your hands!"

Gresham opened his empty palms.

"Nothing," whispered Jarvis. Then his voice exploded through the room. "You mean to say he remembers you? You stinking little half-breed runt, you mean he remembers you?"

There was six feet and a bit over of Gresham: at that he was a runt compared to Jarvis.

Silence followed this; the breathing of Jarvis made the only noise. At last he said: "Call him. Call him and see will he come to anybody but me."

He stood back another long stride.

"Hey, Chris. Come here, boy," said Gresham.

That big fellow turned his head first, looked squarely at his master, and then sneaked across the room to Gresham. He put his head on Gresham's knee and closed his eyes under the hand that was laid on him.

Then the big man broke into a roaring tantrum.

"You do without grub from here to Willow Creek!" he shouted, scooping up what he had left on the table and dropping it back in the tarpaulin. "You done something to Chris. I oughta take and pull the wishbone outta you. You Chris, you damn' fool. . . ."

He took a mighty kick at the dog, but Chris was out of the cabin and into the night like a gray streak of lightning, and Jarvis rushed after him, still cursing.

It took Gresham a breath to come back to himself and the realization that he had been cleaned out of food. Then something else startled him. He ran into the shed with the lantern and stretched out his hand toward the little buckskin sack that contained the gold.

It was gone. It was more than gold. It was nearly two years of his life.

He ran back into the cabin, snatched out the revolver, and plunged into the open. The darkness was laid like a hand across his eyes, but he blundered on until he was deep in the trees. Then the cold knifed him down the back and brought him back to his senses.

He went back into the cabin. He stood in the center of the room for a moment, looking around at the blank walls which had framed those many months. They were empty now. Because he had patted the head of a dog, the fruit of his labor was snatched away from him. He looked down at his right hand curiously as though the magic that had been in its touch might be visible.

Fifty miles of rough ground, snow, and a side-cutting wind would be enough to kill most men, but they did not kill Gresham. He walked till he was tired and then lay down in the snow to sleep.

The legend is that the traveler who lies down must surely die in his sleep; but unless the brain of a man is drugged by exhaustion, the cold will rouse him after fifteen or twenty minutes. So Gresham slogged on and rested and slogged on again; and the aurora borealis grew up out of the dark to set the landscape trembling and light his way. When, actually, he reached Willow Creek, he told himself that he could have gone twice as far.

They had a good big cabin up there. When he pushed open the door and stepped in, the heat, the taste of tobacco, and the sweet fumes of tea in the air made him a little dizzy.

He made out the faces of the men one by one. There were half a dozen of them in the room taking their ease. His mouth watered so that he could not speak at once. That was because of the smell of food and tea in the room.

A big man with a ragged beard stood up and said: "It's that Gresham. What you want first? A drink or a smoke?"

Gresham took a place over by the stove where he could face them all. He said: "Jarvis stopped at my place with a gun. My two dogs are dead now. And my dust is gone. I had thirty ounces. Jarvis took that. He killed my dogs. He cleaned me out of chuck, and he took my dust."

After this speech, he sat down on one of the bunks. For a while no one spoke. Then someone got out some jerked beef, and somebody else began to mix a flapjack with flour, salt, and lard. No one would look at Gresham.

At last the man with the beard stood up and kicked at a burned match on the floor.

"All right," he said. "We gotta do something."

Gresham always paid his way. He suggested: "I'll pay half the dust he stole."

Here the man of the beard looked across at him sharply, frowning. "We won't be needing your dust, brother," he said coldly.

So Gresham knew that he had done something wrong again. He always was doing the wrong thing. Men were creatures of mysterious delicacies. For him it was easier to understand beasts like Jarvis, and Jarvis's dog. He looked down at his right hand and smiled faintly at it.

A moment later an uproar of dogs exploded near the house. When the door was flung open, Gresham saw just in front of it a snarling, worrying heap of Huskies. That heap now burst apart, the savage dogs scattering off to the sides. From under them rose a gray monster with one dead Husky laid at his feet.

"Shoot that damn' wolf! Hand me that gun," said the man nearest the door.

"Hey! Don't shoot!" shouted Gresham. "Chris!"

He called out, though his logical brain kept telling him that it was like summoning something out of a dream. The real Chris was far away with the team of his master. But now the dream materialized in actual fact, for the great brute that walked through the doorway was Chris beyond a doubt. He gave a green look out of his eye to the other men, then he went up to Gresham and sat down at his feet.

The man of the beard said: "That's Jarvis's new leader. He leads Jarvis's team, and he leads Jarvis. How come, Gresham? Could the brute Jarvis be on your trail here?"

The hand of Gresham was wandering idly over the head of the Husky and that strange, new emotion was wakening again in his heart as he answered: "No, Chris must have trailed me here. When he was a puppy, I sold him to Jarvis. That's all. He thinks he belongs to me." He found himself laughing. "Chris thinks he still belongs to me!" he explained.

"That makes you laugh, does it?" asked the man with the beard.

Everybody else was silent. And Gresham knew that he was more of an outcast among his fellows than ever before. Yet he had not meant laughter at all. That had been to cover up something of unspeakable importance, something within him of which he was not exactly ashamed but which unnerved him.

Then he was eating a meal, while three of the men went out to harness a dog team to a sled. He knew that he was making much trouble for them, and this filled him with shame.

Thirty ounces of gold had seemed something infinitely worthwhile. The indifference of these people made it appear no more than thirty ounces of stone. They were setting forth simply because they wanted to see justice done.

Once Gresham put down his hand with a bit of bacon in it. The great teeth of the dog clamped over bone and flesh, discovered its identity, then found and extracted the bacon by use of the tongue alone . . . delicately.

After that he was out with the dogs and three other men and the long sled.

"Get on the sled," said the man with the black beard, whose name was Avery.

"I'll mush with the rest of you. I'm all right," said Gresham.

"Get on the sled, please," directed Avery. "We know that you're done in. Don't be a damned hero."

So Gresham got on the sled. "Do you know how to hit his trail?" he asked.

"If he's going out, we can find him," said Avery.

So Gresham lay back on the sled, and, as the dogs started up, Chris ran beside him with a tireless lope. Gresham lay back and looked at the "merry dancers" in the sky. The aurora borealis was like a standing circle of California tules with big heads of light and incredibly slight, trembling stems that seemed to bow and bend with the arch of the sky. After that he went to sleep.

He wakened to the tune of a howling wolf. It proved to be Chris who stubbornly remained off to one side though the sled was going on.

Gresham jumped off the sled, exclaiming: "Don't you understand? He's found the trail of his man. He's found Jarvis!"

Avery looked at him, said nothing, and then swung the team around. They headed in the direction of Chris. When they came closer, he started on ahead. At every small distance he was found waiting for them and then loping on ahead.

They kept that up for two days, and, though snow often covered the trail deep, Chris still detected it. He would plunge his head deep into the white smother, take a long whiff, and run on.

Gresham, who refused to ride the sled any longer in spite of fatigue, explained this to the others.

"He thinks he's going to bring about a happy reunion between me and Jarvis," he said, and he laughed.

They were silent.

"Because he's split up between Jarvis and me," explained Gresham, "he thinks that he's got to bring us together."

"Perhaps," said Avery dryly.

On the second day they found a sled loaded with bales of fine furs. "We're worrying him," said Avery. "He's dropped his trail sled. He knows we're after him, and he's dropped his trail sled. But it's a funny thing. There are only four of us. Why doesn't he turn back and take a crack at us? What are four men to Jarvis?"

The third day they found a patch of trouble. The lead dog fell, biting at the bullet wound in his breast, and then the clang of a rifle flew out at them from a cloudy patch of trees.

In silence they cut the dead dog loose.

"If he can shoot like that with only the aurora to give him light," said Avery, "why didn't he shoot Chris, instead? He knows that Chris is the only reason we're able to hound him up the trail."

"Don't you see?" explained Gresham. "He's fond of Chris. He's too fond of him to shoot at him. Queer, isn't it? A beast like that, I mean. But he won't shoot Chris, and Chris is running him down."

Avery looked darkly at this explanation. "How do you happen to know Jarvis so well?" he asked. "Ever a bunkmate of his?"

"I don't really know. I only guess," said Gresham weakly.

That was the day he suggested that they try Chris in place of the dead leader. They tried, and the thing worked perfectly so long as Gresham ran at the geepole, singing out orders. But he had to stay there or else Chris turned into a devil. So Gresham stayed, all of that march.

He did his share of the work when they put up camp, also. As he was working down into a sleeping bag for the night, Avery came and sat by him for a moment.

"Look," said Avery. "You're dead on your feet, but you're mushing farther and better than the rest of us. What keeps you going?"

Gresham put out his hand, found the head of Chris, and worried it.

"Ever been dead years in your life? Ever want to bring them to life?" he asked.

"You mean the gold you worked for?" asked Avery. "You mean you want that back? Yes, of course."

"Well, there's the law, too," said Gresham uncertainly.

Avery pointed. "The dog doesn't play any part in it?" he asked.

Chris, jerking his head around, snarled at the pointing hand. Gresham took hold of the muzzle absently. The big teeth closed on his fingers and gnawed at them softly.

"A dog?" said Gresham. "I thought we were talking about robbery and that sort of thing."

"I mean," said Avery, "that you're not wanting to wipe out the man who really owns that dog?"

"I?" gasped Gresham. "Hell, no!"

"All right," murmured Avery, and went away to his sleeping bag.

The next day they found various articles by the trail. Jarvis, hard-pressed, was lightening his main sled. He was making a sprint, now, for the mountains that loomed in the west, while the northern lights played in the sky.

They found queer things among his luggage. They found a *Robinson Crusoe* with grease-marked pages. "My God, he knows how to read! Is he human, after all?" commented Avery.

Then they found some cooking utensils. There were even some beans and a sack of flour.

"He's going to live on his fat part of the way," said Avery.

Before the end of that march they got into the rise of land toward the mountains, and they found the trail of a sled cutting deeply in soft snow which still crumbled into the ruts. They could hardly be an hour behind their quarry. Then they came to a branch of an evergreen laid on the snow and on it buckskin sacks were piled.

"There's a thousand ounces here!" said Avery. "The man's going to have nothing before he leaves the country."

Gresham, staring at the little sacks, picked one up with an exclamation. It was his own gold. He held it in his arms, close to him.

"All right, then," said Avery, "you have your property. We can turn back, then, I suppose? The rest of us are ready to quit. We haven't more than enough grub to see us to the camp again."

Gresham threw his gold sack aside.

"We'll get him tomorrow," he said. "When he tries to get up those slopes, that's where Chris's strength will count double. Lighten the sled of everything we don't absolutely need for one day's march. We'll make a last stab at him. If we miss . . . then it's easy coasting all the way back . . . and we start home."

So they made that last day's effort with Gresham at the geepole, yelling orders, and Chris straining like a mad dog in his harness. They got so close that three times they saw the sled and string ahead of them and big Jarvis herding his dogs on. But they reached exhaustion without overtaking their quarry.

When they sat around the primus stove, Avery sat down beside Gresham with the curious eyes of a doctor making a diagnosis.

"You've had all you want, haven't you?" he asked. "We've made the last try for you. Is it all right if we turn back tomorrow?"

"You've done all I asked," answered Gresham.

But his heart gave a hollow echo to those words, and a fear that had been in him all the way now became a conscious thing. He had known from the start, somehow, that he would have to meet Jarvis and fight it out with him for Chris. This use of numbers did not count. They had to square off man to man.

He took off a mitten and threw it away. "Fetch it," he said.

Chris got up, slunk to the mitten, and brought it back. He sat before his new master and loved him with patiently inquiring eyes.

Avery said: "What do you want, man? A bill of sale? You have the dog, haven't you?"

Everyone was watching and listening. Gresham vaguely was aware of that as he answered: "It's this way . . . I haven't worked it out, but it's this way . . . he belongs to Jarvis. Jarvis is a beast who couldn't own anything, you may say. But Jarvis was fond of Chris. He taught Chris everything Chris knows. How to go and fetch that mitten, for instance."

"Well?" asked Avery.

"I don't know," said Gresham. "I'm going out by myself to think it over."

He took his revolver and went.

The aurora borealis was in big arched bands across the sky. The shrubbery quivered, or seemed to quiver, with electric fire. Chris instantly took the trail, where the snow still was falling into the ruts. Gresham walked behind him. But after a time he called the dog back to him. Chris came and stood before him with his head canted to one side, questioning.

"Look," said Gresham. "This Jarvis you want to bring me to is no good. He's a rotten sort. You like me pretty well. You like him almost as well. But you're wrong. If you bring us together, there's only going to be a fight. Suppose you don't bring us together, are you going to keep hankering for him? Listen, damn you, is that what you're going to do?"

Chris, as though he wished to give the most patient consideration to this important question, sat down and waited for the next remark. It came from the rear, out of a patch of small, crowded trees.

It was the greasy voice of Jarvis, saying: "All right, I guess I got you now, Gresham. Chris, come here, you old fool!"

Chris neither stayed with his new master nor went to the old. Instead, he fled off to the side.

Jarvis, who had the butt of his rifle almost at his shoulder, still eyed Gresham. He said: "I'd kind of like to linger it out. I've thrown away twenty years of work to get rid of you on my trail. And now I'd like to get the taste of killing you all the way down the back of my tongue. Understand, you?"

"I understand," said Gresham, speaking without fear because, he felt, he was too tired to know anything but fatigue.

"What I'm wondering," said Jarvis, "is will he howl and raise hell when you flop down in the snow? Will I have to drag him off howling because he wants to stay here with a dead man?"

"He'll want to stay here," answered Gresham.

"You got my gold," said Jarvis. "Why'd you come after me, when you had that?"

Gresham looked at the face of the man. The only light they had threw strange, trembling shadows that seemed to be a natural darkness of the skin. The thick-jowled face of Jarvis had grown wonderfully lean, with a pucker in the cheeks behind the corners of the mouth. After all, he had worked up the trail as one man against four, and with the four was the majestic power of Chris.

"I don't know why I came after you, but I'm here," said Gresham.

"Go for your gun," commanded Jarvis. "Go and fill your hand before I sock it into you."

"I'll go for my gun pretty soon," said Gresham.

"You wouldn't tell me," declared Jarvis, "but it kind of eats me, wanting to know what you did to him."

Gresham, looking at him still with a curious calm, wondered why the man still seemed superior to him. Perhaps that was why it had been so frightfully important for him to meet Jarvis face to face.

"I'll tell you about it," said Gresham. "When he was a pup, he was sick with distemper, and during his fever I used to set out cold water for him. I didn't know, but he loved me for it. That's the queer thing. He loved me for it. And I didn't know."

It was a word he seldom used, and it troubled him strangely.

"He's gonna forget you, and damn you . . . he's gonna forget you!" shouted Jarvis.

"Take a mitten of mine after I'm dead," answered Gresham, with a strange surety, "and he'll think more of that than he'll ever think of you. Is there room in anybody to love two things at once?"

"You lie!" shouted Jarvis, and jammed the butt of the rifle against his shoulder.

That was when a shadow ran in behind him with a snarl. Gresham could not see whether the teeth of the dog actually touched his master or not, but Jarvis swerved, suddenly, firing blindly into the air, and crying out in a terrible voice: "Chris!"

Gresham had his gun out by that time. He held it with both hands and fired. It seemed to him that he had hardly aimed the revolver before Jarvis fell flat on his back.

He lay there with his huge feet sticking up in the snowshoes as Gresham went up and bent over him. The bullet had gone right home through the left side of the body.

But that was not the important matter. The question was whether or not

Chris had put his teeth into his old master. It would be simple to find out. It meant merely turning the body to one side, but somehow Gresham preferred to keep the question unanswered.

The shadow of the dog was falling across his feet and across the dead man. He held out his gun arm.

"Chris!" he commanded, and the big Husky came instantly under his hand. Gresham dropped to his knees.

Then, without looking, using the sense of touch alone, he picked up handful after handful of the snow and scrubbed the muzzle of the dog. After that he stood up and walked slowly down the back trail. The others could salvage what was left of Jarvis's team and sled.

The dog, as soon as he understood the intention of the master, trotted quietly behind him, his nose never more than an inch behind the hand of Gresham.

Those softly following footfalls seemed to Gresham the only reality in this northern world. The rest, and even his time of labor in the mine, was as dream-like as the trembling of the aurora borealis through the sky.

He began, as he walked, to dream of a southern land where men labored little or not at all, where the sun gave to every soul a blessing greater than gold, and where the women were beautiful forever. He could hear their voices and that imagined sound set him smiling, for they seemed to be hurrying toward him, laughing among themselves, and looking at him with eyes of eternal understanding.

DAN CUSHMAN

The Great Hunger

Dan Cushman (1909–) was born in Osceola, Michigan, and grew up on the Cree Indian reservation in Montana. In the early 1940s his novelette-length stories began appearing regularly in such Fiction House magazines as *North-West Romances* and *Frontier Stories*. The character Comanche John, a Montana road agent featured in numerous rollicking magazine adventures, is the protagonist in Cushman's first novel, *Montana, Here I Be* (Macmillan, 1950), and in two later novels. *Stay Away, Joe* (Viking, 1953), an amusing novel about the mixture, and occasional collision, of Indian culture and Anglo-American culture among the *Métis* (French Indians) living on a reservation in Montana became a bestseller and remains a classic to this day, greatly loved especially by Indian peoples for its truthfulness and humor. Yet, while humor became Cushman's hallmark in later novels, he also produced significant historical fiction in *The Silver Mountain* (Appleton-Century, 1957), concerned with the mining and politics of silver in Montana in the 1890s. This novel won a Spur Award from the Western Writers of America. His fiction remains notable for its breadth, ranging all the way from a story of the cattle frontier in *Tall Wyoming* (Dell, 1957) to a poignant and memorable portrait of small-town life in Michigan just before the Great War in *The Grand and the Glorious* (McGraw-Hill, 1963). His most recent novels, published as Five Star Westerns, have been Northwesterns: *In Alaska with Shipwreck Kelly* (1995) and *Valley of the Thousand Smokes* (1996). Some of Dan Cushman's best Northwestern and Western stories have been recently collected in *Voyageurs of the Midnight Sun* (Capra Press, 1995). "The Great Hunger" was originally published under the byline John Starr in *North-West Romances* (Fall 1946) and is taken from this collection.

The country was an unbroken whiteness. No bird, or wolf, or snowshoe rabbit moved from the frozen hills of the Allakelet to the wide swale of Jack Creek where, that summer, mallards had grown fat on the fish moss. Scrub cottonwoods marked the course of the stream, but their trunks were buried, and the projecting twigs, brittle in the fifty below atmosphere, seemed to have no connection with life. It was as though the cold, the silence, the lifelessness had always been, and would be until the end of time.

Then, over the rim of the void, a string of dark spots appeared and crept by slow degrees along the ridges, and at the deeper grayness that was night they paused in a brushy hollow. As though this miracle of life, once performed, must be repeated, a second string of dots came and followed the same slow descent. They were dog teams, far astray from the winter trail extending northward along the Nanachuk from Reed Lake to Fort Yukon.

Down in the brush where the first string had paused, a lean, bronzed man of thirty, known along the northern trails as Hand-sled Riley, kindled a tiny twig fire, and squatted close, nursing a can of tea to boil. From time to time he glanced up, keeping check on the second team's approach. When it was a mile or so away, he nodded to his companion—a girl.

"Are you sure?" she asked.

"It's Granden." And he added: "Damn him!"

As the attention of Riley and the girl deviated for the moment, one of the malemutes, a gaunt gray and tan, dragged himself on his belly through the loose snow, his small, Oriental eyes on the sled. The other dogs crouched around, watching him intently. When he was a yard or so away, he leaped forward, yellow teeth flashing, and ripped at the tarp.

The girl screamed: "Tan! See Tan!"

Hand-sled Riley rolled out the lash of his dog whip with the accuracy of an aimed rifle. The lash caught the malemute in the hindquarters and turned him over. He still tore at the tarp, but a second swing of the lash sent him away whimpering.

"He's starving," said the girl, looking after the animal.

"They're all starving."

She looked once more at Granden and his approaching team. "I wish he'd stop following."

Riley went back to his can of tea. "I wonder how close he'll come today. Yesterday he was in long rifle range."

Both of them were thinking the same thing. Granden was wanted here on the American side. He would not dare follow them into Fort Alred. But neither would he allow them to escape. He had a gun, and Riley had none. He knew that. There would be a bullet to settle the matter to his satisfaction before the flagpole of Fort Alred came to view.

Riley brought a lump of beans, frozen hard as granite, from the provisions can and laid them near the fire to thaw.

"The last," he said.

They had lost practically all their provisions when shell ice gave way on the Halfanhalf, and since then they'd been going wolf-fashion. The thawing beans gave out an odor of rich pork fat. The dogs whined greedily.

"It wouldn't take much encouragement for those malemutes to jump a man," Riley muttered. "I don't like the looks of that Natuk. He has Siberian blood, and they're always worse. Give me a Husky any day, or one of those Chilliwick half-breeds. I'd even trust a wolf pureblood before a malemute."

"I wish we could feed them!"

Riley smiled. He loved the girl, but he liked her, too. There was a difference. Love was a fever pounding in a man's brain, while liking tingled with a cabin's warmth at the ends of the fingertips. Things were stripped to their elementals in this country of the long twilight and the strong cold. This girl, this unlettered daughter of a French "weasel trader" by a Yellowknife half-breed, had made him feel both love and liking. *There she is*, thought Hand-sled Riley, *half starving, and she worries about the dogs.*

"They'll eat!" he said.

He looked at them, crouched and moaning in their half circle, eyes on the thawing beans, and thought—*Yes, they'll eat. They'll eat Lukla first. She won't last through the next sun. And after her they'll eat Jep. But that damned Natuk . . . he'll keep going.*

Granden was less than a hundred paces away when he trotted forward, kicking up snow powder with his long webs, and collared his lead dog. He looked over at the camp with its miserable fire, and a smile broke apart the reddish growth of whiskers covering his face.

"Eat hearty!" he said.

Although he spoke no more loudly than one conversing over a dinner table, so intense was the winter stillness they could hear him plainly. Granden knew they had lost their supplies back on the Halfanhalf, and it was evident that he considered this "eat hearty" a superb jest. Then, as though to drive in his point, he slowly went about the business of breaking out a half-dozen frozen fish and tossing them to his dogs which waited in a circle.

Led by Natuk, Riley's dogs ran yapping and snarling toward the food. Granden tossed the last fish, and leaped forward, swinging the brutal, frozen lash of his dog whip. He caught Natuk and turned him nose first into the snow. Time after time the whip found its mark until Riley's dogs retreated out of range.

Riley knew the uselessness of words, but in his fury he shouted: "Granden, feeding your dogs in front of mine is the lowest thing a man can do on the trail!"

Granden laughed.

"Keep your malemutes to yourself, Riley, or next time I'll see to it they get food. *Warm* food."

"You kill my dogs and I'll. . . ."

Granden laughed again. He had a gun, and Riley's lay beneath the ice of the Halfanhalf. To emphasize the point, Granden reached beneath a rabbit-skin roll in his sled and drew out a .45 caliber rifle. He worked its lever action to make sure it wasn't frozen.

"It would be easy for me to get the woman back," he remarked.

"You never had her," growled Riley.

Granden went on as though he had not heard. "But I'm not going to. No, Riley, I'm going to let you live. Know why I'm going to let you live? I'll tell you. It's so I can show Lynette the kind of a man she got when she chose you instead of me!"

"I hate you!" the girl cried, in her excitement reverting to the Yellowknife dialect of her mother's people. Then, when Granden seemed not to hear, she repeated in English: "I hate you."

Granden broke twigs and built a fire. He hung a bucket for tea, and cut a chunk of caribou pemmican—pemmican pounded out when the animals were summer-fat, and hence congealed rather than frozen. He propped the meat over the fire, Siwash-fashion. Its grease dripped in the fire, sputtering and smoking, giving off a rich odor that set the starved malemutes to howling. They kept edging closer, but Granden did not seem to notice. He went on humming to himself and stirring the tea leaves in the bucket.

"Tan!" shouted Riley.

Instead of turning at the sound of his name, the dog leaped toward the meat. Granden had been watching from the corner of his eye. He reached the rifle, flipped it to his shoulder, and fired. Tan was knocked backward by the force of the three hundred-grain bullet, his blood making mist and freezing in red blobs across the snow. A second later his starving teammates pounced on him.

The girl hid her face in her mittens while Riley shook his fist impotently and cursed. Granden smiled and worked the lever in short, rapid strokes to prevent moisture from locking the mechanism.

He said: "Well, Riley, I told you I'd feed your dogs."

He squatted down eating slowly, savoring the caribou fat, licking his fingers when the last fragment was gone.

"Maybe you been wondering how I aimed to show you just what kind of fellow your Hand-sled Riley is," he said, speaking slowly, nudging the fire with the toe of his mukluk. "Well, I'll tell you. We're on the Sozokela, aren't we? That means Fort Alred's all of eight sleeps. More than that when your dogs are footsore and dying."

Riley made no sign of hearing, not even when Granden called Jack Creek the Sozokela. The Sozokela was sixty miles to north and west. They had missed it by swinging with the rim of the Allakelet.

Granden went on: "Now a man or a woman can get a trifle hungry in eight sleeps. I went six sleeps without grub one time, and I know."

Granden talked dreamily after the manner of well-fed men. He poked the fire and seemed to be thinking out loud.

"I recall one time over on the Peel. Jack Carney . . . and me . . . and a fellow named Lightfoot were mushing out toward Keno. It had started good, about ten below just like this trip, but it turned cold, and the Peel was filled with rough ice. We only had three dogs . . . a couple of malemutes and a bird dog cross. We went along pretty slow, one man breaking trail, one pushing, one on the geepole. Sometimes it was so bad we only made a mile or two an hour."

Riley started talking to the girl, trying to drown him out, but his words came through anyway.

"Finally we started that long climb up the Ogalvie divide. That's when it got cold. Fifty or sixty below, just like now. The runners seemed glued to the snow, but we fought it through, day after day. Then the grub ran out. First we ate the bird dog, and after that the two malemutes. We threw away all except a couple of rabbit-skin blankets and one rifle. Hungry? I never knew such hunger. We stewed our rabbit-skin blankets, and ate the strips. Hair and all. Tasted good, too. Just as good as this pemmican. And we ate our extra furs. But finally there was nothing left."

Granden looked over and grinned. Riley was still talking to the girl, but in dislocated, meaningless sentences, and by that Granden knew he was listening.

"Now, Jack Carney and Lightfoot were just like father and son. They'd cabined up together ever since Lightfoot first came inside on an H. B. C. steamboat eight years before. Carney'd have died for him, and I guess it would have worked the same for Lightfoot.

"We hadn't seen a living thing except our dogs since leaving the lower Peel, but, just when we were dropping over the rocky ridge on the Keno side of the divide, Carney happened to stumble onto a packrat's nest. The rat got out and dodged around in the scrub spruce with Carney chasing, trying to get a shot. We lost sight of him for a while, and then, bang! We shouted, but he didn't answer. Finally we got down to where he was. Well, Carney'd killed the rat . . . and he'd eaten it. All! He hadn't even left the tail for the man he loved like his own son.

"You see . . . the hunger was greater then either of them. It is greater than any man, or any woman, this hunger of the strong cold. This white hunger. It's stronger than the love of brother for brother, stronger than the love of man for woman, stronger than the love of a mother for her child."

As though there were something humorous in his philosophy, Granden tilted his head back and laughed.

"Lynette!" he said, "back in Delta you told me how much this Hand-sled Riley loved you. In a few sleeps I will prove that he loves his belly more."

Granden yawned, unrolled his rabbit-skin blanket, and went to sleep, trusting the watchfulness of his malemutes to warn of any approach. Lynette watched his form, outlined as a heap in the snow, fearing to go to her own robe when Riley rolled it out.

"He won't bother us," Riley said. "He's not the kind to be satisfied with just putting a chunk of lead between a man's shoulders."

False dawn came. Riley built a fire for tea. There was no food. Granden rolled over, sat up in his rabbit-skin, grinned, and laid back for some more sleep.

In the peculiar, starless darkness following false dawn, Riley and the girl set off along the brush of Jack Creek. Occasionally they would look back and see Granden, trotting easily, three or four miles behind. At the next rest he paused about eighty paces away and fed his dogs generously while Riley's famished team howled and snapped. Again he Siwashed pemmican, and, when he was through with licking his fingers, he said: "On this subject of hunger . . . I met a fellow one time, a college professor. Piloted him in a launch over to Campbell Lake where he wanted to gather soil samples for the geological survey. He was smart, this professor, and he claimed there was nothing could drive a man as much as sex and fear. But he was wrong. He'd never felt the white hunger. I'd seen Carney and Lightfoot, and I knew."

Granden's malemutes were gentle enough, being well fed, and one after another he went over their feet, removing ice lumps. As he worked, he talked on.

"Three sleeps should put us on the Chinoko, and one more to the Simpson. By that time I figure the hunger should get in its work. Not as well as it might, maybe, but good enough. You'll see roast caribou hanging on the cottonwood twigs, and your stomach will be like a cold hand clawing at your brain. Now, when that time comes, when you strike me as being hungry enough, I'm going to cut off one little piece of pemmican." He left the dogs and got the pemmican to measure off a thin slice with his thumb. "See? . . . about so big. Then I'm going to toss it in the snow between you. And Lynette! . . . do you know what he'll do, this fine lover of yours? He'll grab it and eat it all. And if you get your hands on it first, he'll tear it away from you, and he'll eat it all. He'll eat it just like Carney ate the packrat."

By his talk of the Chinoko and the Simpson, Riley knew the man was not familiar with this section of the country. He did not know they had followed the short cut around the Allakelet and hence would touch neither the Chinoko nor the Simpson before arriving at Fort Alred. Instead, in either two or three sleeps, they would reach the Tillimuk, and in one more the Murray River. They would be close to Fort Alred there, while Granden would still believe there was a safe distance. Of course, that was not a solution. There was still that rifle to consider—and the bullet that would come whenever the fort flagpole came to view.

It was a slow climb up an eight-mile slope from the bed of Jack Creek. Following that was a wide plain, as featureless as the sea. After many hours, they rested, but there was no brush—no fire for tea. And hunger tore at their vitals, hunger made even more bitter by the demands of the cold.

Granden had remained in shouting distance, traveling easily on their trail, half the time riding the runners behind his well-fed team. He stopped at his usual distance and built a carbide fire. The odor of the sizzling pemmican made Lynette dizzy from hunger so she lay and buried her face in her robes.

Granden started talking again. "About Carney and Lightfoot . . . we all got to Keno all right, but it was never the same between those two. Carney tried to explain how it was, but Lightfoot hated him for eating the packrat. Just like the woman will hate you, Riley, when you eat the pemmican."

Next day, during the pale sunlight, they made it down to the Tillimuk. And next day brought them to the Murray, which Granden thought was the Simpson. Riley drove the dogs, and he drove the girl. They went on, as in a dream, the awful hunger consuming them. In the false dawn, when Riley bent to fasten Natuk's breastband, the fierce malemute went for his throat. Riley beat him down with his forearm. Natuk struck the snow and twisted over. He hung there, in a crouch. The others circled for the kill, but Riley swung his whip, driving them back. He could hear Granden laughing from his camp.

Granden stayed close all that day as the sleds made a wide swing to the north. At the noonday rest he came quite close, his rifle in the crook of one arm, his long whip around his neck.

"The hunger's got you, Riley. You're headed in the wrong direction."

"We're headed right!" snapped Riley. "We'll sleep tonight in the valley of Jack Creek."

But in five hours they crossed their old trail.

Granden sat on the side of his sled and laughed. "This is the Chinoko again. You're going in circles."

Riley knew he thought the hunger had made him flighty. He watched the man come quite close—scarcely a stone's throw away this time.

"How would you like a little pemmican?" asked Granden.

Granden broke twigs for a fire, and set a can of snow on it to thaw. He laid his rifle a couple of feet away on a scrap of bear robe, hung his whip over his shoulder, and commenced cutting off a thin slice of the meat.

He held it up for them to see. Congealed though it was, its fatty odor set the malemutes to howling. The girl seemed delirious. She laughed and wept at sight of it. Granden came three or four steps, holding it out, and she would have gone to him through the snow had not Riley flung her back.

Granden laughed. "Oh, come! That's no way to treat a woman."

Hand-sled Riley screamed curses, shaking his fist.

"Give the girl a chance!" said Granden with a grim smile. "Maybe she'd like to change men!"

She crawled forward. One of her mittens had fallen off, and she reached with her bare hand. Granden advanced a little more, cocked his arm, and flung the meat, aiming it directly between them.

It curved a little because of its shape, and fell almost within the girl's grasp. She sprang toward it, but Riley was in front of her. She tried to push him from her way, but he scooped it up. Natuk was there, fangs flashing. The other malemutes lunged from either side. Granden roared with triumphant laughter.

"Eat it! Eat it quick!"

But Riley did not eat the meat. He ran toward Granden. Then, with the dogs swinging for his arm, he set himself and hurled it back. It sailed over Granden's head and buried itself in the snow behind the sled runners. The malemutes tore after it. Granden swung his whip at them and cursed. He tried to get to his rifle, forgetting how far he had left it behind. Riley had no chance to head him off, so he stopped suddenly, set himself, and rolled out the longer lash of his dog whip.

He aimed at the can of water. It leaped from the fire with a clang of metal. It overturned, drenching the scrap of bear robe, covering the steel of the rifle's mechanism with an instantaneous coating of ice.

Granden snatched up the rifle and tried to pump it, but it was locked. He could have bent the lever without budging it. Try to thaw it and the magazine would explode. No time, anyway.

Natuk gulped the pemmican; the others tore at Granden's sled, overturning it, spilling the grub can, strewing frozen fish and pemmican across the snow. The malemutes, Granden's as well as the starving brutes of Riley's team, gulped food until their sides bulged, while Granden was on them like a madman, his long lash curling feverishly.

Riley did not fight him then as he was tempted to. There was the woman to be thought of. He dodged among the scrambling dogs, seized a pemmican, and escaped with it to his camp.

His dogs came back in a little while, bleeding from the whip, ready to fall from gorging. He hitched them anyway, and drove them toward Fort Alred.

"I'll catch you!" screamed Granden, who was hunched over his fire trying to thaw the rifle. "It's still five long sleeps to the fort!"

In five hours Riley was at the edge of Gold Bench. Far below, between the purplish cutbanks of Murray River, stood a cluster of little squares and the tall flagpole.

They looked back on reaching the bottoms and saw Granden paused there, at the edge of the bench. He remained still for a long time, watching. At last he heaved his sled around. Although miles away, the silence had such miraculous quality they could hear the cry of its runners. When he swung his dog whip, they could hear the pop of it. And he mushed northward, through the strong cold, into the white hunger.

LES SAVAGE JR.

"Mush Fast or Die!"

Les Savage Jr. (1922–1958) was born in Alhambra, California, and grew up in Los Angeles. His first published story was "Bullets and Bullwhips" accepted by Street & Smith's *Western Story*. Almost ninety more magazine stories followed, all set on the American frontier, many of them published in Fiction House magazines such as *Frontier Stories* and *Lariat Story Magazine* where Savage became a superstar with his name on many covers. His first novel was *Treasure of the Brasada* (Simon & Schuster, 1947) and is still in print. Due to his preference for historical accuracy, Savage often ran into problems with book editors in the 1950s who were concerned about marriages between his protagonists and women of different races—a commonplace on the real frontier but not in much Western fiction in that decade. Savage died young, at thirty-five, from complications arising out of hereditary diabetes and elevated cholesterol. Such noteworthy titles of his as *Outlaw Thickets* (Doubleday, 1951), *The Trail* (Gold Medal, 1951), *Silver Street Woman* (Hanover House, 1954), *Return to Warbow* (Dell, 1956), and *Beyond Wind River* (Doubleday, 1958) have become classics of Western fiction. However, as a result of the censorship imposed on many of his works, only now are they being fully restored by returning to the author's original manuscripts. Among recent restorations of Savage's great Western stories are *Fire Dance at Spider Rock* (Five Star Westerns, 1995), *Copper Bluffs* (Circle V Westerns, 1996), *Medicine Wheel* (Five Star Westerns, 1996), and *Coffin Gap* (Five Star Westerns, 1997). Much as Stephen Crane before him, while he wrote the shadow of his imminent death grew longer and longer across his young life, and he knew that, if he was going to do it at all, he would have to do it quickly. He did it well, and now that his novels and stories are being restored to what he had intended them to be, his achievement irradiated by his powerful and profoundly sensitive imagination will be with us always, as he had wanted it to be, as he had so rushed against time and mortality that it might be.

Savage wrote a total of eight Northwestern stories of varying length. All of them will be gathered together in a collection titled *In the Land of Little Sticks* (Five Star Westerns, 2000). "He wrote action stories of the barren, wind-swept North, the snows and rocks of granite," Dan Cushman observes in his Foreword to this collection. "His North does not yield to the men and women who contend with it. It is linear and unrelenting, as are the snows they cross. But there are other aspects . . . something unexpected to tie the *babiche* of unity around a frigid tale . . . people with a past who know their own humanity in a land where the odds are always against them." The story that follows first appeared in *North-West Romances* (Fall 1945).

I

Eddie Kopernick jumped up and back from the fire and snapped open the lever on his Winchester, all with one startled motion, and then stood there, peering covertly into the dark poplars filling the air with their heady spring scent all around his camp. It had been this way the past three years. It was how a man got. Jumping at every sound within a mile of him, the butt of his carbine slick and oily from the constant contact with his hands.

In place of a coat he wore a tattered Hudson Bay blanket, a hole cut in the center poncho-style for his head, the four ends dangling like tails beneath his belt. His corduroy trousers were patched all over with greasy buckskin, and his moccasins consisted more of the rawhide whangs he had sewn on them for repairs than the original moose hide. Black snow glasses hid his eyes, and his shaggy mane of unkempt black hair and hoary curling beard gave his head a massive, leonine look.

"Eddie?" said the man who staggered out of the trees.

"Hell, Smoky," said Kopernick, and moved angrily toward the old sourdough. "I wish you'd make some sign before you bust in like that. Where are they?"

Smoky's gray hair fell over his pouched, dissolute face like the frizzled ends of a mop from beneath a battered black hat that had seen the inside of every saloon from Edmonton to Yukon. He tried to say something, but only smacked toothless gums, and took another step before he fell forward. Still holding his Winchester in one hand, Kopernick caught the man before he went clear down.

"Where'd you get the money?" he said caustically. "I told you. . . ."

"Listen, Kopernick, lissen . . ."—Smoky's hand on Kopernick's arm was a gnarled claw—"I ain't drunk. Fust time in my life. I swear, I ain't drunk. He's right behind me, Eddie. Thought he done me in for sure, but I got away. . . ."

"What are you babbling about," snarled Kopernick, shaking Smoky's hand off his arm and standing up over the crouched man. "You've had some red-eye. Ten beaver pelts against a sour bannock you talked while you were swilling. I'm getting out, Smoky. Andover's around here, and, if he gets word I was near Resolution, he'll be on my trail like a bear after honey."

"No, Eddie." Smoky threw his arms around Kopernick's legs, holding him there, sobbing like a baby now. "Lissen. I'm not drunk. You've got to. I went into town to meet 'em like I promised. They weren't there, and he cornered me in the Alaska Light before they came. . . ."

"Who cornered you?" asked Kopernick, trying to kick free. "Let go, you old *moonyass*. You're drunk, and I'm through. I don't know what you're talking about. I don't know why I came down here in the first place. Putting my head in a jump trap, that's all."

"For your own good, Eddie," bawled Smoky, puffy cheeks gleaming with his tears. "I told you. Meet me here and I'd have something that would clear you of that murder charge. You're the only man ever treated me decent, Eddie. I'd do anything for you, Eddie. . . ." Smoky broke off to cough weakly, and Kopernick suddenly quit trying to free himself of the sourdough's grasp, and looked down at him with a strange, taut expression on his face. "Lissen, Eddie, I'm not drunk. Maybe I was when he cornered me in the Alaska Light, but I'm not now. A man couldn't be, the way I am now. It ain't lignite, see. It ain't lignite or bituminous or anthracite. They think it is, but it ain't. I know. I got the map to prove it. Not really a map. They think it's a map, but it ain't really a map. In my shirt, Eddie. He's right behind me."

Kopernick was on his knees now, catching the old man as Smoky started to cough again. "Will you make sense, Smoky? Lignite? What are you talking about? What map? I. . . ."

Kopernick broke off, stiffening to stare across the old man's bent head toward the trees. Another man stood there. Maybe six feet tall, the singular bulk of his upper body set grotesquely on a pair of short, bandy legs, like a pot of tea propped up on snubbed ski poles. In the Northwest Territories, fat on a man, as on a dog, was considered a weakness, and to anyone who didn't know him, the evident avoirdupois on this man's belly might have been taken for that weakness. Kopernick knew him.

"Well, Caribou," he said.

When Caribou Carnes chuckled, it puffed his fat cheeks up till they almost hit his eyes, giving his face a sly, puckish look. "*Si-tzel-twi*," he said in Chippewayan.

"I haven't got any tobacco," said Kopernick, and he was watching the man warily now, still holding up Smoky.

"Then how about the horns of a deer in velvet?" chuckled Caribou, coming out of the trees like a great, awkward Cupid. "I would give my right arm for the horns of a deer in velvet."

He was born of a white father and a Chippewayan mother, this Caribou Carnes, and some of the heft of his upper body came from hauling York boats up the Athabaska, and the rest had come from eating. Where most men only wore leggings during the winter to keep their pants dry, he wore them all year around. Dog-rib leggings of soft, embroidered caribou hide, tied on his buckskin pants as high as the knees. He rubbed his heavy jowls, gleaming and blue with an unshaven stubble, and grinned enigmatically at Kopernick.

"Sort of dangerous for you to be this near Fort Resolution, isn't it, Eddie?

Couple of Mounted Police here last Tuesday. Andover was one. He hasn't given up, Eddie."

Then it was both of them, turning to the rattle of rabbit brush on the opposite side of the clearing from which Caribou had come. Kopernick had one of his hands on his Winchester when the man showed. He wore a gray suit, the pants stuffed into muddy, laced boots, and the brush tearing at his clothes must have irritated him, because his narrow dark face was flushed. Seeing Caribou and Kopernick seemed to surprise him; he stopped abruptly, and his hand slid spasmodically beneath his coat. Then he pulled it out again, and his forced grin showed chalky white teeth beneath a small black mustache.

"Ah, *m'sieurs*, I hope you are the ones."

"That's Smoky," said the girl, coming up behind the man. "They *must* be the ones."

"Ah, yes, Smoky," grinned Caribou Carnes. "Poor, poor Smoky. Always drinking. He must be having the dt's again, eh, Eddie?"

Smoky was a dead weight against Kopernick's arm now, and he suddenly realized how wet his palm was. He pulled his hand from beneath Smoky, and looked at the viscid red blood on it.

"No," he said, "Smoky isn't having the dt's, Caribou."

After Kopernick had pulled his other four point blanket over the body, he squatted there with his hand still holding one corner, eyeing the girl. It had been a long time since he had seen a beautiful woman, and he couldn't help a certain sullen appreciation of the way her honey blonde hair swept down about cheeks colored high by the winds. Big blue eyes, too, that could do things with a man if he would let them. Body like the neat, trim frame of a racing *odabaggan*, with curves in all the right places to shed the snow. The breeze caught at her thin yellow skirt, whipping it about the curving lines of her legs, and he grabbed his Winchester and stood up suddenly. The hell with that.

"You with Caribou?" he asked the man in the gray suit.

"Caribou?" the man looked blankly at Kopernick. Then he looked toward Caribou Carnes. "Oh, him. *Non, m'sieu*, Miss Burdette and I are alone."

"Burdette!" Kopernick whirled to face the girl squarely, that taut look crossing the cracked, chapped skin of his cheeks.

"Yes." She was frowning at him, puzzled. "Arlis Burdette. And this is Jacques Brazeau. We are trying to get a man to guide us into the Barrens. You undoubtedly heard of William Burdette, who was supposed to have been murdered up north of Slave Lake three years ago. He was my father, and last month I received irrefutable proof that he is not dead. This Smoky . . ."— she stopped, looking at the blanket-covered body, and bit her lip, forcing the rest out—"Smoky contacted us at Edmonton. He said he'd lead us to the only white man living who had been to the Barren Grounds. Smoky was to meet us today in Fort Resolution with this man. We saw Smoky about half an hour ago, but he was acting strangely and wouldn't even stop to talk. We followed him out here."

"Acting strangely?" Caribou Carnes chuckled and pulled a hunk of dried backfat from his pocket, taking out his *besshath*. With this wickedly crooked knife of the Chippewayans, he began to pare off a piece of the meat. "I should think so. You know, Eddie, next to beaver tail there is nothing better than *doupille*. This backfat, now, is from a yearling caribou, and as succulent as when I first stripped it off." Smacking his thick, sensuous lips, Caribou turned with an affected innocence to Arlis Burdette. "Did Smoky tell you the name of this man he was going to show you?"

"Shut up, Caribou," said Kopernick.

The girl's face held a growing speculation as she stared at Kopernick. "No, Smoky didn't tell us any names. Only that this fellow was the only white man living who had been into the Barren Grounds."

"He-he . . ."—laughing like a sly old squaw, Caribou licked his plump finger—"he-he. I should think so. What about you, Eddie? Did Smoky tell you what he wanted to see you about here?"

"Will you shut up?" snarled Kopernick, leaping across Smoky's body to belly up against Caribou Carnes, one hand bunching the man's plaid shirt.

The grin on Caribou's face didn't fade, but it had suddenly lost its mirth. Carefully, he put away the chunk of *doupille*, and his little eyes, almost hidden by fat cheeks, were focused on Eddie Kopernick's hand.

"I think you better let go, Eddie," he grinned, staring at the hand almost cross-eyed. "You seem to forget how many men have spilled their brains over my moccasins. Do you wish to add your gray matter to the list? I could kick your head off your neck from where I stand, Eddie. You wouldn't have to remove your hand from my shirt, even. I could. . . ."

"I'm asking you to shut up." Kopernick's voice was flat. "I'm leaving here now without any more hot air being blown out. I'm asking. . . ."

Only Caribou could have done it. Without having moved his upper body a fraction of an inch, he brought his right leg out and up and around in a kick that would have felled a musk ox. Kopernick jumped back with a grunt, released his hold on the huge half-breed's shirt with his left hand, using his right hand to slash downward viciously with the Winchester. Caribou's kick met the gun with a sharp, bony thud, and Caribou screamed in pain, lurching sideways, and then falling over on his face. He twisted around and was up to his knees almost before he had hit, but the pain in his leg caused him to fall over on his other side. Kopernick stood there with his Winchester held across his belly, cocked, watching the half-breed without much expression showing on his face beneath the black snow glasses. Breathing heavily, Caribou rubbed his leg, the pain still contorting his mouth. It was a long moment before he could bring back that grin.

"I will kill you for that some day, Eddie." Chuckling he stood up, putting his great weight on the leg gingerly.

"Why not now?" said Kopernick.

Caribou looked at the gun, then pulled the fat from his pocket, still chuckling. "*Kompay*, maybe. Tomorrow. Or the next day. It doesn't matter. Someday. I am the king of savate on the Slave Lake, and nobody can do that to me and live. Someday I will get you without that gun and kick your brains out."

"*M'sieu*," said the man the girl had called Jacques Brazeau, "am I to take it that you are the fellow this Smoky was leading us to?"

"You better not take anything," said Kopernick.

Caribou was licking his fingers with a loud smacking sound, watching Kopernick with sly little eyes. "How else could you construe it, Brazeau? You are looking at the only white man living who has entered the Barren Grounds. Other white men have been there, but they are no longer alive."

The girl was staring at Kopernick. "Then . . . who are you?"

"He-he . . ."—Caribou sliced off another piece of backfat—"he-he. It would seem Smoky was playing a joke on all parties concerned. Smoky didn't tell you the name of the man he was bringing you to, Miss Burdette? Smoky didn't tell you he was bringing Miss Burdette here to meet you, Eddie? You ask who this is, Miss Burdette? I want you to meet. . . ."

"Caribou!"

Kopernick's voice turned Caribou. The huge man swallowed the last of his *doupille*, grinning down the bore of the Winchester pointed at his belly. With a chuckle, he deliberately went on.

"He is Eddie Kopernick."

The girl's face went dead white, and for a moment she tried to speak without any success, and, when it did come finally, it had a hoarse, strained sound. "Eddie Kopernick! Then you're . . . you're . . . ?"

"Yes," chuckled Caribou Carnes. "The man who murdered your father."

II

The Indians called it *tud-de-theh-cho*, which was Great Slave Lake, and its shores were still swampy and green with late summer, the conies and suckers so thick along the inlets that the latter could be scooped out with a dip net.

The calendar of the Territories was divided into dog season and canoe season and with the snow yet weeks away, the two Peterboro canoes were drawn up on the strip of white beach below the timber, tattered and patched with birch bark from their long haul north of Fort Resolution. Eddie Kopernick squatted with his head in the swirling gray smoke of the campfire to escape the maddening swarms of bulldog flies, cutting a ten-pound sucker into strips and hanging the strips on a spit above the flames. Caribou Carnes sat with his back against a tree, as oblivious to the flies as only a man with Indian blood in him could be, smoking a cutty pipe full of the Indian tobacco called *kinnikinnik*, made from the inner bark of the willow.

"You still thinking about Arlis Burdette, Eddie?" Caribou asked, chuckling pinguidly. "You shouldn't have left in such a hurry, after I told her who you were."

"What point in staying?"

"Maybe she would have told you what that irrefutable proof was of her father being alive."

"Don't be crazy. How could William Burdette be alive, when I . . . ?" Kopernick broke off, dark head jerking from side to side in a bitter, frustrated way.

"When you saw him dead three years ago?" grinned Caribou. "You should know, Eddie. I imagine it would be hard to believe a man was alive again after one had killed him. I never did get the whole story, Eddie. William Burdette was a research engineer for Anacosta Coal, wasn't he?"

"Let it go," said Kopernick stiffly.

"Yes," grinned Caribou. "As I understand it, Anacosta had sent Burdette up here to locate coal fields comparable to those estimated by geologists in Alaska."

"You use a lot of big words for an Indian."

"I am white, Eddie," pouted Caribou, holding the same dislike of most half-breeds for their Indian blood. "My father was Peter Carnes. At least almost white. How can I have any Indian blood when I am so erudite? I should have a Ph. D."

Kopernick scratched his black beard. "A man can get too smart for himself."

"I have begun to reach that conclusion, too, Eddie," chuckled Caribou. "It is much easier to sit on one's hams and eat beaver tail than to read all the books in the Athabaska library. You wouldn't believe it, Eddie, but I have read all the books in the H. B. C. library at Athabaska. I am a scholar and the king of savate on *tud-de-theh-cho*, and I can consume more unborn caribou calves than any ten men along the Slave River. I'll bet William Burdette never ate an unborn caribou calf." Caribou looked up under his bushy brows at Kopernick, little eyes sly. "As for discovering the coal fields up here, I understand Anacosta was interested in finding a practical way of exploiting what they found. With snow up here eight months of the year and the Indians so lazy they wouldn't even look at a coal shovel, much less pick it up, that would constitute a major problem for any corporation, wouldn't it? I imagine that's why the Alaskan coal fields haven't been utilized. There are also problems of transportation. Is that the fuss you had with William Burdette, Eddie? Over a problem of transportation?"

"Don't ride your sled too hard," said Kopernick.

"Is my *beth-chinny* going pretty fast now, Eddie?" grinned Caribou, using the Chippewayan word for sled. "I never did hear your side of the story, Eddie. Only what Constable Andover told. William Burdette and Nils Glenister hired you to guide them into the Barren Grounds? Smoky went along to pack for you over Pike's Portage. You made your base camp at Sithor's village on McLeod Bay. Nils Glenister and Smoky stayed at the Indian village while you and Burdette made your dashes into the Barrens. There had been trouble with poachers south of the Land of Little Sticks, and Constable Andover had come to Sithor's village investigating. Andover was there when you came back after the third run into the Barrens and had that row with Burdette about more pay for another trip."

"It wasn't that. He. . . ." Kopernick stopped suddenly, his mouth twisting bitterly. "Will you shut up? I don't want to talk about it."

Caribou chuckled. "So, you did have a fight with Burdette. And the next morning they heard a shot behind Sithor's lodge, and Constable Andover and Nils Glenister found you bent over the body of William Burdette. Your Forty-Four-Forty had several fired shells in its magazine. You claimed you'd been hunting. . . ."

"I had, I had!" exploded Kopernick. Then, cursing, he stuck his head back in the smoke and began working viciously at the fish again. Caribou's chuckle was satisfied.

"You're touchier about it than you like to admit, aren't you, Eddie?" The half-breed got out his inevitable hunk of backfat and began paring off a slice with his crooked-bladed *besshath*. "There's a lot of queer angles to that business, Eddie. Whatever became of Glenister, for instance?"

Kopernick spat it out. "How should I know?"

"Glenister was Burdette's partner? You'd think he would have gone with Andover and you when the constable started back to put you on trial at Edmonton. Yet Glenister stayed at Sithor's village, and, the day before you and Andover left, Glenister left, telling Sithor he was heading for Resolution.

They never saw him anywhere. He just disappeared." Caribou took a succulent bite of backfat. "How did you get away from Andover, Eddie? He
won't ever tell. I guess he's ashamed."

"I got away."

"He-he." Caribou's laugh was sly. "You sure did. I guess nobody will ever
know except you and the constable. I guess nobody will ever know what
happened to William Burdette's body, either."

Kopernick whirled, still squatting. "Will you get off that sled? I told you I
don't want to talk about it."

"Just disappeared. Like Glenister . . . disappeared. Is that why you're
going north, Eddie? Because you don't know what happened to the body of
William Burdette? Why not admit it?" Caribou sucked the grease off one
plump finger with a loud, smacking sound. "The body disappeared some-
time between the morning you were found with it and the following evening. Sithor's bucks took it to one of their lodges and that's the last they saw
of it. And now, when Burdette's daughter comes, claiming she has positive
proof her father is alive. . . ."

"But I saw him, damn you, I saw him!"

"Yes, didn't you," grinned Caribou. "That's what you can't get over, isn't
it, Eddie? You want to believe the girl, because Burdette being alive would
clear you of a murder charge. Yet you can't believe her because you did the
killing yourself. And yet, you can't stop yourself from going north to make
sure, because you don't really know what happened to Burdette. It's ironic,
isn't it? Of all the men in the Territories, you should know. And you don't.
One thing I don't see, though, Eddie. If you used a gun on Burdette, how is
it Smoky was killed with a knife?"

Kopernick rose slowly from the fire, his hands closing into fists. "You're
going too fast now, Caribou. You better jump off that sled, before it tips
over with you."

"I never tipped a *beth-chinny* in my life," chuckled Caribou. "Did you get
what you wanted off Smoky . . . ?"

"You've tipped this one, Caribou!" Kopernick jumped to where Caribou
sat, standing above him with his bearded face turned dark by rage. "When
Smoky came to me, he was running from whoever had put that blade
through him, and he told me that they were right behind. Next minute you
showed up on one side of the clearing, and that Arlis Burdette came on the
other side with Brazeau."

"And we found you bent over Smoky, the same way Glenister found you
bent over Burdette," said Caribou, getting ponderously to his feet. "My
sled's still going first rate. You ain't got that gun, Eddie. Remember what I

told you I'd do, when you didn't have it? My *beth-chinny*'s still going, but, if you want to try and turn it over, go ahead. Now, who were you intimating put that blade through Smoky?"

"Caribou . . . !"

Kopernick broke off, seeing Caribou's little eyes go past him toward the timber behind. For a moment, the snapping fire was the only sound. Then Caribou's voice came, a hoarse shout.

"*Ma-a-rche*, Eddie!" yelled Caribou. "It's Constable Andover!"

It was all confused to Eddie Kopernick after that, a running, shouting, brawling insanity of those two scarlet-coated Mounties looming at him from behind, Andover in the lead, a big, red-faced man in his early thirties with a thick blond mustache riding his bleak mouth like hoarfrost on a ridge of muskeg. He had his gun out, its thong flapping from the weapon's butt to where it was attached around his neck. Nine out of ten men would have tried to escape Andover's rush like that, but Kopernick's jump toward the constable was the thoughtless jump of a man who had been hunted till his reactions were those of a wild animal, and the very unexpectedness of it must have been what made Andover miss his first shot. With the roar of the gun deafening him, Kopernick went into the constable's solid bulk. They made a thick, fleshy sound, meeting, and then the ground was hard against Kopernick's back, and he was rolling beneath Andover. He sprawled into the fire, scattering smoked fish and burning brands everywhere, the sudden heat giving his struggles a spasmodic violence. He twisted Andover's gun around, and with it still in the man's hand beat at Andover's face.

"Damn you, Kopernick. . . ."

Andover's desperate curse was cut off by his own shout of pain as the gun butt smashed into his brow. Kopernick got to his knees, straddling the man, shaking the burning sticks and coals off his back as he fought to tear the revolver completely free of Andover's desperate grip. The second constable had been blocked off from firing by Andover's running body, and now he was moving to get the two struggling men from between him and Caribou so he could shoot without fear of hitting Andover.

"Myers," yelled Andover, struggling to keep Kopernick from hitting him again. "Don't let that man get at you with his feet. Keep away from Caribou's feet!"

Caribou caught Myers off guard by jumping directly across Andover and Kopernick, one foot striking Kopernick's head. Constable Myers tried to whirl toward Caribou as the huge half-breed came down on one foot. That left his other foot free to swing, and Kopernick knew what was coming. Even as Myers got his gun around that way, Caribou's first kick flashed out.

It knocked the revolver up as it went off. With an amazing agility, Caribou followed up, dropping his kicking leg and throwing his weight on it and lashing out with the opposite foot all in one smooth swift motion, so fast Kopernick couldn't follow it. The second kick caught Myers in the belly and sent him crashing back into a tree, doubled over.

All this time Kopernick had been wrenching desperately at the gun to get it free of Andover's grip. Finally he tore it completely out of the constable's hand, and hit him again in the face with the butt.

"I am the king of savate on *tud-de-theh-cho*," roared Caribou Carnes, "and I have spattered the brains of men with more guns than you,"—he had his third kick coming—"all over my moccasins."—and it smashed Myers's head back against the tree trunk.

Caribou then executed an amazing follow-up, kicking the Mountie's gun out of his hand, and then caught the constable with a head-high kick that sent him slamming sideways from the tree trunk to roll over and over like a birled log till he came up against a spruce tree farther away and stopped and lay still.

The Mounties tied their guns on that way for good reason, and the best Kopernick could do was empty Andover's weapon into the sky before he got up. "Let's mush, Caribou."

Caribou was standing with his *besshath* in his hand, looking mournfully down at the constable he had kicked into unconsciousness. "I am tempted to take out his tripe with my crooked knife. But, then, I would be running like the little *nakee* all the rest of my life, just like you are, and sooner or later the little red fox gets caught, doesn't he?"

Kopernick grabbed him by the arm, and they were running when they reached the two Peterboro canoes. Kopernick jerked the towline attached to the lead canoe to test it, then shoved the craft into the water, and Caribou had the second one out after it. They both jumped into the lead craft, Kopernick in the stern.

"Pull that paddle, you big *moonyass!*" shouted Kopernick. "Andover's got his own canoe somewhere."

There was nothing a caribou-eater hated worse than to be called a tenderfoot in Cree, and, smarting under the gibe, Caribou bent over his paddle. "Don't talk to me, you Athabaska *teotenny*. I'll be pulling this canoe when you're dead in its bottom from exhaustion."

"Don't put that in my cariole," laughed Kopernick harshly. "You've got the streak of fat, Caribou. Big dogs, big men, it's the same thing. Packing or sledding or canoeing, the big one goes down first."

"You're a dirty Klincha liar," shouted Caribou apoplectically. "I'll take twice your load on my packing board and reach the finish an hour ahead of you on an hour's run. I'll drive dogs three times as big as any *kli* in your team and beat you in a snowstorm with my mittens tied to my snowshoes. And I'll be paddling this canoe up here when they've given you a scow to tow on the Styx. I'm no caribou-eater that can't go in a straight line. I was pulling a paddle when you were riding around on your mother's back in a moss bag."

It was true. One of the paradoxes of the Territories was that, though the Chippewayans had for untold generations utilized the water for their transportation during every canoe season, they were still execrable boatmen. The Chippewayan paddles were clumsy things, thick and broad, and the caribou-eaters themselves had apparently never conceived the idea of learning to paddle so dexterously on one side that the canoe would be driven in a straight line, preferring to paddle two or three times on one side, and then shift sides, sending the boat in endless zigzags. But Caribou Carnes, as he so willingly admitted, was not a common Indian, and Kopernick felt the boat surge forward under the huge man's drive and saw their wake streak out behind them, white and gurgling and straight.

Back on the beach, Andover had risen to his knees, pawing the blood feebly from his eyes as he sought to reload his gun. He must have realized he could never do this in time, for he raised his hand suddenly, lowering the weapon, and his shout came over the rapidly widening breach of water to Kopernick.

"I'm not through, Kopernick. You can't find a pushup in any river far enough away to hide from me. I'm after you on two counts now. I'm after you for Smoky. I'll get you, Kopernick. I'll get you if I have to follow you to hell!"

III

They belonged to the Dene nation, the Indians native to the Canadian Northwest Territories, and their origin was as mysterious as the origin of the winds they worshipped. The tribes speaking Chippewayan roamed the region north of Resolution, and those living near the Barrens had come to be called the caribou-eaters because their very existence depended upon the caribou to which they looked for their main source of food. Caribou Carnes had been born in Sithor's village, on McLeod Bay, and he had come north with Kopernick, returning to his people. Chippewayan was harsh and caustic to the ear compared with Cree, and it was this guttural tongue that filled the lodge of Sithor, punctuated by the lonely yap of a wolf dog from outside, or the snap of a spruce bough in the fire.

The encounter with Constable Andover was two weeks behind them, and Kopernick and Caribou sat among the fetid, greasy Indians, listening to Sithor.

"Your affair with the one called William Burdette is of no concern to us," he told Kopernick. "When one of our men is killed in a personal feud, we don't want the whites to interfere. Our only concern is that Constable Andover is known to be on your trail, and, if he found you here, we might be deprived of our treaty money this year for harboring you."

"Forget the constable," said Caribou Carnes. "Am I not in the lodge of my brothers? Kopernick comes with me. All we ask is that you sell him a good sled and enough dogs to run with."

Sithor was dressed in a caribou-hide coat, embroidered with porcupine quills down the front, epaulets fringed with musk ox hair. His face was seamed and wrinkled, and his eyes held the narrow, wind-marked look of a man who had spent his life staring across vast distances.

"You aren't going into the Barren Grounds?"

The words caused the bucks to shift around Kopernick, murmuring and grunting darkly, and he felt cold suddenly. "You never did find William Burdette's body?"

Sithor shook his head, braids of gray hair bobbing against his shoulders. "Nobody knows what happened to it."

Kopernick bent forward, that intense look drawing the chapped, reddened skin taut across his cheeks. "Sithor, you were with Nils Glenister when he came on me and Burdette. Could you swear Burdette was dead?"

Sithor's brow wrinkled in a frown. "You should be the one to know that."

"Could you swear he was dead?"

"We carried him back to the village." Sithor took a sharp breath. "He is dead, isn't he?"

Caribou chuckled. "Are you asking us, Uncle Sithor?"

Sithor waved a grizzled hand impatiently. "But even if he were not dead, a man in that condition does not just rise and walk off of his own accord."

"Perhaps he had something to hide," smiled Caribou. "We have never heard the whole story of what happened between Kopernick and Burdette. Glenister might have told it, but he disappeared three years ago. Smoky might have told it, but he is dead. Burdette, alive or dead, is, at the present, in no condition to tell it. Kopernick. . . ."

"If Burdette is alive somewhere in the Barrens . . . ," said Kopernick, and stopped, because that ominous muttering had risen among the bucks around him again. He stared at their dark faces. "What is it?"

"You aren't going into the Barren Grounds," said Sithor. "For your own good, Kopernick. Don't go."

"Why do you speak like that?" said Kopernick. "If Burdette is there, he can clear me. Your own hunters have been there."

"For the last two years," said Sithor, "the men who have sought caribou in the Barren Grounds have not returned. Seven of our bravest warriors left the village, at one time or another. We never saw them again. If you seek Burdette beyond the Land of Little Sticks, you will find nothing but death."

The braves muttered and nodded, and then they all began talking and shouting at once. A buck slipped in from outside and whispered in Sithor's ear. The caribou-hide tom-tom they called a *hali-gali* was sitting in front of him, and he beat on it for silence.

"There is another *teotenny* outside," he told Kopernick, "another white man."

"You mean white *woman*," she said, coming toward Kopernick through the crowd.

It was Arlis Burdette.

From the swamps north of camp came the low *kick-kick* of a secretive yellow rail, and somewhere a partridge was drumming on a balsam poplar. It was the only sound Kopernick heard as he stood there at the door of the lodge, holding the skin flap back with one hand, gripping his Winchester with the other. The minute Arlis Burdette had spoken, he had been on his feet, jumping past her to the door.

"Did I surprise you that much?" she said.

"Where's Andover?" he asked, tight-lipped, peering out the door.

"What do you mean?" Then she must have understood, and she flushed angrily. "Oh, don't be a fool. I didn't bring the Mounted Police. I never saw such a suspicious man."

He stepped out the door and moved down the wall to stop there with his back against the hair-cap chinking the undressed spruce logs, sweeping the camp from behind his black snow glasses. Arlis Burdette followed, dropping the skin flap behind her, and from inside the lodge the Indians began shouting and talking among themselves.

"Look," said Arlis, coming up to Kopernick, "Brazeau and I have been trying to find a guide all the way from Fort Resolution up here. None of the Indians will go into the Barrens, and it looks as if what they say about you is true . . . you're the only white man living who's been past the Land of Little Sticks. We were a day's trek south of here when we passed a caribou-eater who said you were in his camp. . . ."

He was looking at her now, and she must have seen the puzzled expression crossing his face, for she suddenly grabbed him by both arms, something desperate in her voice.

"Oh, don't you see? I can't help it if you tried to kill my father. . . ."

"*Tried* to kill?"

"Yes, *yes*," she said swiftly, almost crying. "If there was anyone else who could take me into the Barrens, do you think I'd ask you? I'd do my best to see the Mounties get you. But there isn't anyone else. I despise you for what you did, but I need you. What you did can't have any significance. All I care about now is finding my father. If you guide me to him, I'll do anything for you. I'll even help you escape the Mounties. I've got money. Enough money to take you to China if you want."

He was rigid against the wall, painfully aware of her nearness, not wanting to look at those wide blue eyes. "You really believe your father's alive, don't you?"

"I've got to believe it. He isn't dead, I tell you. This letter proves it."

She fumbled a tattered piece of paper from the front of her mackinaw, shoving it into his hand. Automatically he took it; then he shook his head, thrusting the paper back to her. She looked at his snow glasses.

"Andover was on my trail last winter," he said uncomfortably. "He had me running across the ice too long without glasses. The glare. . . ." He shrugged, indicating the paper. "You do it."

Her eyes remained on his face another moment, something indefinable passing through them, then lowered to the letter. "It's dated August First, Nineteen Twenty-Eight. Not much of a note, really. 'Dear Arlis . . . I've found it at last. Something big. Something bigger than Anacosta ever dreamed, or I ever dreamed, or any of us. As you know, I've duplicated all the data I collected up here during the last months, and sent the extra copies to you. Somehow, all the originals disappeared, and I can't make any official reports till I've corroborated my findings. I'll need that data to do it. Please get Anacosta to send those duplicates as soon as possible. If you need any help, look to Jacques. Your loving father . . . William Burdette.'"

It had been hard for Kopernick to concentrate on the letter. She was standing so close to him her honey-colored hair was almost brushing his beard—like the perfume poplars give off in the spring. It was hard to concentrate on anything. He swallowed something in his throat and edged down the wall to get away from the scent of her hair.

"That data . . . ?" He made a vague gesture with his free hand, still not quite back on the sled. "That data . . . ?"

"Maps, charts, weather reports, geological findings," she said. "You know. Dad made this his base camp, and, whenever he returned here from a run into the Barrens, he compiled everything he'd found into reports, sending duplicate copies of each one to Anacosta. He is a scientist, primarily.

Whatever coal deposits he found would have to be cross checked with all those other reports, before he could make any final, official report to the company. He couldn't locate his discovery exactly enough for the company, in the first place, without the maps he'd made. You can see how necessary all this data was to him."

"Three years. Then up he pops and writes you a short little note, with no explanation of where he's been or what's happened." Kopernick shook his head. "I can't eat those bannocks. Would there be any reason for someone else . . . ?"

"No, no." She had his arms again, looking up at him. "I had the handwriting checked by experts. It's his. He wrote this letter three months ago. You can see the date." Suddenly she was pleading with him like a child. "Tell me he's alive, Kopernick. Tell me you aren't sure you killed him. There could have been a chance, couldn't there? Nobody knows what happened to him, really. There could be a chance he's still alive. You of all people should know that."

"Everybody takes it I'm the authority on the subject," said Kopernick bitterly. "Suppose I'm not. Suppose I don't know any more about it than you? Suppose I didn't shoot him?"

"Oh, don't joke with me."

"That's what Andover said," muttered Kopernick.

Yes, that's what they all had said. *Don't make me laugh. You were bent over him with fired shells in your .44–40 and a bullet the same caliber in him. Out hunting? That's a little thick to swallow, isn't it? Out hunting? That's funny. Or unfortunate. Or don't make me laugh. Or don't joke with me.* Until he had quit telling them he was out hunting. Until he had quit telling them anything. Until he had just run like a wolf runs, without any particular goal except to avoid human beings and to keep one jump ahead of Andover.

"It's not so funny he should write a note like that." Arlis was talking more to herself than him now. "Dad is a scientist. You don't know men like that, Kopernick. They get so wrapped up in their work they forget time or space or life. Probably wasn't even thinking how funny it would seem for the note to pop up like that when he wrote it. He'll explain when we find him. Very logically. He's alive. Tell me he's alive. Some Indian must have taken him away. Sithor and his bucks carried Dad to the lodge and then one of them took him away. That's how it happened, isn't it, Kopernick?"

She was crying against his shoulder, and his arms were around her somehow, and he was surprised at how small and soft she was. Like a snowshoe hare. Yes, small and soft and trembling against him like a little snowshoe hare. Then he became aware of how many Indians had come out the door after him, and of how long they must have been standing there, watching them.

"Maybe you'll take her into the Barrens now, Eddie?" chuckled Caribou Carnes. "I would take her into the Barrens, if she cried on my shoulder like that."

Kopernick pulled his arms from around the girl. "Shut up."

"He-he." Caribou's giggle drew his fat cheeks up till they almost hid his little eyes. "Sithor tells me he has a nice long Cree toboggan he got from Athabaska last year. That would make a good sled for you. And his *klis*, Eddie, the dogs. He has a spitz leader that makes you wish it was winter already."

Kopernick looked at the girl for a long minute, then jerked his head toward Caribou. "Let's go see the dogs."

In the summer, the Indians treated their dogs as carelessly as they treated their canoes in the winter, and the dozen Huskies lying around behind Sithor's lodge were gaunt and nervous, rising to their feet and bristling as Kopernick came toward them. Caribou pointed out the spitz leader, a black male with the wolf showing in his prick ears and sharp nose.

"Maybe goes eighty pounds now," grinned Caribou. "But he'll run a hundred easy as soon as you start feeding him regular. Sithor says he led the team that won the races in Athabaska last year."

"Too big," said Kopernick. "How about that gray bitch? She looks like she'll make eighty at her top."

"Too big?" scoffed Caribou. "The bigger the better, I say. I already got my team picked out. Not a one will weigh under a hundred after I feed them up."

"And a smaller team will wear them out on the long run every time," said Kopernick, studying the gray female. "Streak of fat, Caribou, men and dogs."

Caribou's laugh shook his belly. "Wait till we get to running. I'll show you. I'll lead you all the way and have your dogs so gaunted up they look like the wrong end of a hard winter. Streak of fat. He-he. I didn't see any streak of fat in that canoe race with Andover."

"What's her name?"

Caribou looked at the lean, wolfish bitch. "Kachesy. It means Little Hare. Because she runs like one, I guess."

"Kachesy," said Kopernick, squatting down and holding out one hand, "Kachesy"—and the sudden velvet of his voice made Arlis Burdette look down at him in a certain surprise.

"You don't think she'll come to you?" said Arlis. "A strange dog."

"He-he," chuckled Caribou. "Down in Athabaska they say Eddie Kopernick is part dog. He doesn't drive them in a sled. He gets in the harness and pulls with them."

"Don't be fantastic," said Arlis.

"He doesn't sleep in a bag at night like ordinary men. He digs himself a cabane in the snow, just like the dogs. It wouldn't surprise me if he hid a tail down one leg of those corduroys."

"Oh, stop it."

"Kachesy." The female had come in slowly, hesitantly, snarling softly and bristling, but now Kopernick had his hand on her ruff. "Kachesy. I think I'm going to like you. Little Hare? How would you like to run in a toboggan? None of this gang hitch these caribou-eaters have been using on you. Nome-style, Kachesy."

"Nome-style," laughed Caribou. "Tandem hitch. I wouldn't drive my dogs that way if the horns of a deer in velvet depended on it. You do everything wrong, Kopernick. I don't see how you ever kept ahead of Andover last winter. Half dog, and you still do everything wrong."

Kopernick felt the gray's forelegs, and she relaxed under his touch. Straight and not too long, with a light spring in the pasterns that was good. He pursed his lips, nodding slightly, and ran his sensitive fingers down her hindquarters, a faint smile catching momentarily at his mouth as he felt the singular development of the thigh, and second thigh.

"This is my king dog," he said finally. "Sithor got a price?"

"My God!" Caribou threw up his hands in mock despair. "A female for a king dog. I've seen everything. He-he. I suppose Sithor has a price. He would sell his grandmother for two years' worth of treaty money."

"Pick out the best you can get," said Arlis Burdette. "It's on me. While you're looking, I'm going down to get Brazeau. He's unpacking our canoes."

The two men watched Arlis go off, the lilt of her walk tapping her wool skirt against bare legs with each step, and finally Caribou looked down at Kopernick, chuckling. "I guess I'd go north, too, if a girl like that asked me."

Kopernick turned back to the dog abruptly, lips tight. "If I can find Burdette alive, it'll clear me of the murder."

"I'd go north, too, if a girl like that asked me," repeated Caribou, grinning slyly, and turned to go after Arlis.

It was dark before Kopernick had finished picking his team. Tying the five dogs apart from the main group, he turned toward the lodges. A bunch of gray jays came wailing through the gloom, heading south before a chill wind that presaged early snow. A silent squaw passed Kopernick, papoose carried in a moss bag on her back, caribou-hide skirt rustling softly against her bright red stroud leggings. Most of the Indians had gone into their lodges, and Kopernick could see streaks of light showing through the crack in the walls of Sithor's lodge where the hair-cap chinking had come out from between the logs.

The silence that descended over an Indian village after dark had always oppressed him, somehow, and Kopernick shivered a little, pulling the Hudson Bay blanket closer around him. He'd have to get a parka out of the stake the girl was putting up for an outfit. First snow come, and this damned blanket wouldn't provide any more protection than a caribou hide with bot holes in it.

He was going down the narrow lane between Sithor's lodge and the next one when the scraping sound across the roof made him look up. There was a black shadow above him, and he hadn't even jerked up his gun when the weight struck his face, hot and resilient and stunning.

Kopernick went down with a shout that was muffled against the man's body, his head rocking to a blow. He tried to get his feet under him, but the passage was too narrow to straighten his twisted legs, and the man's weight held him down. He grabbed his Winchester with both hands, jamming it upward viciously. The man on top grunted, shifted violently, lifted an arm. Kopernick tried to roll aside from the blow. But he was jammed in too tightly. Something hard struck his head, knocking it back against the log wall, and he heard his own yell of pain.

He jammed the rifle up again, spasmodically, but it was a feeble thrust, and the man tore it from his hands, striking again. Kopernick threw up one hand, and the blow caught him there, knocking the fingers back into his face and smashing them against his jaw. The third blow struck him full across the forehead, and after that whatever sensation remained was dim and unreal in the whirling vortex of pain screaming through his brain. He felt the man's hands go beneath his blanket, feeling around on the inside of his belt against his skin, then he sensed the pockets of his corduroys being pulled out, tobacco and rawhide whangs spilling onto the ground.

"Damn you," he heard the man say, and felt his body jerk as he was rolled over. At first he thought he was struggling again, then realized it was only the desire to struggle in his mind. His body refused to answer that desire. He tried to sob in a sort of frustrated anger, and couldn't even do that.

"Kopernick?" It came from somewhere far away, hardly intelligible at first. "Kopernick, was that you? Where are you?"

The man crouching by Kopernick cursed again, and rose to slip down the alley way and disappear. The girl came from the opposite direction, and it must have been her calling. She knelt beside him, and he could hear her saying something fearful and compassionate, and her hands were soft against his face. He was coming out of it now, the pain growing more intense as his consciousness returned.

"Stunned me," he mumbled, shaking his head. "Stunned me." He tried to sit up.

"Why?" she said. "Who was it?"

He fumbled beneath the broad belt which held in the four corners of his blanket, and pulled out a piece of paper. "I think they were after this. When Smoky first contacted me on the Slave Lake, he told me if I met him at the poplar grove north of Resolution on the tenth, he'd have something that might help clear me of the murder charge. You know what happened when he did meet me at the grove. Before he died, he babbled a lot of trash I couldn't understand about lignite and bituminous and how they thought it was a map, but it wasn't really a map."

"Lignite," she said. "That's coal. Who thought it was a map?"

"I don't know who he meant by *they*." Kopernick unfolded the paper. "Smoky said he had it in his shirt. I got it out without you or Caribou seeing me. This."

She acquainted her eyes in the darkness to see what was drawn on the paper. "Looks like a picture of a tree."

"Lobstick."

"Lobstick?"

"You find them all over the Territories," said Kopernick. "Whenever something noteworthy happens along the trial, the men cut a lobstick to commemorate it. They choose a good-sized tree and shave the branches off the trunk in a pattern. Like Commander Webb's lobstick on Caribou Island. You must have seen it if you came up Slave Lake. Webb saved a whole boatload of caribou-eaters from drowning, and they chose a pine growing near the water and shaved all the branches off one side about halfway up to mark the event."

"And you found this drawing of a lobstick inside Smoky's shirt?"

He nodded. "The only paper there. It must be what he was talking about. No two lobsticks are alike. If you ever saw the real one this picture represents, you couldn't miss it."

"But Kopernick," she said, "what could it mean?"

IV

Pike's Portage between Sithor's village on Great Slave Lake and Artillery Lake was thirty miles of packing for Kopernick and the others, wooded land interspersed by nine smaller lakes. Even the dogs carried a load, thirty-five or forty pounds packed into the panniers formed by a strip of canvas slung over the animal's back, held on by a breast strap and belly band. The men's packing boards were carried on their backs in such a way that the two hundred and fifty pounds of weight rested on the body's center of gravity, the board itself held by a broad strap around the head. Before the first day was over, Jacques Brazeau had lightened his load by half, and every few minutes he had to stop and rest his back. They reached Weeso Lake in early afternoon, but there he squatted down with his board, slipping the strap off his head with a bitter curse.

"*Sacre*," he panted, "don't you beasts know the meaning of fatigue? I can't go any farther."

"We'll go until it's dark," said Kopernick. "Andover's behind us somewhere, and he'll be traveling lighter than we are."

"Oh, let the poor *moonyass* rest, Eddie," chuckled Caribou Carnes, setting down his load and rubbing the great smooth muscles of his neck, developed from countless portages like this.

"You wearing out already?"

"Wearing out?" Caribou bridled. "I'll pack you to the Mackenzie Delta and be carrying both our loads when you're crawling along behind on your hands and knees."

"Streak of fat," said Kopernick.

"Streak of fat, my grandmother's moss bag. I'll outlast you on any portage from here to the Yukon. You can't. . . ."

"Oh, put on your mukluks and go after the sled. We'll leave Brazeau here, and maybe he'll be rested up by the time we get back."

They hadn't been able to carry everything in one trip, and had left the dismantled sleds and canoes in a cache three miles back. Caribou unloaded the panniers on his huge black Siberians and started off before Kopernick was finished unloading the last of his own smaller sled dogs.

"Do you and Caribou always have to fight?" Arlis Burdette asked Eddie Kopernick.

"I don't particularly like him," said Kopernick. "I don't particularly trust him. I wish you'd hired one of the other Indians at the camp."

"I didn't hire Caribou."

He looked up from his butt dog. "I thought you did."

"I thought he was with you," she said.

Kopernick turned to Brazeau. "Did you sign on Caribou?"

The Frenchman rubbed the stubble beard on his lean pale face, sloe-eyes not meeting Kopernick's. "He seemed to know the country. We needed another man. *Bon Dieu*, why make so much of it?"

"Sort of a private deal, wasn't it? Not even consulting Miss Burdette."

Brazeau flushed. "I was William Burdette's best friend, *m'sieu*. I have been his daughter's confidante and advisor since his disappearance. I do what I think best for her interests."

"Then you must know a lot about William Burdette," said Kopernick, "and what he was doing. Maybe even more than Arlis knows. Nils Glenister, for instance."

Something passed through Brazeau's dark eyes. "Nils?"

"You knew him that well? What happened to him?"

The Frenchman shrugged narrow shoulders in his plaid mackinaw. "How should I know? You should know better. Nils was with you and William on that last trip, wasn't he?"

"And Smoky," said Kopernick. "Smoky's dead because he knew something. What about Nils Glenister? Nils was supposed to have disappeared right after Burdette was . . ."—he stopped, glancing at the girl—"after what happened to Burdette. The general consensus of opinion seems to be that Glenister is dead, too. How about that, Brazeau? Smoky died because he knew something. How about Glenister?"

"Will you stop asking me? How should I know? All I know is Glenister was last seen in Sithor's village, the day after Andover started out to take you down to Fort Resolution. Glenister left the village then and never showed up at Resolution or any of the other posts farther south." Brazeau was fumbling in his pack for something. "What are you driving at, Kopernick? I. . . ."

"Don't pull that out with the dogs free!"

But Kopernick's shout was too late. Brazeau had pulled a big chunk of smoked whitefish out of the pack, and the five dogs leaped forward in a howling, snarling bunch. The Frenchman went down beneath them with a loud cry, rolling over beneath their bodies as they tore at him to get the meat. He came to his feet among them, fighting to stand up in the mad, yapping tangle, and Kopernick saw the big Grant-Hammond automatic in his hand.

"*Pour l'amour du bon Dieu!*" screamed Brazeau, and whirled about to bring the .45 to bear on Kachesy.

"Brazeau!" shouted Kopernick, and scooped up a loaded pannier from where he had dumped it on the ground, and slung the whole pack saddle at the Frenchman, blankets and stroud wrappings falling out of the pockets as the pack saddle flew through the air.

The pannier struck Brazeau as the Grant-Hammond exploded, knocking the gun upward. Staggering backward under the impact, Brazeau was unable to keep his balance under the whirling turbulence of the fighting dogs, and he went down again. Grabbing a heavy tent pole from another pannier, Kopernick leaped among the animals, beating at them viciously.

"Kachesy," he swore, "get back, damn you, get out of here . . . !"

It was brutal, but most of them were half wolf anyhow, and the only way a man could control them when they were maddened and fighting like this was to beat them almost insensible. Kopernick laid about him with the clubbed tent pole until the dogs fell back, so Brazeau could roll over and get his feet under him. He still had his Grant-Hammond and, while he was yet on his knees, he turned, cursing viciously.

"I'll kill them!" Brazeau shouted frenziedly. "I'll kill them all."

His first shot went above the head of Kopernick's butt dog. Kopernick quit beating the dogs and turned to slug Brazeau across the back of the neck. The Frenchman went forward with a hoarse cry, rolling over on one shoulder and onto his back. He pulled his gun arm from beneath him, and Kopernick saw the intent stamped in his rage-twisted face.

"Don't, Jacques!" cried the girl.

Kopernick threw the tent pole fully in Brazeau's face, and jumped after it, kicking at the man's gun while he was in mid-air. He heard the weapon go off and felt the hot leap of it against his foot, and then he was on Brazeau. The dogs were back in again, fighting each other for the shredded piece of whitefish and tearing at the two men to find more. Kopernick lurched up beneath their furry bodies, surprised to see the gun still gripped desperately in Brazeau's hand. He caught the .45 and twisted it around sharply, hitting Brazeau in the face with his free fist.

Kachesy and another dog crashed into Kopernick, knocking him off Brazeau. Partly freed of Kopernick's weight, the Frenchman got to his knees, throwing Kopernick over onto his back. The dogs rolled across Kopernick's face, hot and furry, claws ripping him, and another spitz jumped in. Kopernick tore at them, swinging his leg around in a blind kick at Brazeau. He heard the man grunt, and kicked again, and then he had the dogs off and could see, and still lying on his back that way he lashed out with his foot a third time, catching Brazeau fully in the face.

It knocked the Frenchman backward almost off his knees, and, while he was still twisted over, Kopernick shoved the last dog off his arm and rolled over and jumped Brazeau, snarling like one of the Huskies. He hit Brazeau in the mouth, knocking him flat, and tore the gun from his hand, and hit him again in the face when he tried to rise, and kept hitting him, sprawled across his body, until the man ceased to move. Then he staggered to his feet, finding the tent pole, and belayed the dogs till they were scattered about him in a circle, snarling sullenly and licking their wounds. Brazeau groaned feebly, and Kopernick turned to him, standing there with his face clawed and bleeding, his black hair down in a matted tangle over his snow glasses.

"You aren't doing any killing, Brazeau," he gasped. "Next time you try to use that gun on those dogs, it's you who'll be killed, I swear!"

They were on Aylmer Lake when the first snow fell, and they cached the canoes on the shore and bolted the runners on their sleds. Driving the heavy sledge called a *komatic* by the Eskimos, Caribou Carnes started right off at the five-mile pace adopted by the trippers over a good run.

"Hold them down, Caribou," Kopernick called to him. "They've been starving all summer. You'll run their legs off the first day."

"He-he." Caribou's laugh shook his belly against the bright red L'Assumption sash he had tied around his waist. "No wonder you want to go slow, with that crazy toboggan you picked. All it's good for is the woods, Kopernick. All my friends tell me the same thing. A man's crazy to ride a toboggan past Last Wood. All prairies up there, hard-packed snow, just like the Eskimos ride."

"Your friends never hunted as far as I took Burdette." Kopernick was jogging beside the woodland sled called a toboggan by the Indians, from the Algonquin word *odabaggan*, and he caught the tail line to steady it as the nose struck a rock. "There's more muskeg up there than you ever saw in your life. You need a toboggan for that."

"Muskeg, my grandfather's moss bag," laughed Caribou, lashing his dogs. "*M-a-a-arche*, you *klis, marche!* I'll be coasting over that muskeg like a beaver down a slide while you're all tangled up in your broken runners. And when we're on the level, you'll see how good that damn' ski of yours is against a decent pair of runners."

Kopernick spat disgustedly. Well, maybe the toboggan did look like a ski. Instead of runners, it had two flat strips of birch bolted together and curved up at the nose. The cariole, where the load was stowed, looked like a canvas bathtub, extending the whole eight feet of the sled and held in place by a sling extending from the curved nose to the blackboard.

"Try climbing a hill with that *komatic*," said Kopernick. "You'd spill the whole load right in your lap."

"*Chanipson*," shouted Caribou, using the Chippewayan to turn his dogs right around a tree. "*Chanipson*, you crazy *klis, chanipson!* Listen, Kopernick, my dogs are big enough to climb any hill with any load."

"And wear out before they reach the top."

"*Unipson*," bellowed Caribou, turning the dogs left this time, his voice growing louder as his irritation increased. "They won't ever wear out. You never proved that streak of fat on me yet. I wore you out on the lake, didn't I? I packed you out on the portage."

"You didn't wear me out."

"Will you two stop fighting," panted Arlis Burdette. "I don't see how you have enough breath left to speak a word."

Jacques Brazeau jogged sullenly beside her, narrow chest heaving, face covered with perspiration. The fight with Kopernick was a week behind, but the Frenchman still eyed him with a vindictive anger.

They settled down to a steady trot now, and the toboggan made a soft crunching sound through the hoarfrost coating the reindeer moss atop the rises. They crossed the tracks of a marten, made in neat little pairs across the trail, each set oblique to the other. Then they broke through a narrow passage in the brush, knocking frozen clusters of cranberries off either side, and entered a long open stretch.

"Kopernick," called Arlis suddenly, and he saw where she was pointing.

Caribou Carnes looked around from up ahead, chuckling. "A lobstick, Miss Burdette. You must have seen them on the way up from Athabaska. Not truly a natural phenomenon."

"Is that the one?"

"Is which the one?" asked Caribou.

"She wasn't talking to you," said Kopernick.

"Oh," said Caribou, a sly grin crossing his face as he slowed his stride to drop back toward them, "are you interested in a particular lobstick?"

V

It was then the shot came—sharp and clear on the cold air—followed almost instantly by Brazeau's shout. The Frenchman was running beside Kopernick's toboggan, and he lurched over, smashing into it. The sled swung sideways beneath his weight. He clawed at it to keep from falling, dragging for a few feet, one of his long Seauteax shoes ripping out of its footstrap. Kopernick caught the tail line, but Brazeau's weight had already tilted the sled too far over.

"Whoa," shouted Kopernick. "Kachesy, whoa . . . !"

But the frightened dogs had speeded up, the overturned sled bouncing and bumping along behind them, blankets and food dumped from it with every foot. The second shot came just as Kopernick's steer dog rammed into Caribou's sled. Caribou yelled something, and stumbled, and rolled forward into the snow. Kachesy got mixed up in the flapping tail line of Caribou's traces, and the number two dog rammed into her, tangling the moose-hide traces, and Caribou's sled went over on them. With the whole team in a yapping, baying tangle, the third shot rang out. Kopernick felt the hood of his parka jerk, and heard the thud of the bullet going into the packed snow at his feet, and knew how it had to be now.

"Dive for that brush!" he screamed at the girl, and bent to reach inside the overturned cariole of his sled, still bouncing over the ground, pulled by the frenzied, tangled dogs. But Arlis Burdette continued to run by his side, face twisted in a puzzled, frightened way. "Dive for the brush, damn you, dive for it . . . !"

With a bitter curse he yanked his .44–40 out of the cariole and jumped for her, catching her around the waist just as the fourth shot barked. The two of them rolled into the snow with the bullet of a high-caliber rifle making its mordant whine above them. Then Kopernick half lifted Arlis onto her feet and shoved her ahead of him toward the rabbit brush and stunted spruce trees at their right. He pumped two shots in the direction he thought would do the most good, and then threw himself after the girl into the cover.

They lay there, panting, Kopernick levering his rifle for a third try. Then the girl caught his arm, and he saw Caribou dragging Brazeau in from where the Frenchman had gone down.

"Cover me, Kopernick," called Caribou. "He's in that timber on the rise ahead of us. Cover me."

His voice was drowned out by Kopernick's .44–40. Kopernick raked the trees methodically until his magazine was empty, and by that time Caribou was in beside them.

"You're one up on me, Caribou," said Kopernick ironically. "I didn't think you had it in you."

"Oh, don't be like that now!" The girl's face was flushed with anger. "He might have been killed, stopping to drag in Brazeau that way."

"He-he." Caribou's face was bathed in sweat. "I couldn't leave him out there, could I? Sniper got me in the arm somewhere. I think Brazeau's worse."

Kopernick had Brazeau's coat opened, and saw how thick and viscid the blood was blotting the man's plaid shirt, and Brazeau reached up to paw feebly at Kopernick's arm, nodding dully.

"*Oui, oui, c'est fini*, eh? All right. I don't complain. Listen, Kopernick. It isn't lignite or bituminous, *comprende*? I studied all the data William sent back to us, and I've been checking the geological formations as we came north, and I know. It can't be lignite or bituminous. He thought it was, but he must have realized he was wrong even when he was sending the data down. Not lignite, or bi . . . bi . . . tumi. . . ."

"That's the same thing Smoky said," urged Kopernick, catching at Brazeau's hand. "What do you mean? Brazeau?"

They hunkered there a long silent moment after that, and then Kopernick took off the Frenchman's bloody coat and put it over his dead face. Caribou was sitting, holding his thick arm, but his eyes were on Kopernick. That strange feral expression had come into Kopernick's gaunt face, the little muscles along his bony jaw bunching up and drawing the flesh so taut across his flat cheekbones that faint cracks began to show in the chapped, reddened skin.

"The same thing Smoky said down at Resolution," he muttered, almost inaudibly. Then he searched for his rifle. "You stay here."

"Kopernick . . . ?"

With the girl's call following him, he crouched out onto the flats. The dogs had dragged the sleds almost to the fringe of trees ahead, and were snarling and fighting among themselves. One of Caribou's black Huskies had broken free and was running toward timber. Kopernick reached his overturned toboggan and began rummaging for a box of .44–40s, throwing things heedlessly out on the snow till he found it. He snapped open his lever and began jamming the center-fires home, then moved in a swift run toward the stunted spruces. He had on a pair of Ungava shoes, shorter and broader than most men liked to wear for any speed, but more wieldy in thick timber where a longer shoe would have kept running into the close-set trees.

Almost immediately he found where the man had crouched, and the tracks leading away through the trees. They had been made by the triangular shoe used farther north. Andover? Following the prints in a wary crouch, Kopernick shook his head. The constable wouldn't wear Eskimo snow-shoes, or do the thing from ambush like that.

The timber showed the effect of the short summers up here. They had passed from the Canadian zone down around Resolution, and these trees were stunted and scrubby, most of them standing less than fifteen feet tall. For a while, the only sound was the soft *sluff-sluff* of Kopernick's shoes in the snow, barely audible even to him. His breath fogged before his face in the chill air, and he moved like a tense, wary animal, head never still. He was rising a gentle slope when he heard the dim yap of a dog from ahead. He speeded up, reaching the crest, then stopped. Below the crest was an open field of tundra, stretching northward as far as he could see. The sled was a mile or so ahead of him, barely visible now. Kopernick whirled suddenly to a sound from behind him, jerking up his rifle.

"You're the most nervous man I've ever seen," said Arlis.

"He-he," chuckled Caribou. "You get that way when the Mounties have been after you three years."

"I thought I told you to stay back there." Kopernick's voice held impatient anger.

"We couldn't do any more . . . back there." The girl's face darkened a moment, but she was looking after the sled. "You're not going to follow it?"

"He's riding the runners," said Kopernick, almost sullenly. "We'd never catch a ridden sled on snowshoes."

"Kopernick." Her big eyes were wide and frightened on him. "Kopernick, who could it be?"

It was the real Barrens now, the Land of Little Sticks, where spruce trees over three hundred years old grew only eight or nine feet high, the timber spread in straggling groves, each grove separated by miles of treeless, empty prairie.

The girl was weakening under the trip, hardly having the strength to mutter one word during the whole day, stumbling doggedly behind Kopernick when the country became too rough for the dogs to pull her extra weight. Kopernick himself was running like some hunted animal, the gaunt lines of his face accentuated by exhaustion, haunted by the knowledge that the inexorable Andover was somewhere on their back trail, keyed up every moment of each long run for that rifle to begin crashing from some ambush again.

Only Caribou seemed unaffected. He had an incredible endurance, and seemed as fresh and strong after a twelve-hour run as when he had begun it, still full of that sly, chuckling humor, laughing even when he lashed his huge dogs unmercifully. Kopernick didn't know exactly when that day he first began to notice that Arlis was limping. They were crossing a stretch of swampland the Crees called muskeg, its brooding hummocks and ridges frozen over now to form a corrugated madness for sledding, and the girl in the sled would have been too hard on the dogs, so she was jogging along behind Kopernick.

"*Marche*, you stupid *klis*," shouted Caribou, sending his rawhide lash cracking across the back of his steer dog. "You won't get any whitefish tonight, if you don't do any better than this."

"What's the matter, Caribou?" said Kopernick. "I thought that Eskimo sledge could take the muskeg."

"Who said I'm not taking it," laughed Caribou. "I just have to touch my dogs once in a while so they don't forget I'm here."

"Put that lash on them much more and they won't have any hides left," said Kopernick. The girl cried out behind him, and he whirled around in time to catch her before she went clear down. She gasped a thanks, and tried to start running again.

"How long have you been limping like that?" he asked.

"I don't know," she panted. "It isn't anything."

"You wearing duffels?" he said. She nodded dully, and he turned to call after Caribou. "We're stopping here a minute."

"What's the matter? Those *klis* of yours wearing out already? Streak of fat, Kopernick, streak of fat."

Kopernick hardly heard him. He had set the girl down on the side of his toboggan and was removing her snowshoes. Caribou had turned his big sledge around and brought it back broadside to the toboggan so he could hunker down against it facing the girl. His big black dogs lay down in the snow, and Caribou took off the mitten over his right glove, and then the glove itself, reaching inside his parka for his big *besshath* and a piece of back-fat. With the crooked knife, he pared off a chunk for himself.

"No wonder you've got foot trouble," he said, smacking his lips. "Your duffels are all the same size. You get them all too large that way and your socks wrinkle and the wrinkles freeze and then your snowshoe strings freeze and begin to cut into your toes and instep, and you're crippled up good."

Kopernick was holding one of her small, pale feet in his hands, and he saw how deeply the flesh had been impressed by the frozen wrinkles of the duffels. "How long have they been like this?"

"I don't know. I didn't think it was worth bothering you about. I didn't want to complain."

He was looking up at her, and a strange, new emotion welled up in him. He hadn't expected that from a girl, somehow. Then, with a jerk, he reached into the cariole for some fresh duffel, and began to cut it into strips.

"Oh, no, Kopernick," groaned Caribou, stuffing the last of the *doupille* into his mouth. "You aren't going to give her Indian duffels. That's only for some dirty Klincha. Make socks for her, at least. Do it like my squaw does and you never get wrinkles. Four pairs, each pair smaller than the next, so they fit inside each other. Snug as a papoose in a moss bag."

Kopernick began winding the strip of duffel he had cut around her foot. "We haven't got time to sew socks. This is better than any duffel you ever wore, anyway. If you'd admit a little more of your Indian blood, you might learn something. You can thaw these strips out at night twice as fast as socks. I've seen you put on wet socks more than one morning."

"I haven't got any Indian blood," pouted Caribou. "My father was Peter Carnes."

It had begun to snow before they were started again, and soon they were mushing through a soft white swirl. Kopernick began hunting for a sheltered spot to pitch camp before they lost their direction completely. It was then he heard the dog yap from somewhere on their left flank.

"Caribou?" he shouted.

"What is it now?" answered Caribou from the white fall, and it came from ahead.

"Whoa!" shouted Kopernick, and his dogs came to a stiff-legged halt, and he turned to catch Arlis. "Crouch down in the lee of the sled. Don't move no matter what happens."

He had his .44–40, whirling toward the flank, head cocked for that yapping again. Andover? Kopernick began moving away from the toboggan. The snow beat softly against his face, and he kept pawing it off his dark glasses with a mitten. It seemed he was climbing a rise, and he began to breathe harder and to sweat inside his heavy parka of caribou hide. Then it was the yapping again, so much nearer this time that it startled him, and, even as he was stiffening, he heard the shout of a man.

"Andover?" Kopernick yelled into the snow, and then had his rifle up and going, because the other man was shooting.

The .44–40 jerked in his hands with the first shot, and, when he levered it, the empty shell flew out and hit the snow with a soft sizzle, and that was drowned out by the soft clattering of the other man's gun, and then Kopernick felt the blow in his belly, like someone hitting him there with all their weight behind the punch, and after that, just before he fell, the awful pain shooting through him. He felt himself rolling back down the slope toward the sled, and then he brought up against something hard, and stopped.

It seemed an eternity that he lay there in a stupor of pain, but it couldn't have been very long, because, when he could move again, he brushed dazedly at the snow on his glasses, and then made out the man standing above him, holding a rifle. Through the pain flooding his body came the surprise, so strong it was like a physical shock. Kopernick raised up spasmodically, and his voice had a hoarse, incredulous sound.

"Nils Glenister!" he said.

The dogs stood with their brushes down like wolves, huddled together in their moose-hide traces, staring owlishly into the falling snow. Caribou was still on the runners of his sledge, face blank with surprise. The girl squatted pale and tense beside Kopernick, looking up at the man above him. It was his own toboggan Kopernick had rolled into off the hill. Caribou had come back about the same time Glenister had come down off the rise after Kopernick, and now they were all held by Glenister's rifle.

He was almost as big as Caribou—Nils Glenister—the slope of his great shoulders thrusting his whole body forward slightly, his moose-hide parka tattered and patched, strips of duffel wound about his legs as high as the knee in place of regular leggings. Ice had frozen on his beard and was breaking off in chunks, and his eyes had a feverish burn beneath the fox-fur lining of his hood. Kopernick saw the Eskimo snowshoes he wore, shorter than the Chippewayan, triangular.

"It was you sniping us the other day, then," muttered Kopernick.

"Did you find my tracks?" said Glenister. "I tried to get you all at once, but you dove for timber too soon. I knew I'd get you sooner or later. When it started snowing today, it gave me just as good an ambush as that timber. If my damn' dogs hadn't yapped, I could have finished you before you knew what happened. Nobody'll find what's up here, Kopernick. Not even the Indians. They wonder what happened to their hunters who came into the Barrens? They should wonder. Seven of them, Kopernick. I kept count. And now you. All I want is the girl. She knows where it is."

"Where what is?" Kopernick could hardly speak with the pain in his stomach.

Glenister jerked his gun toward Caribou Carnes. "You stand still!"

"I wasn't doing anything," chuckled Caribou fatuously, and then his eyes were on Glenister's rifle. "Well, a Forty-Four-Forty. That's the same caliber Kopernick packs. How coincidental."

Glenister's feverish eyes seemed to glitter a little, and Kopernick stared at him, beginning to sense something in the man. He had seen the Barrens do that to other men before, the utter desolation, the loneliness. Three years? That was long enough for the strongest mind.

"Glenister," he said slowly. "Who killed Burdette?"

Glenister turned toward him, grinning thinly. "I knew Burdette had found it on that last dash you and he took into the Barrens, Kopernick."

"Found what?" said Caribou.

"Burdette wasn't going to let me in on it," said Glenister. "His own partner . . . and he wasn't going to let me in on it. I took all the data he'd kept and tried to find it on the maps, but it wasn't there."

"So that's what happened to the originals." Arlis's voice was strained, as if she had begun to sense the implication of it now.

"Yes," smiled Glenister mirthlessly. "That's why William sent to you for the duplicates. After I couldn't find it in the data, I caught him out behind Sithor's lodge and tried to force it from him. The old fool put up a fight and grabbed at my gun. It was his own fault. Then I heard you coming, Kopernick, and ran down that alley between the two lodges. Sithor and Andover had heard the shot, though, and met me before I was completely through the alley. I tried to head them off, but they wouldn't take that. But when we came back, you were crouching over Burdette."

"He-he." Caribou's chuckle drew his fat cheeks up until they almost hid his eyes. "So you really were out hunting, Kopernick. How ironic."

"You. . . ." Arlis had one small hand up to her mouth, eyes wide and horrified on Glenister. "You killed Dad. Nils. You. . . ."

VI

A sudden virulent anger swept Glenister. "Yes, me. Who else? He was holding out on me, wasn't he? I was his own partner, and he wouldn't share it with me. I got his body out of the lodge they had taken it to that night, loaded him on a sled, and headed for the Barrens. I thought he'd have the map on him. But all he had was a letter he'd written to you and hadn't sent."

"Letter?" Arlis fumbled in her parka. "You sent . . . ?"

"Yes," snarled Glenister, his eyes blazing fanatically now. "I found it on William's body. But when I'd taken him away from Sithor's, I didn't have a chance to load my sled up for any extended trip. I'd only carried him a day's run north of camp, so I could search his body without the Indians finding me, but the snow caught me up there, and I got turned around. I would have frozen to death if a band of Dogribs hadn't found me up north of the Land of Little Sticks. It took them the better part of that year to nurse me into health again, and they didn't let me go till summer. I guess I was still delirious. There are blank spots. I don't remember much. I do remember killing every Indian who set foot past the Land of Little Sticks. I guess I must have spent the whole three years out in the Barrens, hunting for it."

"For what?" said Caribou, grinning slyly.

"Only last January did I come out of the fog finally, and piece things together. I still had the letter, and I realized I would never find it hunting blind like that. It was easy enough to change the Nineteen Twenty-Five to Nineteen Twenty-Eight on the date of the letter so nobody would notice it. Your father always made his fives like an 'S' anyway. As for the month, all I had to do was wait till August to send it so that postal date on the envelope would match the one on the letter."

"But why send the letter at all?" The girl's voice was hollow.

"Isn't it obvious?" snapped Glenister. "In this letter William asked you to send the duplicates of all that data. But after his being thought dead for three years, I knew you'd come personally, when you got the note. And I knew you'd bring what he asked you. William didn't have the map along with the other maps and data he'd kept, and didn't have it on his person. He must have sent it to you with those duplicates. Now tell me where it is, Arlis."

"I don't have any map," she told him, frightened tears welling up in her eyes. "Are you crazy, Nils? We can't just sit and talk like this while Kopernick is. . . ."

Glenister took a vicious step to grab her shoulder, tearing her away from Kopernick and forcing her to remain on her knees. "Don't lie to me, Arlis. Your father must have made a map when he found it. He couldn't have come back to it any other way in the Barrens. Where is it?"

Caribou Carnes's complacent chuckle made Glenister raise his head. "Mister Glenister, has it ever occurred to you that William Burdette might have entrusted this map you speak of to someone besides his daughter?"

Glenister's face darkened. "How could you know? You weren't even with us."

"Smoky was," grinned Caribou. "Smoky packed over Pike's Portage for you, remember? Smoky stayed with you at Sithor's camp while Kopernick and Burdette made their trips into the Barrens. I met Smoky in the Alaska Light at Fort Resolution a month ago. He was drunk. I guess he was always drunk. Things spilled out of him, like they usually spill out of a drunk man. He told me how he had heard Arlis was at Athabaska with proof that her father was alive. He told me he had effected a meeting between Arlis and Kopernick at the poplar grove south of Resolution. Kopernick was the only man who had ever treated Smoky decently. I guess Smoky wanted to help Kopernick clear himself.

"Ah, friendship. Smoky didn't tell Arlis he was taking her to Kopernick, and didn't tell Kopernick he would be meeting Arlis. I guess he realized neither of them would come if they knew who they were going to see. Smoky was waiting in the Alaska Light to take Arlis to the poplar grove, when I found him."

Kopernick tried to roll over on an elbow and raise himself, and groaned with the pain that it caused him. "It was you put that blade through Smoky. . . ."

Caribou took out his keen-edged *besshath* and began slicing at a portion of backfat, chuckling. "There is nothing like *doupille*, Kopernick, unless it is the horns of a deer in velvet. But it takes a sharp knife to cut it right. I had always thought William Burdette was going into the Barrens after something more than coal. . . ."

"But he wasn't," flamed the girl. "He was a scientist."

"And Smoky corroborated my opinion," went on Caribou, ignoring her. "He didn't tell me in so many words, but the way he was acting and talking whetted my dormant curiosity. I got him in the back room, but he turned sly. I guess my *besshath* wasn't as sharp as it should have been. He escaped me. That must have been when you and Brazeau saw him, Arlis. He was running down Dogrib Row toward the poplar grove. He must have given it to you before he died, didn't he, Kopernick?"

"Given what?" said Glenister. "I think you're stalling. I'm going to kill you."

Caribou's chuckle was unperturbed. "I tried to get it off Kopernick down at Sithor's village. Were you surprised when I came down off the roof on top of you, Kopernick? Arlis came before I could search you thoroughly. You don't think I know where the map is, Glenister? Why don't you look in Kopernick's parka?"

It was instinctive for Kopernick to try and roll away from Glenister, and that was what caused the big man to jump at him, a savage eagerness crossing his face. That eagerness took Glenister's attention from Caribou.

"*Nezon!*" roared Caribou, "savate!" He leaped across Kopernick's sled to crash boldly into Glenister before the man could jerk straight. The two of them went to the ground, and Kopernick screamed with the pain of Glenister's weight on his wound. Caribou was on his feet like a rubber ball, and, as Glenister lifted himself off Kopernick, whirling with the rifle coming up, Carnes launched a kick from the hips that smashed the weapon out of Glenister's hands, and brought his kicking leg down with a thump and pivoted on it and lashed out with the opposite one to catch Glenister in the belly, doubling him over, and recovered that kick while the man was still bent, and had another one smashing into Glenister's chin.

Glenister went over backward with a shout of pain, but rolled over and caught the toboggan as Caribou rushed him. He leaped up and took Caribou's next kick full in the face and went right on in, screaming insanely. He got Caribou around the waist, trying to jam a knee into his groin. Caribou jerked sideways, blocking the knee with his own knee. Face twisted savagely, Glenister clawed at the half-breed with broken, dirty nails. Caribou got his weight beneath him and brought his leg up in a circular swing to kick Glenister in the ribs. Snarling like a wild animal, Glenister let go with one arm to slug at Caribou's face.

"*Nezon,*" shouted Caribou gleefully, "he's crazy," and caught Glenister's fist, straightening the man's arm and levering him back that way. Screaming fanatically, Glenister tried to keep his hold on Caribou with his other arm, but he finally had to let go. He kicked wildly at Caribou. Caribou avoided the foot numbly and caught it while it was still in mid-air, heaving Glenister over with it. The man went onto his back, and Caribou jumped after him.

"Damn you," howled Glenister. "I'll kill you. I've killed them all. Nobody finds out where it is. . . ."

Caribou kicked him back down as he tried to rise. Glenister rolled over on his belly, and Caribou jumped after him, kicking him in the head and face with a thick, drumming sound. Bawling with the pain, Glenister turned fully into the kicks and rose deliberately to his knees, his face a bloody mess. He caught Caribou about the knees. Caribou tried to twist away, jerking Glenister's head back with a blow to the chin. But Glenister clung to him with the bestial strength of a madman, snarling and cursing, tears of pain and rage streaking his mashed cheeks. Glenister was trying to climb up Caribou and gain his feet, arms twined desperately about Caribou's legs to keep him from kicking. But Caribou bent to jam the heel of one hand under Glenister's chin, forcing his head back. Glenister grunted spasmodically, bent backward like a bow under the strain, and Kopernick thought the man's back would break before he finally let go of Caribou's legs. The very instant Glenister released his hold, Caribou snapped all his weight onto one leg and lashed out with the other. Still on his knees, Glenister took the kick in his face.

"Oh, Caribou," screamed the girl, "stop it, for God's sake, stop it!"

But Caribou jumped on in, pivoting to kick again, dropping that leg back and shifting his weight onto it and lashing out with the other. Pivoting and shifting and spinning so fast Kopernick couldn't follow each separate movement, Caribou kept Glenister rolling and jerking over so he couldn't rise, raining brutal kicks into him. Glenister tried to get up a last time, his face an unrecognizable blur, inarticulate, animal sounds escaping his pulped lips, bloody hands pawing at his eyes.

"Savate," shouted Caribou, "*nezon*," and jumped in again, and this time Glenister went down for good. Huge chest heaving, Caribou bent over and rolled the body over onto its back. He stopped to peer at the wreckage of Glenister's face, then he pulled open the parka and thrust his hand in to put it against Glenister's chest. Finally he straightened up.

"He was crazy, wasn't he?" chuckled Caribou. "I guess he's better off dead."

He turned to pick up Glenister's rifle, wiping the snow off it. Then he shuffled around in the white drifts till he uncovered the paper Glenister had taken out of Kopernick's parka. Caribou stared at it.

"So you were interested in lobsticks," he said, and glared at the girl. "What does this mean?"

She bit her lip, barely able to speak. "I don't know."

"This what Smoky gave you, Kopernick?" Caribou waited for an answer, and, when it didn't come, said it again without the question. "This is what Smoky gave you. What does it mean, Arlis?"

"I don't know, I tell you."

"I think you do," he said, and the sly jollity of his chuckle only made it more evil. He went to his big Eskimo sledge and began unloading the extra blankets and spare gear; then he took the food in Kopernick's sled and loaded it into the space left on his own. After that he took out his *besshath* and walked toward Kopernick's team. Kachesy's ruff stiffened, and she snarled softly. Kopernick jerked spasmodically, trying to roll over and get to his hands and knees, but the agony that it caused him was too much. Arlis crouched over him, watching Caribou in a fascinated horror.

"Come here, Kachesy," chuckled the half-breed, holding out his hand. "Come here, Little Hare."

"Caribou . . . !" Kopernick gasped.

"Oh, I'm not going to kill your *klis*, Kopernick," said Caribou. "Just cut them loose. No food, no dogs. If that bullet in your belly doesn't kill you, starvation will. I sort of hate to do it, Kopernick, old friend. I've grown so fond of you during this trip. I guess there really isn't anyone up here quite like you. It will be the passing of an era. Come here, Little Hare."

With a sudden, vicious snarl, Kachesy leaped at him. Caribou jumped to one side, caught the dog about its thick neck as the traces brought it up short, and with two skillful slashes of his *besshath* had the moose-hide harness cut. He leaped away as Kachesy whirled. The dog stood there stiff-legged, fangs bared, brush up. Then she became aware that she was free, and moved to one side experimentally. Caribou cut the other dogs loose the same way, then turned to the girl.

"All right, Arlis, get into the sled."

She rose, trying to comprehend. "In . . . the sled . . . ?"

"Yes, my little green-winged teal. You and I are going to find that lobstick and you're going to tell me what it means. It's a singular lobstick. I know we haven't passed it on the way up. See it and I'd know it. It must be somewhere in the Land of Little Sticks. Get into the sled."

"No." A wild look widened Arlis's big eyes. "No, no. . . ."

She turned frantically and started to run, then stopped, looking back at Kopernick. Caribou jumped after her, and she turned again, breaking into a stumbling run. He caught up with her, catching her arm and spinning her around. Kopernick saw the kick coming, and cried out with his inability to rise. Caribou did it as neatly as a man would with his fist, his moccasin catching Arlis on the point of her chin. He recovered and caught her even before she fell, carrying her to the sledge. Then he slipped his big Yukon snowshoes back on, uncurling his dog whip.

"Caribou," groaned Kopernick. "Don't be a fool. That lobstick doesn't mean anything."

"Oh, yes, it does," chuckled Caribou Carnes. "Everything. Burdette wouldn't trust it to the mails, because by that time he was beginning to suspect Glenister of intercepting everything he sent down and examining it before sending it on. So Burdette gave it to Smoky to take to his daughter. Burdette had meant to include the letter with it, asking her to send the duplicates of that data up. But Smoky got drunk and left too soon. I guess Smoky sincerely intended taking the paper with the lobstick on it to Arlis, but you know how that is. He got drunk and forgot about it for a while. Then, when he was sober enough to remember and start out again, he needed another little drink to fortify himself, and that drink led to a second, and so on. He never did get any farther south than Edmonton. Lucky he was sober when he heard Arlis had come north with proof her father was alive. Smoky wanted to help clear you, Kopernick. Ah, friendship. When Smoky told me down at the Alaska Light, I thought he was talking about a map. I guess this is sort of a map, all right. A map only Burdette and his daughter would know how to decipher."

"But what good will it do you?" asked Kopernick, fighting for consciousness. "Coal? What can you do with that?"

"Not coal, Kopernick, don't you remember? Not lignite or bituminous. It's the old story, Kopernick, but it's always new, every time it's told." Laughing, Caribou lashed his dogs into a run, and shouted it back over his shoulder as they swept away: "Gold, Kopernick. Gold!"

VII

Kopernick didn't know how long he lay there, his spirit hovering in an agonized stupor, the blood on his belly congealing and freezing. Crazy things kept spinning dimly through his head. Arlis, mostly—soft and small and trembling like a snowshoe hare he had held once. The things he had felt when she was near. The softness in him that had come after so many years of hardness and bitterness and loneliness.

"Kopernick?"

He didn't know whether he opened his eyes, or they had been opened. The man had a lean, adamantine face, burned a reddish hue by the sun and the wind, eyes as cold and blue and humorless as the glacial ice on Caribou Island. It came to Kopernick suddenly that this wasn't in his mind, and he reached up to grasp at the man's leggings.

"Andover?" he said.

"Just wondered if you were still with us," said the constable, and nodded at Glenister, lying in the snow farther off. "You really messed up his face. Was that after he put the bullet through your belly?"

"Andover?"

"Yeah. I guess you're groggy." Andover took off his mittens and began to open Kopernick's parka away from the wound. "I came on ahead, Kopernick. Constable Myers stayed back in timber with the sled. We hit Sithor's village about a day after you left. This isn't as bad as all the blood indicates. Didn't hit you dead center. You'll make it back to Resolution for trial with some to spare. I've put some whitefish out for your dogs. Looks like somebody cut them loose. That other fellow? They'll be back for it soon."

He found the flask of whiskey down in the bottom of the cariole on Kopernick's sled and gave Kopernick a drink. It was pain, at first, but Kopernick reached up for another drink, feeling lucidity return.

"Andover?"

"Yeah." The constable was working at his wound now, swabbing the blood away with the whiskey. He nodded at Glenister. "Who is he?"

"Listen, Andover," said Kopernick, and the whiskey had given him strength enough to sit up part way, hanging onto the constable's arm. "Listen. Caribou got away with Arlis. Gotta go after him. The lobstick was the only thing they had to go by, see? Burdette had lost his original maps, and he sent Smoky south with the lobstick to give his daughter. She had duplicate maps. You know the Barrens. Helluva time trying to find where you've been a second time. Even the Indians can't. Burdette couldn't without the maps he'd made. All he had to go on was the lobstick. Man could spend his life hunting that alone up here. . . ."

"You're raving like a lunatic. I'd better put these on you before you start something else."

Kopernick looked dazedly at the handcuffs on his wrists, jerked his hands too late, then he reached up to catch Andover's parka in both hands. "Andover. Don't be a fool. You can't let Caribou get away with Arlis. He'll kill her as soon as he finds that lobstick. He's got all the maps now and the drawing. He'll kill her. Damn you, Andover, listen. Let me at least get them. I'll do anything for you after that. I'll go back and stand trial. Just let me stop Caribou. She's with him, I tell you!"

"You're in no condition to stop anybody. Shut up now while I bandage you. You're out of your head, Kopernick. Get back to Myers and we'll build a fire and make you some tea and bannocks. Wrap you up good."

"No." Kopernick tried to rise against the man's hands, the whiskey burning a false strength through him. "I swear, Andover, you aren't going to stop me now."

Andover tried to jerk free, pawing beneath his parka for his revolver. "Kopernick. Cause me any trouble and I'll put you out. Without compunction. I know you, Kopernick, and I'll knock you out."

Kopernick had him around the waist, trying to rise. He got his knees under him with his face buried in the acrid pithy smell of the wolverine fur lining the hood of Andover's parka. He felt Andover's right arm jerk outward with the gun. With a desperate gasp, he let go of the constable and drew back both hands, the chain on the cuffs rattling. Andover saw it coming and tried to throw himself backward and use his gun butt and shout all at the same time.

"Kopernick . . . !"

Kopernick crouched there on his hands and knees a long time after he had done it, shaking his head, trying to find the strength to move. Finally he crawled over till he was straddling the unconscious constable, fishing inside his parka for the key. The chain of the cuffs had made an ugly welt across Andover's forehead, and blood was starting to seep through the contusions. Kopernick unlocked the cuffs and snapped them open; then he put them on the constable. The hardest thing was to drag Andover to the sled and lift him in.

He didn't want to take a chance of Andover's using the cuffs on him the way he had on Andover, and he lashed the constable into the cariole with *babiche*, the untanned strips of caribou hide the Indians used for rope. Kopernick slumped over the sled, clinging to the lazy board with numb hands. Funny. They used *babiche* for everything. Toboggan was lashed with it. Dog's harness. Moss bags. Snowshoe straps. Everything.

He jerked his head up, realizing he had started to wander. Not knowing he was groaning with each movement, he turned away from the sled, one hand across his belly. How could anything hurt so much? Kopernick didn't remember when it had stopped snowing, but on the chill, clear air the dogs could scent things an amazing distance, and the whitefish Andover had put out had drawn Kachesy back first, and now the butt dog was slinking in, sniffing the air.

"Kachesy? Come here, Kachesy. Good dog, good *kli*. Little Hare. Put you in the moose hide. We'll make this last run a good one."

Harnessing each dog was a separate agony. He had to tie the sliced ends of the smoked moose-hide traces together and then place the saddle on the dog, slipping the traces through the loops on either side of the saddle, then hitching them up to the withy collar which was lined with caribou hide and packed with moss to bring the weight of pull on the dog's shoulders without galling. Finally he had them harnessed. He cut the lanyard on Andover's revolver, and stuffed the gun into his parka. Then he drank the last of the whiskey, slipped his mittens on.

"All right." He grabbed the lazy board to keep from falling. "I'm going to have to ride the runners, understand? Kachesy? Not much running. All riding. Think you can do it. All right. Mush!"

Their legs stiffened and the enormous muscles of their hindquarters stood out through the master hair and then the toboggan moved beneath Kopernick, and the snow began its soft *phlutt-phlutt* beneath the spruce runners.

Most of it was hazy and unreal after that. Most of it was pain. Sometimes there would be the stunted clumps of trees passing by in a frightened black pattern against the white drifts of snow. Jackpine, maybe, or dappled spruce, or birches, standing like slim, pale Indian maidens awaiting the return of their bucks. More than the trees, though, was the snow. *Phlutt-phlutt* all the time. Fluffing up behind and sprawling out on either side. The tail line tapping across a bare spot of rock. The spruce runners crunching through hoarfrost covering the caribou moss on a rise.

Funny. Caribou moss. Caribou Carnes. I'm not an Indian. Trees like Indian maidens. Pain. Oh God, the pain. Funny. Phlutt-phlutt. *Funny. . . .*

He jerked himself up, realizing it would be fatal to let it get him like that. He was so sleepy, though. He wanted to lie down in the white snow and go to sleep. Sleep in the white snow and forget pain and bitterness. Sleep.

Arlis?

It brought lucidity back in a shocking flash, and his whole body trembled to it. Arlis. It was what drove him on, through the pain, through the terrible lethargy. He swept past another bunch of stunted grandfather trees, limbs bearded white with dripping icicles. The dogs were running stretched out now with their shoulders whitened by snow kicked up by the animal in front of them.

"Are you crazy, Kopernick. Let me go. Untie me, you fool."

"Caribou Carnes, Andover. You can't stop me. He's got Arlis."

For the first time, Andover must have realized Kopernick wasn't raving. The constable tried to twist his head around, still groggy with having just recovered consciousness.

"You mean you're actually trying to catch Caribou Carnes?" he asked, stupefied. "Kopernick, even you can't do that. Not with a bullet through your belly. You couldn't catch him under normal circumstances. I've seen those dogs of his."

"Streak of fat."

"What?" he asked. "Listen, Kopernick, you'll kill yourself. You won't last another mile. Look, you're bleeding again. Let me up, Kopernick. Let me run it for you."

"I don't trust you, Andover. I don't trust anybody."

Bleeding again. As long as he stayed quiet the cold would have congealed his blood, but it was flowing out with his sweat now, darkening the front of his parka, wet and sticky against his belly. He had been following Carnes's trail in the fresh white snow almost since the beginning. Now his eyes wouldn't focus on the tracks, and, whenever he bent to see better, he almost fell from the runners. The dogs were running with the down brush of exhaustion, tails sagging like wolves, flanks heaving.

"Come on, Kachesy. Last run. *Unipson*, you *klis*, *unipson* . . . !"

The wheel dog steadied down with his forefeet to check the momentum of the toboggan, and Kachesy started the left turn around the snow-covered rise. They rounded the hill and passed another clump of trees, and Kopernick realized what was in Caribou's mind. Every time a grove appeared ahead, the trail immediately turned and pointed directly toward it.

"See what he's doing," babbled Kopernick dazedly. "Hunting for that lobstick. Hitting every bunch of trees he sights."

"What?" asked Andover. Then the sled jerked as he tried to sit up, staring ahead. "Kopernick!"

It took a long time for Kopernick to see it. He pawed at his snow glasses, thinking they were dirty. Then his eyes finally focused on that black dot moving so slowly across the snow field ahead of them. Miles ahead. No telling how far. Distances were deceptive. Funny. Miles ahead. . . .

Arlis!

Sobbing with his pain and exhaustion, he shouted hoarsely at the dogs. "Mush, you *klis*, mush."

He didn't know exactly when Caribou began shooting at him. The sound of the shots began to come dimly through the fog, then more sharply. He heard something whine past his head, and Andover was shouting and writhing from side to side in the cariole, trying to break free, the sled tilting dangerously with his struggles. Kopernick began pawing for the revolver he had taken from the constable. Then he realized he couldn't return Caribou's fire for fear of hitting the girl, and he sobbed in a bitter frustration, cursing Caribou Carnes.

Caribou must have emptied his rifle, because he was running along all humped over and his elbow kept jerking as if he were reloading it. But it slowed him down, and without his lash over them the dogs weren't running so fast; and, when he looked around and saw how Kopernick had closed in on him, he quit trying to reload and jumped on the runners of his own sledge.

"*Ma-a-a-arche*, you Klincha *klis*, you Dogrib dogs, you sons of wolf bitches and pileated woodpecker fathers, you execrable crosses between an albino musk ox and a purple caribou. *Ma-a-a-arche*, or I'll stuff you in my rogan and drown you in the Slave!"

They topped a rise. Kopernick was beyond any sane reasoning, and he hardly heard his own mad screams as he clung to the lazy board with the snow pluming up on either side of him. "Streak of fat, Caribou, streak of fat! Fat man with fat dogs, and I've run you down."

"Streak of fat, my grandfather's moss bag," roared Caribou. "*Ma-a-a-arche*, you *tel-ky-lay-azzys*. . . ."

He broke off to twist around on his runners as Kopernick's toboggan swept up beside the huge *komatic*. They had started down the other side of the rise and were running into a long sloping field, jagged rocks thrusting up through the snow on every side. Kopernick knew if he jumped Caribou, the dogs would run away down that field and eventually tip over the sleds.

"Jump before we get going too fast," he shouted hoarsely at Arlis, and then bent to cut the lashings on Andover.

The constable must have realized what Kopernick intended, for, as soon as his bindings were cut, he rolled over the side of the toboggan and bounced through the hard-packed snow, shouting hoarsely with the pain of coming up against a rock. The girl rose in the *komatic*, but Caribou reached forward and struck her down with the butt end of his empty rifle. The excited dogs were galloping faster and faster down the field, and Kopernick could hardly stay on his bouncing, switching toboggan.

"Jump," he screamed, "jump . . . !"

Arlis tried it again, but once more Caribou beat her about the head with his rifle, and she sank back, sobbing. "I can't, Eddie, I can't."

With a savage curse, Kopernick yelled at his dogs— "*Cha, cha!*" and they swerved to the right, bringing the toboggan up beside the *komatic*, and Kopernick jumped.

Caribou tried to catch him with the rifle, but Kopernick had leaped for the cariole instead of the man, landing sprawled out over the girl, hands clawing for holds on the *babiche* lashing the slides. Caribou's gun butt thudded into Kopernick's head, but Kopernick caught the girl and got his weight beneath her and heaved.

"Eddie!" she cried, and then was gone, rolling away out of his sight through the snow. The dogs were baying with their wild run, and the sled was moving faster and faster down the slope, equipment flying from its cariole every time it bounced across the rocks. Kopernick tried to stand erect to jump at Caribou, clinging to the sides. Then he saw the huge man climbing over the jerking, swaying lazy board. Caribou had dropped his rifle and his dog whip, and he was chuckling.

"Now," he said, and Kopernick could barely hear him over the whipping snow and rattling, crashing sled, "we'll see about that streak of fat."

Kopernick ducked to meet the man's jump, throwing himself to one side from that first kick. The *komatic* lurched over with his weight, tilting dangerously.

Kopernick was almost thrown out, but Caribou retained his balance with an amazing agility, riding the sledge as if birling a log, leaning toward the opposite side to compensate for the *komatic*'s tilt and keeping his feet under him enough to jump on toward Kopernick and launch another kick. Kopernick was off balance, and he couldn't duck it. The foot caught him in the stomach, and he doubled over it with all the air exploding from him. The *komatic* was racing madly down the slope now and whoever was thrown out at this speed would stand little chance of living. Caribou jerked his leg out from beneath Kopernick's bent torso and pivoted to kick again.

"Savate!" he roared, and it came.

Gasping, Kopernick threw himself on that leg before it had gained its full momentum, and the aborted kick made a dull, fleshy sound against his chest, and he carried Caribou backward with both his arms twined around the man's thick leg. Caribou was down on the tarp-covered pile of supplies in the back end of the cariole, with Kopernick sprawled on top of him, the sledge leaping and jumping beneath them, snow puffing in a cloud from beneath the runners. Kopernick drew back his fist and slugged at Caribou's heavy middle, and heard the man's air explode from him with the blow.

"Streak of fat," he said, and his voice was muffled against the fetid heat of Caribou's parka, and he slugged again.

Caribou tried to thrust Kopernick off him, but the smaller man hung on with one arm, his other arm pistoning into Caribou's belly. Grunting sickly with each blow, Caribou finally twisted over to one side so he could ram his knee into Kopernick's belly. It caught him in his bullet wound, and the sudden shock of pain blinded Kopernick. Caribou levered a forearm across his neck and shoved him up and back. Kopernick caught at the sides of the cariole to keep from falling completely over and saw the huge man rise above him, swaying and lurching with the sled, shifting his weight for another kick. Kopernick tried to twist his legs beneath him and get onto his knees, but he had no strength left. He tried to shout something, and only a hoarse, animal sound escaped his numb lips. He didn't even see the kick when it came.

It felt as if his head had been jerked off, and he heard the sharp crackle of his broken snow glasses. He knew his body was dangling over the edge of the cariole, the snow shooting all over his face, and he felt the dull shudder of the sledge as Caribou brought his leg down and shifted his weight over to free his opposite foot for that last kick. With a guttural cry, Kopernick caught the sides of the cariole, fighting up through the terrible lethargy of pain. He saw Caribou's face above him, swaying back and forth, thick, sensuous lips spread back from his white teeth in a puckish grin, little eyes almost hidden by his fat cheeks. He saw the big man's body sway as he launched that last kick.

Without knowing how, Kopernick threw himself beneath the lashing foot, his body responding spasmodically to his will, carrying him up against Caribou's pivot leg. And before Caribou could recover his kick, Kopernick twined his arms about that pivot leg and, with the man's other leg still caught in the air above his body, heaved.

Caribou Carnes shouted something as he tumbled out of the racing sledge, but it was drowned in the din of baying dogs and clattering runners and rattling canvas, then he was gone, lost behind the sledge in the white snow and jagged black rocks.

Kopernick hauled himself weakly erect, panting, calling feebly to the dogs—"Whoa, whoa"—and then he saw it up ahead, through his cracked snow glasses, what Caribou must have seen from the top of that first rise before he realized Kopernick was behind, what he must have been going toward when Kopernick caught him. The lobstick.

Andover had kneaded the flour and water and grease for the bannocks and shaped the dough an inch deep inside the frying pan, and now they stood browning before the crackling fire. Kopernick sat with his back against the oddly shaped lobstick, the pain of his wound soothed, somehow, by the nearness of Arlis Burdette. On one of the maps included in the data she had brought her father, they found the lobstick labeled. No one could have told what it meant on the map itself, for Burdette had labeled many landmarks, but now that they knew its significance, they had been able to follow a line charted from the lobstick northward for a quarter mile to an outcropping of rock on the slope of a line of rocky hills. Andover held one of the samples he had taken, turning it over and over so the firelight caught on the streaks of yellow in the rock.

"I'd say a hundred dollars to the ton at the least," he muttered. "Soon's we get back to Resolution, we can have it assayed. I wouldn't have believed anyone who told me they'd found gold in the Barrens. The geological formations are all against it."

"The sourdoughs have an old saying," grinned Kopernick. "Gold is where you find it."

Arlis smiled tremulously. "Andover, don't you think it would be better to start back with Eddie tonight?"

"Rest'll do him good," said Andover, shifting the teapot above the flames. "That wound isn't as serious as it might be, and, if we wait till morning, the snow'll be frozen over for better running. You don't have to worry about Eddie Kopernick, Arlis. If he can run down Caribou Carnes over a twenty-mile stretch with a hole in his belly, he can do a simple little thing like riding back to Resolution over smooth ice all wrapped up in four-point blankets."

He turned to the bannocks, and Kopernick slid his hand out of the blanket to catch the girl's fingers. "I know I must have seemed sort of wild to you, but a man gets that way, I guess, after three years of running and hiding. I used to be respectable enough, up here. I had a string of trading posts started, and an idea going for organizing the rivermen. Maybe this isn't exactly your country, but, if you lived here a while, you'd learn to love it. What I mean is . . . if you had something that you wanted to stay for."

"I've got something to stay for."

"I wasn't talking about the gold."

"I know you weren't," she said, and her face was so close her hair brushed his cheek like spun honey.

"Tea?" said Andover, turning with the pot and a collapsible tin cup. Then he looked up and saw what they were doing, and turned his back on them uncomfortably, pouring the cup full. "No, I guess not. I'll drink it myself."

JAMES B. HENDRYX

Cheechako Trouble

James B(eardsley) Hendryx (1880–1963) was born at Sauk Center, Minnesota. He was enrolled at the University of Minnesota for two years before he quit to become a newspaper journalist. The most formative experience of his life, however, came when he ventured into the wilderness of the Far North. Virtually all of the fiction he came to write is set there. If as in *On the Arctic Rim* (Doubleday, 1948) a novel does open in the American West, the scene soon changes to Saskatchewan, and from there this story travels even farther north. Hendryx created a number of series characters who returned in story after story: Connie Morgan in a long-running group of young adult books, Corporal Downey of the Royal Mounted, and Black John of Halfaday Creek, an outlaw who somehow always manages to break the law in the interests of justice. Hendryx's son, James B. Hendryx Jr., initially followed his father's career into writing for the magazine market—"Partners of the Siwash" in *North-West Romances* (Winter, 1942) was one of his earliest stories—before moving to the other side of the desk as a story editor for Standard Magazines. Later in life Hendryx divided his time between Lee's Point at Sutton's Bay, Michigan, and Thessalon in Ontario. He is at his best in providing a vivid sense of place in his stories, and he had an ear for Canadian voices and the polyglot that came to live in the reaches of Alaska and the Canadian Northwest Territories. The story that follows features both Corporal Downey and Black John and is among the very last Hendryx wrote for the magazine market.

I

Murder at Elbow Rapids

It was late in the afternoon of the day after Christmas when Black John Smith and Lyme Cushing stepped into the Tivoli Saloon in Dawson to be greeted heartily by the little group of sourdoughs that had foregathered near the end of the bar. Swiftwater Bill eyed the big man with a grin. "Speak of the devil an' up he pops! We was wonderin' if you'd show up this Christmas, John, but we sure never expected you'd fetch Cush along."

Black John returned the grin. "Hell, it was him that fetched me! Personally, I prefer the peace an' quiet of Halfaday, but Cush got his mind set on the bright lights an' was rarin' to go, so I give in."

Old Cush, the lugubrious proprietor of Cushing's Fort, the combined trading post and saloon that ministered to the wants of the little community of outlawed men that had sprung up on Halfaday Creek close against the Yukon-Alaska border, scowled. "Huh, it was him that was rarin' to go. One mornin' when he come in the saloon an' we was pourin' our drink, I says how the squaw that does my cookin' an' cleanin' around the place was aimin' to go 'way off in the hills somewheres where her folks is goin' to have a big potlatch.

"I know them damn' potlatches is apt to last for two, three weeks, an' I tried to talk her out of it. But I might've know'd better. A man can't talk no woman outta nothin' once she gits a notion in her head.

"Then John, he starts in about what a hell of a good time we could have down here to Dawson, what with everyone in off'n the cricks an' all, an' how I hadn't been nowheres in a hell of a while, an' what a hell of a lot of work it would be if I had to take care of things without that gal to help . . . an' he went at it till I kinda seen it that way myself. So, bein' as how no one but me and John knows the combination of the safe, I give in, an' hired Pot-Gutted John an' One-Armed John to run the place till I got back. John warned 'em if they stole any more'n we figgered they ought to, we'd call a miners' meetin' an' hang 'em higher'n hell."

"Looks like you got here a day late, at that," Burr MacShane said.

"We never got here no day late," Cush replied. "By God, the way John put them seven big dogs of his'n over the trail you'd thought the devil was after us! We got in yesterday mornin' an' put up at the Fairview Hotel an' rolled into bed. We never woke up till ten, last night. So we got supper over to the Northern Restaurant, an' then we went over to the Pavilion an' danced all night. I'm gittin' old for sech doin's. My feet hurt, an' I couldn't've got no tireder if I'd've stayed to home an' done my work an' the squaw's chores on top of it."

Old Bettles, dean of the sourdoughs, grinned. "I'm buyin' a drink. Cheer up, Cush, we'll be startin' a stud game pretty quick, an' you can rest up."

As the drinks were poured, Moosehide Charlie joined the group. "I was jest talkin' to Constable Peters. Accordin' to him, young Bill Amberdahl's wife found him layin' dead on the portage trail around Elbow Rapids up there on Johnson Crick with a bullet hole in the back of his head. The day before Christmas, Bill went down to Clem Orkey's roadhouse at the mouth of the crick for some supplies, an', when he didn't come home that night, she hit down the crick, figgerin' they was probably a bunch in Clem's place an' Bill had got soused. It had snowed durin' the night an' damn' if she didn't trip over Bill's corpse layin' there under the snow."

Art Harper, a sourdough who had been in the country longer than any of them, spoke up. "Young Bill ain't the man his dad was, by a damn' sight. Old

Ben Amberdahl was some man, anyway you look at him. God, I'll never forget the day he cleaned up on them Roosians down at the mouth of Seventy-Mile, on the American side. Ben, he was a cowpuncher that got shanghaied in 'Frisco an' woke up aboard a whaler. He deserted at Saint Michael an' come on upriver. I come into the country in 'Seventy-Three, overland from the Mackenzie, an' Ben was snipin' the bars on Forty-Mile when I got there.

"I rec'lect it was the day before Christmas of 'Seventy-Four I was mushin' upriver with a sled load of trade goods when I met Ben comin' down hellbent, ridin' an empty sled draw'd by six big Siberian dogs. He'd got soft on a Siwash gal, an' they aimed to hit down to Fort Yukon an' get married, come spring, an' he told me the Roosians had kidnapped her.

"A big Roosian name of Ivan had built that log tradin' post at the mouth of Seventy-Mile. There was always three, four Roosians hangin' out there, an' they was a damn' tough outfit. The Siwashes would fetch in their fur, an' Ivan would get 'em drunk, take the fur, an' claim he'd paid 'em for it, an' then kick them out. An' they'd steal Siwash girls an' run 'em down river an' sell 'em to the whalers.

"There wasn't no law in the country them days, an' Ben was alone. I told him he better not tackle them Roosians single-handed, but he claimed he wasn't afraid of 'em, an' hit on downriver. I hated to think what would happen to him, so I turned around an' follered him down. It wasn't only a little ways back, an', when I got there an' was slippin' my rifle out from under the lashin' of my load, I seen Ben shove the door of the tradin' room open. Before I got up the bank, there was the damnedest volley of shots I ever heard, an' a couple of minutes later, when I busted into the room with my rifle cocked, Ben stood there shovin' shells into the cylinder of his Forty-Four Colt, an' four Roosians laid dead on the floor . . . three of 'em with guns in their hands. Ivan an' another one was layin' behind the counter, an' two was in front of it. Ben, he'd fired five shots. Each one of them Roosians had a bullet hole in his forehead, an' one bullet had missed an' hit the picture of the Roosian King right between the eyes."

"Did he get the girl?" Camillo Bill asked.

"Sure he did. They had her locked in a back room. He got her out an' loaded her onto his sled an' shoved on down to Fort Yukon an' they got married without waitin' for spring."

"I've heard about that fight in that Roosian tradin' post," Bettles said. "It's the post that Joe Turner runs now."

Several others had heard of it, and Burr MacShane asked: "What became of Ben Amberdahl?"

Art Harper shook his head. "Don't no one seem to know. He ain't been around for years. Made him a stake on Forty-Mile, I guess, an' went outside."

"I've seen his gun . . . that Colt Forty-Four. Joe Turner had it hangin' on his wall. It had Amberdahl's initials carved in the wooden grip."

"That's right," Harper said. "Joe bought the layout from Ivan's Siwash wife, an' later he bought Ben's gun an' hung it on the wall right under that picture with the bullet hole between the eyes. But it ain't there now . . . it nor the picture, neither. I come through there not long ago, an' Joe told me someone had stole the gun a year or so back."

"Ain't they got no idea who shot Bill Amberdahl?" old Bettles wanted to know.

"Accordin' to Peters," Moosehide replied, "along in the forenoon of Christmas he got to Clem Orkey's roadhouse on a reg'lar patrol. They was a bunch in there from up the Klondike an' some of them cricks that runs into it above Bonanza. Clem didn't have no complaints an' neither did the others, an' Peters was about to pull out when Amberdahl's wife come bustin' in complainin' she'd tripped over his corpse, there at the Elbow Rapids, an' he'd been shot in the back of the head. She stayed there with Clem's woman while Peters an' Clem an' a couple of others went up an' fetched Amberdahl down an' heisted him up on the meat cache.

"Clem give Peters a list of everyone that was to the roadhouse the day before. There ain't only three claims on Johnson Crick. Amberdahl an' his wife was the first ones to locate on the crick. They filed a claim a year ago last spring a couple of miles above the Elbow Rapids. Couple months later Duff Regan an' his 'breed wife located a mine farther up, an' in the fall a young feller name of Jack Manners located above Regan's."

Harper observed: "Duff Regan must've abandoned his claim on the Kandik. He married Ivan's 'breed daughter Sonia, after Ivan got killed, an' they located on the Kandik. Had a pretty good layout there, it looked like."

"Accordin' to what Clem told Peters," Moosehide went on, "some of the boys was already there when Amberdahl come in about the middle of the forenoon. Duff Regan's wife come in a little later, an' along about noon this here Jack Manners drifted in. Drinks was had, an' after while Amberdahl got kinda ugly an' accused Manners of seein' too much of his wife. Manners told him he was a damn' fool. Told him that he never was down to Amberdahl's when Amberdahl wasn't there hisself. Claimed it was lonesome up there on his claim alone, an' he'd come down now an' then to play cribbage. Claimed Amberdahl hisself had invited him down, an' so had his wife, an' they'd play cribbage, an' then he'd hit out for home. He told Amberdahl that, if he wasn't soused, he'd never accused him of seein' his wife.

"Clem says that Amberdahl told Manners to stay away from his place from then on . . . or he'd shoot him. An' Manners got mad, an' told him that two could play that game. Then he turned around an' walked out. Clem said that Amberdahl got his supplies an' pulled out later, an' then some of the others pulled out.

"The way things looked, Peters hit out fer Manners's place to question him, but Manners wasn't there, an' hadn't been since the snow. So he went back to Clem's, an' they loaded Amberdahl's corpse on Peters's sled, an' he fetched it here to Dawson, Amberdahl's wife comin' along. An' damn' if they didn't meet Manners right here on Front Street! So Peters took him an' Amberdahl's corpse over to headquarters, an' Amberdahl's wife went to the hotel. Peters says Corporal Downey took over there, an', when they searched Manners, they found a Forty-Five revolver on him with an empty shell in the cylinder. Manners claimed he'd shot at a wolf. But they locked him up."

Swiftwater Bill frowned. "Damned if I'll believe Jack Manners shot Amberdahl . . . leastwise not in the back of the head. I know Manners. He's a cheechako, but he's a damned good kid. Worked for me for a while. Hell, I was talkin' to him last evenin' over to the Fairview Hotel, an' he didn't seem like a man that had jest pulled off a murder, by a damn' sight. Accordin' to what you said, there was plenty of others in Orkey's place that could have had it in for Amberdahl. I know him. He don't get soused very often, but, when he does, he's apt to get mean. An' as for Manners runnin' after his wife . . . that's all bunk. I know Maybelle Amberdahl . . . know'd her when she was a kid, down there on the Porcupine. She's a damn' fine young woman. Manners told me about stoppin' in at Orkey's place for a couple of drinks, an' then he come on here for the Christmas jamboree."

"A hell of a jamboree he'll have locked in a cell over to headquarters," Moosehide said. "Accordin' to Peters, it looks damn' bad for him. An' besides which, that wife of Amberdahl's is a damn' good looker. A man couldn't hardly blame this here Manners for makin' a play for her if he got the chance."

Black John grinned. "I fear your ethics are open to question, Moosehide," he said.

"Ethics . . . hell! I ain't got no ethics . . . wouldn't know one if I seen it. All I says . . . it looks damn' bad for Manners."

Cush glanced at the clock. "It's goin' on six," he said, "an' I'm goin' to the hotel. I ain't goin' to play stud on no empty stummick. An' neither I ain't goin' to be late for supper an' have to take no leavin's, neither."

"Me an' you both," Black John said, and turned to the others. "We'll be back in an hour or so, an' it ain't no more'n right I should warn you damn' gravel hounds that on Christmas night us Halfaday Crickers plays 'em high, wide, an' handsome.'"

II

Lady in Distress

As they waited for their order in the dining room of the Fairview Hotel, Cush noticed that a good-looking young woman seated at a table across the room kept glancing at Black John. Finishing her meal, she rose and headed for the door, pausing beside the table at which the two were seated. "Pardon me," she said, glancing into the big man's face, "but aren't you Black John Smith?"

"That's right, ma'am. But you have the best of me. I don't rec'lect ever seein' you before."

The woman's lips smiled, accentuating the look of tragedy in the dark eyes. "You probably haven't seen me since I was a little girl. I have changed . . . but you haven't. I'm Maybelle Bolton. My father, Sam Bolton, has a location on the Porcupine. You and Corporal Downey stopped overnight with us the time you went up to Taylor's Post and arrested that horrible Cronin who murdered Mister Taylor and robbed the safe, and tried to lay the blame on Tom Keith. Mamie Taylor knew Tom was innocent even though Cronin had used Tom's knife to stab Mister Taylor to death with, and then left it where the police could find it. Mamie's my best friend. She and Tom are married now, running the post, and they both say that, if it hadn't been for you, even Corporal Downey would have believed Tom was guilty."

"Oh, sure," Black John replied. "I rec'lect Sam Bolton an' you, too. This Mamie Taylor an' Tom Keith are a mighty fine pair of young folks. But Corporal Downey's the one that deserves the credit for solvin' that murder. I ain't connected with the police. I was jest an unofficial observer . . . jest went along for the ride."

"You could never make Mamie or Tom believe that," the woman told him. "I know most people think you're an outlaw. But they can't make me believe it, because I know Corporal Downey would never have anything to do with an outlaw, except to arrest him."

White teeth flashed behind the black beard. "Thanks for the vote of confidence."

"My father says you are smart . . . smarter even than Corporal Downey. And he, too, believes that, if it hadn't been for you, Tom Keith would have been hanged for Mister Taylor's murder, and Cronin would have gone scot free. I recognized you the minute you stepped into the room, and I've been trying to get up courage to . . . to ask you if . . . if you couldn't help me out."

"Why, sure, ma'am, I'll do what I can. What's your trouble?"

"I married Bill Amberdahl, and we have a location on Johnson Crick a few miles above Clem Orkey's roadhouse. On the day before Christmas, Bill went down to Orkey's for some supplies, and, when he didn't return that night, I went down to find out why, and I . . . I tripped over Bill's body lying there under the snow on the portage trail around the Elbow Rapids. I hurried on to the post and found Constable Peters there. Clem Orkey told me that Bill had been drinking and had accused young Jack Manners of seeing too much of me. The accusation was perfectly absurd, and Bill would never have made it, if he hadn't been drinking.

"They brought Bill's body down to the trading post. He had been shot in the back of the head. Orkey said that, when Bill accused Jack, Jack denied it and called Bill a fool for saying such a thing, and they had words back and forth, and finally Bill told him that, if he ever showed up at our place again, he would shoot him.

"Of course, Bill would never have done it, and Jack knew he wouldn't. Bill was drunk, and Jack was mad. But they locked Jack up, and Corporal Downey intends to remove the bullet from Bill's head . . . and, if it's a Forty-Five, I'm afraid Jack will be in a terrible position."

Black John nodded. "Yeah . . . it would kinda look like that, wouldn't it?"

"It certainly would. And I know he never shot Bill. He is a fine young man, and Orkey said he was perfectly sober. Bill would have been sorry when he sobered up . . . and Jack Manners knew that. He certainly would never have laid for Bill and shot him. There were others in Orkey's that day he had quarreled with at times . . . maybe one of them shot him, knowing that Jack would be blamed for it.

"I swear to you that there was absolutely nothing in Bill's accusation! I never even saw Jack when Bill wasn't present. You do believe me, don't you? Oh . . . you must!"

"Why . . . sure I believe you," the big man said gently and, drawing a well-filled pouch from his pocket, tossed it onto the table. "So you're broke here in Dawson an' need some dust to tide you over till this thing is straightened out, eh? Well, there you are. Take it an' welcome."

"No! No! I don't need any dust! Bill and I did well there on our claim. We have money in the bank here . . . plenty of money. What I want you to do . . . if you only will . . . is to help Corporal Downey . . . as you did there on the Porcupine. If he removes that bullet, and it should be a Forty-Five, they might even hang Jack Manners. And I know he never killed Bill."

"How about robbery?" Black John asked. "Did Bill flash a heavy poke there in Orkey's place?"

"Yes, Bill had a well-filled poke with him, and I suppose he did flash it. But he wasn't murdered for his dust. His poke with the dust in it was in his pocket when they brought him down to Orkey's. Whoever shot Bill hated him. The quarrels Bill had from time to time with the prospectors and trappers that frequent Orkey's place were never very serious ones, so I'm wondering if whoever shot Bill did it to avenge something that happened years ago. If so, the murderer might kill me, too. I'll never feel safe there on the claim alone until the murderer is caught.

"You see, I hadn't known Bill very long before I married him. I've heard that he was pretty wild in those days. But, since we were married, he settled down. He drank now and then . . . maybe once or twice a year. But he soon sobered up and was always sorry. He was a hard worker and really a perfectly wonderful man."

"Hmm. Well," Black John replied, pocketing the poke, "I'll do what I can. I ain't promisin' anything, though. Policin' is Downey's business . . . not mine. But in a case like this . . . if it will make you feel any easier, I'll drop into detachment headquarters tomorrow an' see what's goin' on."

"Oh, thank you!" the woman cried, in a voice that was half a sob. "I have every confidence in you." And, abruptly, she turned and left the room.

Cush slanted the big man a scowling glance. "I'll be damned if I kin figger out how every good-lookin' woman that comes along picks you out to have confidence in, an' tell their troubles to . . . when everyone knows you're the damnedest outlaw in the country."

Black John grinned. "The reason is ondoubtless owin' to the benign an' confidence-inspirin' contour of my features, coupled with the subtle aura of virtue that emanates. . . ."

"If them damn' words means anything, you better talk 'em to someone that knows what it is!" Cush interrupted. "By God, any woman kin git anything she wants outta you! Hell . . . tossin' out your poke . . . a good eighty ounces . . . jest 'cause she stands there an' claims she's got troubles. If she'd've grabbed up the poke, it would've served you right. An' damn' if I don't wish she had! Like I say, it would've served you right . . . an' mebbe learnt you somethin'. Her claimin' there weren't nothin' goin' on betwixt her an' this here Jack Manners . . . when anyone would know that any young feller would've fell for her . . . husband, or no husband! An' when some woman likes some young guy which ain't her husband, an' claims he's a fine young man, it's jest too damn' bad for the husband. I've had four wives . . . an', by God, I know what women are like!"

Black John shook his head slowly. "Your viewpoint on women is incontrovertibly pessimistic an'. . . ."

"An' if you say jest one more big word, you'll git this here cup right between the eyes!" Cush exclaimed, waving the item mentioned under Big John's nose. "An' what's more . . . I'm bettin' that, if this here Manners gets turned loose, like she wants him to, she'll be makin' a play to marry one of you two . . . or mebbe both before the snow melts on Bill Amberdahl's grave."

Black John's grin broadened. "A man might do worse, at that. Good-lookin' young woman . . . good location . . . money in the bank."

"Yeah . . . an' hell a-poppin' on Halfaday all the rest of your life! Come on, let's git over to the Tivoli. What with all the folks they is in town, we mightn't get no seat in the stud game."

Along toward the middle of the following morning, Black John stepped into the office at detachment headquarters and greeted Corporal Downey seated behind his flattop desk. "Well, how's things goin' in the ranks of the sinful?"

"Oh, not too bad for the number of people that's in for the Christmas hell-raisin'. Draw up a chair an' sit down. Town detail keeps busy with drunks, an' fights, an' whatnot. We've got one murder on our hands, though, that don't look so good."

The big man grinned. "Well, takin' 'em by an' large, as the Good Book says, damn' few murders do look good to the casual observer."

"What I mean . . . a fellow by the name of Bill Amberdahl was. . . ."

"Yeah," Black John interrupted, "I've heard the particulars . . . everything up to how you found a Forty-Five gun on Manners with one empty shell in the cylinder, an' Manners claimed he'd shot at a wolf."

Downey nodded. "An' on the face of it, it looked bad for Manners. But here's somethin' else . . . I got the bullet out of Amberdahl's head. He was wearin' a twill parka, an', whoever shot him, slipped up behind him on the trail and fired the bullet into his skull, low down. He slipped up damn' close, too. There's flecks of burnt powder around the bullet hole in Amberdahl's parka . . . black powder. The cartridges in Manners's gun were smokeless. I got the bullet where it had plowed through his brain an' stopped against his skull, high up in front, about where the hair starts. It was a soft lead bullet . . . mushroomed a little, but in pretty good shape.

"I fired a bullet out of the gun we took off Manners into a tub of mud an' took the two bullets over to the hospital where they've got a good microscope, an' it didn't take but a few minutes to see that it couldn't have been fired from Manners's gun. The butt end of the bullet that killed Amberdahl measured a mite smaller than the other . . . prob'ly a Forty-Four. The two bullets were a different shape an' weight. The lands an' grooves were different, too. But the thing that mattered most is that the bullet I took from Amberdahl's head was fired from a left-hand twist gun, and Manners's gun is a right-hand twist. The Colt is the only left-hand twist I ever heard of . . . all the rest are right-hand. The lands an' grooves show the twist of the barrel the bullet was fired from. One other thing . . . the course of the bullet slanted upward, showin' that whoever fired it was shorter than Amberdahl, who measured five-foot ten. Manners stands six-foot one in his socks."

"So you turned Manners loose, eh?" Black John asked.

"I'm goin' to in a few minutes. I jest got back from the hospital a half hour ago an' ain't finished my report yet. Manners seems like a nice young fellow . . . not one that would sneak up an' shoot a man from behind. I'm glad he's in the clear."

Black John filled and lighted his pipe. "So, the case is closed, I guess."

"Closed . . . hell!" Downey exclaimed. "It won't be closed till the one that murdered Bill Amberdahl is hung!"

"Might be quite a chore to locate the party. Accordin' to what Peters told Moosehide Charlie, there was quite a few in Orkey's place that day that didn't like Amberdahl none too well. Any one of them might have shot him."

"That's right," Downey agreed. "An' the chances are, one of 'em did. My job is to find that one. I'm hittin' out for the Johnson Crick country as soon as I turn Manners loose."

"Yup . . . quite a chore," Black John repeated. "What with them trappers an' prospectors scattered all over hell, an' the new snow like it is, an' the strong cold due anytime. Some of 'em might still be hangin' in Orkey's, but the chances are most of 'em have pulled out."

"Sure, it's goin' to be quite a chore . . . an' 'most likely nothin' will come of it. He was shot with a revolver, all right. A rifle would have drove the bullet clean through his head."

Black John nodded. "Yeah, an', when whoever done it finds out you're on the job, it won't be long before that revolver is damn' well hid, or throw'd away."

"If Orkey or one of the others don't know who owns a Colt revolver, the chances are I never will locate the gun. It's prob'ly a hopeless case. But I've got to make a stab at it. It was a grudge killin' . . . no robbery. Amberdahl's poke with around seventy ounces in it was in his pocket when his wife found him there on the trail." The officer paused and shrugged. "One of them prospectors or trappers done it, all right . . . but which one?"

"Damn' few trappers or prospectors pack revolvers."

"Manners packed one. An' so do you."

"Yeah, but Manners is a cheechako. Time he's been here a while he'll sell it, or throw it away, or leave it home. Me . . . how the hell could I keep Half-aday moral without it . . . what with the disreputable characters that keeps driftin' in on us?"

"Someone besides Manners was packin' one," Downey persisted.

"That's right." Black John shrugged. "An' that one held a grudge that called for murder. Your job is to locate the one that had both the grudge, an' the gun, an' the opportunity to use it."

"Yeah . . . some job!" Downey exclaimed.

"Oh, I don't know," the big man drawled, smiling.

"What do you mean . . . you don't know?"

"Meanin' I've got a sort of a hunch, that's all."

Downey eyed the other narrowly. "An' you'll help me out on this case?"

"You know damn' well, Downey, that I never neither help nor hinder the police in their work."

"Yeah, I know. An' I know, too, that there's been plenty of times when, if it hadn't been for you, I'd never have solved a case. How about it . . . will you? Or, won't you?"

"You rec'lect the time you went down on the Porcupine on that Taylor murder, an' I sort of trailed along, an' how we stopped overnight with Sam Bolton? Well, Sam's little girl . . . Maybelle her name is . . . is Bill Amber-dahl's wife. I was talkin' to her over to the hotel, an' she claims she's afraid that maybe the one that murdered Bill might take it out on her, too. An' she wondered if I wouldn't help find the one that done it, rememberin' that I was along with you that time on the Porcupine. I told her I'd do what I could . . . but not bein' in the police, it prob'ly wouldn't be much. So, if you don't mind, we'll foller this hunch I've got. But I'm warnin' you, we ain't workin' together. Just what you might say . . . parallel. You from the police angle, an' me just sort of keepin' my promise to Amberdahl's wife."

Downey grinned. "Okay, John. What's your hunch?"

"This here land an' groove stuff you was tellin' about, s'pose you got holt of a bullet that was fired quite a while back . . . say twenty years, or so? . . . from the same gun that killed Amberdahl, would that microscope up to the hospital show it was the same gun?"

"It would show whether or not the lands an' grooves were the same. An' it would show whether the gun that fired it was a right-hand or left-hand twist. An', yes, I believe in this case it would show it was the same gun, be-cause all but one of the lands show clean-cut edges. That one sort of slants down into the groove. You see, a bullet is slightly larger than the diameter of the barrel, and the hot lead, forced through the barrel, carries the marks not only of the twist but of any irregularity in the last inch or so of the barrel. The gun that fired that bullet that killed Amberdahl had one land that had been damaged near the muzzle."

"Okay . . . let's go."

"Go! Go where?"

"Down to Joe Turner's tradin' post an' roadhouse there at the mouth of Seventy-Mile."

"Joe Turner's! Seventy-Mile! This murder was committed on Johnson Crick, not Seventy-Mile!"

"That's so, ain't it?" the big man grinned. "An' the rookus started in Clem Orkey's place . . . not Turner's."

"Sure it did! I'll throw an outfit together, an' we'll hit out for Orkey's."

"If that's where we're headin', we ain't runnin' parallel no more. 'Cause here's where I split off. I'm headin' for Joe Turner's."

"But, hell, man . . . that's 'way over in Alaska!"

"Sure it is. An' there's a good trail on the river. Not like wallerin' through the deep snow huntin' up them prospectors an' trappers that was in Orkey's that day."

"But I've got no authority on the American side."

"You won't need none. All you need is a dog outfit, a hand saw, a pick an' shovel, an' enough grub for the trip."

"What the hell do you mean?"

"Meanin' that we're goin' down to Turner's an' saw a bullet out of a log, an' maybe a couple of more out of the skulls of a couple of dead Roosians. Hell, Downey, ain't that clear enough?"

"Clear as mud," grinned the officer. "I'll have the stuff ready in an hour."

III

Time to Kill

The following day the two stepped into the trading room at Turner's post to be greeted heartily by the proprietor, who grinned at the officer as he cast a sidewise glance at Black John. "Congratulations, Downey! I see you've run the old reprobate down at last!"

The big man nodded. "Yeah, he run me down, all right. But I outsmarted him. I hit hell-bent for the line, an', when he caught up with me, he was in Alaska without no authority whatever."

All three joined in the laughter, and Turner set out a bottle and three glasses. "Where you two headin'?" he asked as the drinks were poured. "What's on your minds?"

Ignoring the questions, Black John fixed his gaze on the wall behind the counter. "What became of that picture that used to hang there? Used to be one of them Forty-Four single-action Colt revolvers hangin' under it from a peg drove into the wall."

"Oh, that! Someone stole the gun, a year or so back. An' the picture . . . it was some old Roosian . . . it got all blacked up, what with the flies an' smoke an' all, an' I throwed it into the stove."

"Accordin' to Art Harper, this used to be a Roosian outfit."

"That's right. A big Roosian name of Ivan owned it. There was always three, four Roosians hangin' around here, them days . . . as ornery a bunch of sidewinders as ever got together. There wasn't no law in the country, then. But Ben Amberdahl, he didn't need no law. When they stole his gal an' locked her up in the back room there, Ben come b'ilin' down the river. He. . . ."

"Amberdahl!" Corporal Downey exclaimed. "I knew I'd heard that name before! That fight happened long before I came into the country. Before any police hit the Yukon. But I heard about it years ago. This Ben Amberdahl must have been some man."

"I'll say he was," Turner agreed. "They didn't make 'em no better. It was Ben's gun that I had hangin' there on the wall under the picture. I was snipin' the bars on the Kandik, an', when I heard about the fight, I come down an' bought the outfit off'n Ivan's Siwash wife. An' later I bought that Colt Forty-Four off'n Ben. Claimed he was hittin' outside an' didn't have no use for it, so I hung it there on the wall."

"So Ben got his gal an' married her, eh?" Black John asked.

"That's right. They had one kid, Bill his name is. He was a kind of hell-raiser when he was a youngster. But couple of year ago he married old Sam Bolton's girl over on the Porcupine, an' I heard they'd gone over on the Yukon side an' was doin' all right."

"He was doin' all right till the day before Christmas," Downey said. "Then someone murdered him . . . shot him in the back of the head on the trail."

"Well, I'll be damned!" Turner exclaimed. "That's sure too bad. I know Maybelle Amberdahl. She's a fine young woman. Know'd Bill, too."

"That gun of Ben's . . . when was it stole off'n the wall there?" Black John asked.

"Oh, about a year or so ago. That's when I noticed it was gone. I remember I was gone about a week down in Nulato, an', when I come back, the gun was gone."

"Maybe whoever you left in charge here stole it?"

"No, my wife run the place while I was away. There was quite a few in an' out, an' she never noticed the gun was gone, till I come back an' missed it."

Black John nodded slowly. "Quite a lot of coincidence, eh, Downey? Bill Amberdahl an' his wife locate there on Johnson Crick. A little later, Duff Regan an' his Roosian 'breed wife pull stakes an' locate there, too. Just about the same time, Ben Amberdahl's gun disappeared from its peg there on the wall. Ivan was shot by Ben Amberdahl with that gun the day before Christmas. Bill Amberdahl is shot the day before Christmas. Bill Amberdahl was Ben Amberdahl's son. Sonia Regan is Ivan's daughter."

"By God, I believe you've got it, John!" Corporal Downey cried. "I believe you've hit the nail on the head. But if she did it, she sure bided her time . . . avengin' a murder twenty-three years old."

"Them 'breeds are patient, Downey. They're canny, too . . . damn' canny. She was in Orkey's roadhouse that mornin' an' heard the row between Amberdahl an' Manners . . . heard Amberdahl threaten to shoot Manners, an' heard Manners tell him that two could play that game. It looked to her like a perfect setup."

Downey nodded. "An' if we can get hold of some of the bullets Ben Amberdahl fired that day, an' compare them with the one that killed Bill, we've got an open an' shut case . . . if we can find the gun in Sonia Regan's possession." He paused and glanced at Turner. "Do you know where those Roosians were buried?"

"Hell, yes. I helped bury 'em. They're out back . . . an' not more'n two, three foot down. The ground was froze, an' we didn't go in very deep."

"An' would you mind if we got that bullet out of the wall . . . the one that went through the picture? We'll saw out around it an' put the plug back."

"Go to it," Turner said. "To hell with the plug. I can fit one in place."

"We'll dig up them graves, too," Downey said. "I sure hope them bullets didn't all go plumb through every one of them Roosians' skulls."

"None of 'em did," Turner said. "Every one of 'em had jest one hole in his head . . . in his forehead, jest above the eyes. An' I sure hope you git the goods on that gal. No one likes her. Hell, even Duff Regan's afraid of her."

With the bullet taken from the wall and the three from the skulls of the dead Russians in their possession, the two thanked Turner and headed upriver. In Dawson, the following afternoon, the bullets were taken to the hospital where the microscope showed beyond doubt that they had been fired from the same gun as the bullet that killed Amberdahl.

"OK," Downey said, as they returned to headquarters. "Tomorrow we'll hit for Johnson Crick. But tell me, John, how in the devil did you figure it was Sonia Regan that knocked Amberdahl off that night at Orkey's?"

"I didn't really figure it. Like I said, it was just a hunch. I was in the Tivoli when Art Harper was tellin' about Ben Amberdahl cleanin' up on them Roosians. He told about Ben Amberdahl's gun bein' stole off'n Joe Turner's wall. Then Moosehide Charlie come in an' spilled what Peters had told him, about Bill Amberdahl gettin' murdered an' all. An' he mentioned that this Sonia Regan was there in Orkey's, when he had the run-in with Manners. Art said that her an' Regan had left a good thing on the Kandik an' settled on Johnson Crick soon after Amberdahl did . . . so, puttin' two an' two together, I got a hunch, that's all. I sure hope the hunch works out."

Downey grinned. "The hunch has worked out already. It's the gun we want, now. Come on over to the Tivoli. I'll buy a drink."

They joined Burr MacShane and Gordon Bettles at the bar. As the glasses were filled, Duff Regan stepped into the room, and Black John motioned him to join them at the bar.

"Come on up, Duff. Wet your whistle. Downey's buyin' one. I just been askin' the boys here where in hell I can get holt of a Thirty-Eight revolver. We hung a feller up on Halfaday a while back, an' amongst his estate was eight, ten boxes of Thirty-Eight ammunition, an' I'd sure like to get holt of a gun that would fit 'em. It's a damn' shame to waste 'em. But I don't know what else to do."

As Regan filled his glass, he shook his head.

"I ain't got no Thirty-Eight gun. Ain't got no revolver. The woman's got a Colt Forty-Four. Had it couple of years or so. What the hell she wants with it's more'n I know. She never shoots. It's one of them old-fashioned ones that you've got to cock with your thumb. Got some initials carved on the butt. I'd ought to throw the damn' thing in the river . . . the way she looks at me sometimes."

Corporal Downey tossed off his drink. "Well, so long, you birds. Have a good time. I've got to get back to detachment and take care of things."

Shortly thereafter Black John sauntered from the room and, a few minutes later, joined Downey in his office.

The officer greeted him with a grin. "Well, what are we waitin' for? Let's go! But tell me one thing . . . why the devil did you ask Regan about a Thirty-Eight? You knew damn' well that Amberdahl was shot with a Forty-Four."

"Sure I did. An' if I asked him about a Forty-Four, he might have got suspicious an' shut up like a clam. Askin' about a Thirty-Eight that way, he just never give it a thought."

"If it wasn't for some . . . er . . . eccentricities in your makeup, John, you'd make a wonderful policeman."

"Oh, hell, Downey, I'd never make a policeman. A policeman's got to be smart. It takes everything I've got to keep Halfaday moral . . . while you've got to handle the whole Yukon."

They arrived at the Regan location just on the edge of dark. The door opened to their knock, and Regan's 'breed wife eyed them sullenly.

"The jig's up, Sonia," Downey said. "You're under arrest for the murder of Bill Amberdahl. We've got evidence enough to hang you, and it's my duty to warn you that anything you say may be used against you. Get your things together and let's go."

The woman gasped and stepped aside as they entered the room. "Yes, I'm keel Amberdahl. Amberdahl papa keel mine papa, long tam ago. W'en I'm leetle girl, I'm say I'm git even . . . I'm gon' keel Ben Amberdahl. But Ben Amberdahl gone 'way before I kin keel heem. So I'm gon' keel hees boy . . . git even. I'm keel heem wit hees papa gon . . . de gon dat keel mine papa. So I'm steal hees papa gon off Joe Turner wall. I'm always car' dat gon in mine pack, so's wait for chance to keel Bill Amberdahl. W'en Bill Amberdahl git marry an' com' Johnson Crick, I mak' Duff Regan quit Kandik an' com' here, too. He no want to com' . . . but I'm mak' heem. He 'fraid of me . . . 'fraid som'tam I'm keel heem."

"What made you pick that day?" Corporal Downey asked.

"I wait for chance. Day befor' Chris'mas, I'm go to Orkey for supply. Bill Amberdahl dere. Git dronk. Git in row wit Manners. Den Manners go out. I'm go pret' queek. I'm wait by de rapids, an', w'en Bill Amberdahl com' 'long, I'm sneak up behine an' shoot heem in de head . . . lak hees papa shoot mine papa . . . day before Chris'mas. I'm got even wit Ben Amberdahl after long tam. Som'tam I'm mebbeso keel Bill Amberdahl woman, too. Git mor' even. How you p'liss know it me keel Amberdahl? Me, I'm t'ink you arres' Manners, 'cause he say he keel heem."

"We figured it out, all right," Downey said. "We'll pick up the gun, now, an' you get dressed for the trail. We're hittin' for Dawson."

"I git de gon," the woman said and swiftly slipped into the bedroom. Black John loosened the buttons of his shirt and grasped the butt of his Forty-Five, and Corporal Downey drew his service revolver, both with their eyes on the bedroom door. The next moment the sound of a shot roared out, and both men rushed to the door to see the woman collapse on the bed. She had placed the muzzle of the gun in her mouth and pulled the trigger.

"Well," Downey said, eyeing the big man. "It looks like the case is closed. I'm glad it happened this way. Somehow, I'd hate to have to hang a woman . . . even one like her."

Color at Forty-Mile

Tim Champlin is the *nom de plume* of John Michael Champlin (1937–). He was born in Fargo, North Dakota, and graduated from Middle Tennessee State University, subsequently earning a master's degree from Peabody College in Nashville, Tennessee, in 1964. He began his career as an author of Western stories with *Summer of the Sioux* (Ballantine, 1982). This became the first in a series of novels about the adventures of Matt Tierney who begins his professional career as a reporter for the *Chicago Times-Herald*, covering an expeditionary force venturing into the Big Horn country and the Yellowstone. His second series character is Jay McGraw, who is plunged into outlawry at the beginning of *Colt Lightning* (Ballantine, 1989), but who soon finds himself working as an agent for Wells Fargo & Company. More recently Champlin has departed from series characters to concentrate on historical fiction, such as *The Last Campaign* (Five Star Westerns, 1996) which is concerned with the final pursuit of Geronimo in the Southwest, and *Swift Thunder* (Five Star Westerns, 1998), a story that takes place during the days of the Pony Express. In all of Champlin's stories there are always unconventional plot ingredients, striking historical details, vivid characterizations of the multitude of ethnic and cultural diversity found on the frontier, and narratives rich and original and surprising. His exuberant tapestries include lumber schooners sailing the West Coast, early-day wet-plate photography, daredevils who thrill crowds with gas balloons and the first parachutes, Tong Wars in San Francisco's Chinatown, Basque sheepherders, and the *penitentes* of the Southwest. Long an admirer of Jack London, Tim Champlin was gracious enough to provide the following story to conclude this fictional odyssey to the Northwest.

Bill Carmody burst out the back door of McGrew's Saloon in a panic, his sudden fury dissipating faster than the smoke from the Bisley in his hand. Shock and the chill night air of mid-May sobered him quickly as he sprinted instinctively toward the Dawson waterfront.

His mind was temporarily blunted to the full realization that he had just put two bullets into his partner, Cache Swenson. His only thought was to get away—fast—before one of those yelling witnesses behind him went for a Mountie.

The Yukon River. It was the quickest way to escape. Carmody thought of it as the only way. There were dozens of places to hide in Dawson City, but he knew he would be ferreted out before long. Distance would provide the only refuge. As he ran, the two sounds that still echoed in his head were the blasts of the gunshots and the scream of Rachel Hampton, his former fiancée, as she rushed to the falling Swenson.

He darted across the main street and between two buildings, knowing he had to find Chilcoot Charlie, the Indian packer he'd left only hours before. Together they'd steal an unattended boat and disappear into the night.

Panting heavily, he leaped up the wooden steps to a prostitute's crib and banged on the door. "Charlie! Charlie! You in there?"

He heard a muffled curse from within.

"Charlie, get out here! Hurry!" He kept his voice low, but urgent, mouth close to the warped door casing.

The door opened and a sloe-eyed woman in a chemise regarded him with a hard look.

"Where's Charlie?"

Before she could reply, the dark, broad-shouldered Indian shoved past her, buttoning his shirt. Carmody caught a whiff of raw alcohol on his breath as he grabbed the Indian's arm and pulled him down the steps. "I'm in trouble! I just shot Swenson!" he hissed in the big man's ear.

There was no change of expression on the dark features as they passed the lamplight streaming from a storefront. The Indian was a bit unsteady. From experience, Carmody knew this was probably due to the effects of a load of hooch, usually enough to render two ordinary men unconscious.

"Mebbe we go," Charlie mumbled, looking quickly around.

"You damn' betcha we go," Carmody replied.

"Get boat. Go downriver," Chilcoot Charlie said, lurching ahead into the darkness.

With no questions or comments, the aborigine had grasped the situation and, even half drunk, had come to the aid of his friend. It was what Carmody had counted on as he followed, dodging the clutter of freight piled on the waterfront wharves.

A nearly full May moon etched inky shadows where the two men worked along, looking for a boat. A sense of urgency was lent by the excited voices Carmody could hear from the direction of the main street.

White men murdering each other meant nothing to the Indian, Carmody knew. Nor did stealing a boat. Charlie's knife blade flashed in the moonlight as he slashed the painter of a big rowboat. The two of them half tumbled in with much loud clattering, and Carmody took several precious seconds trying to get the oars shipped as Charlie shoved away from the pier. Carmody, though much smaller than the Indian, took charge of the rowing. Charlie had never seemed to master the knack of pulling a boat. And, drunk as he was now, he would probably row them around in a circle. The Indian was much better in a canoe.

Before they reached the middle of the river, Carmody knew Charlie had erred in his choice of a boat. The craft was one of many homemade boats put together from whip-sawed green lumber and caulked for the trip to Dawson by some stampeder. It was a heavy, leaky, cross-grained craft built by landsmen. The boat was out of plumb and balance and required more effort on one oar than the other to force it ahead in a straight line.

But it was too late now to pick out another one as the current of the swift-flowing Yukon began to grip them. He rested on his oars to catch his breath and looked back. Behind, along the mud streets among the wooden buildings, he could see figures running. A couple of torches flickered, and the sound of excited voices carried to him across the water.

Pursuit would be coming; he was sure of it. And most likely it would be in the form of Constable Vernon Douglas of the Northwest Mounted Police. The long-limbed, tireless Mountie was the only white man, besides Carmody himself, for whom Chilcoot Charlie had ever shown any respect. Douglas's dogged adherence to principle and his athletic prowess had become legendary in the Yukon Territory.

Carmody bent to his oars again. In spite of his exertions, he shivered in the chill wind that blew off the water. Even though it appeared placid enough, the icy flood still ran high and dangerous with spring snowmelt. The broad, flat surface of the river looked like quicksilver, sliding along in the moonlight.

Dawson City, anchored to the flat benchland, receded quickly. But, before they were carried out of its sight around the first big bend, Carmody thought he saw a boat edge into the river from behind a docked steamboat. He ceased rowing and watched intently for several seconds. Was the dark spot moving, or was it their own drift that made it seem so? He couldn't be sure. Perhaps it was just a snag of driftwood, or a fearful imagination deceiving him. Why would anyone pursue him at all? Swenson, except when he was weighing out dust to set up drinks for the house, wasn't very well liked. For years he'd been suspected of raiding other men's caches with no effort to restock them, or prepare any of his own—a serious breach of the Northland's unwritten law. Nothing could ever be proven, but the old sourdoughs had begun calling him "Cache" Swenson—at first among themselves and, later, to his face. The big Swede never flinched or gave any indication that he knew, or cared, what they meant.

In his rush to escape, Carmody had come away with no food, water, or extra clothing. The river would provide drinking water, and he had a few wooden matches in his pocket. Even though he had no extra ammunition, his Bisley still held four .45 caliber cartridges. With a good shot, he might be able to kill something to eat. But this time of year there was little real danger. After all, Forty-Mile River was only forty-five to fifty miles downstream from Dawson. Then, less than twenty miles farther, in the Alaska Territory, was the town of Eagle. He gauged the current was running at least six or seven miles an hour. He would be near his claim above the town of Forty-Mile by noon. There was a Mountie post on an island at the mouth of the river, just opposite the town, so he dared not stop. But once in United States territory, he would be safe from the jurisdiction of the Dominion of Canada and its intractable Mounties. There was no telegraph to send a message ahead of him, and he began to feel he would be able to get away into the interior of Alaska and evade the law. With Chilcoot Charlie to help him, he had no fear of the wilderness. He was too busy rowing and thinking ahead to have any feelings of remorse for his deed.

Charlie slouched on a stern thwart, half dozing. Carmody knew the Indian understood English very well, yet he couldn't, or wouldn't, speak it often. The deep-chested Indian had earned his nickname during the hard winter by packing loads on his back, up to one hundred and twenty pounds, over the snow of Chilcoot Pass for hundreds of cheechakos stampeding to the interior gold fields. For some unexplained reason, he had taken a fancy to Carmody who had hired him for packing and trailing years earlier when he and Swenson had first filed their claims on a feeder creek above the mouth of Forty-Mile River.

Carmody tried to dull his mind of all thought as he braced his feet against a thwart and continued stroking with the oars. But the left oar required more effort than the right, and he couldn't settle into a comfortable rhythm. Before long, his left arm and shoulder were aching.

The boat was about nineteen feet long and had two sets of oarlocks, but only one set of oars. Charlie now slept soundly in the stern, his feet drawn up out of the several inches of bilge water that sloshed around in the bottom of the leaky craft.

The dark sky gradually softened to pearl. Days were quickly getting longer and nights shorter as the earth tilted toward the Arctic summer. Unconsciously grasping an excuse to rest on his oars, Carmody paused to watch the beauty of the coming day. His gaze drifted over the dark spruce that grew down the hillsides to the water's edge. As the terrain lightened and the moon paled, he saw an early-rising bald eagle perched atop a hundred-foot dead snag, watching the swift river for its breakfast. The wild, haunting cry of a loon swept across the flat water, and from somewhere deep in the forest echoed the hollow staccato of a woodpecker's rapping. As he turned his head, a moose lunged noisily out of the shallows along the far shore and disappeared into the woods. The natural world was going quietly about its business as dawn crept up over the misty river.

To the casual eye, nature seemed at peace, as did Carmody. But, beneath a placid exterior, he was in turmoil. The rush of adrenaline had ebbed at least two hours before, and the liquor had worn off even earlier. He had been up all night, and his shoulders and back felt as if he'd been rowing this balky boat for years. Carmody's mood was as gray as the early morning. The specter of his dead partner crept up and hunkered just beyond his consciousness until Carmody finally cried aloud: "I shot you, dammit! You been asking for it for years!"

He paused, surprised at his outburst. Was guilt causing him to lose his grip on sanity? No. It was this violent land, so big that it overwhelmed any human act. He'd been justified in killing Swenson, he reasoned. After all, the man had cheated him of many thousands of dollars of gold over the years.

But it had not started out that way. He'd met the big Swede in a San Francisco saloon in 1886 and, with a small inheritance, had agreed to grubstake him for a year for an equal share of any discoveries. Only three months later, Carmody had received a letter telling him to come and see the claims Swenson had staked where he'd found good color in the vicinity of Forty-Mile River.

But now, twelve years later, Carmody wished he'd never heeded those words. "Color at Forty-Mile," he muttered with a deep ache of regret. He hated the sound of it. "None of this would've happened if I hadn't come to this accursed place!"

He thought of all the men who had groveled and fought and died for gold here—froze, drowned, rotted with scurvy in lonely cabins, betrayed and debauched one another and the women who followed them for the sake of the yellow metal that washed down from the mountains. They didn't call it *gold fever* for nothing. It was a form of madness.

But Carmody had been immune from it at first. Since he couldn't stand the cold, he'd taken his half and gone outside each winter to purchase supplies and tools and clothing—even a few books—then hauled it all back by steamer after the ice breakup in the spring. He and Swenson were very different physically and temperamentally, but they worked well together through the short summers, operating a long Tom, sluicing the gold from their jointly held and adjacent claims, then carefully dividing the take. They had struck no bonanzas, but the creeks had provided a lot more than wages, even given them a moderate amount of wealth after all expenses were paid. Carmody had stashed as much of his as possible in a California bank, while Swenson had squandered his share in riotous living. Carmody had made no judgments of his partner. If that's the way a man wanted to enjoy his wealth, so be it.

Only after Carmody had met Rachel Hampton last winter in California and she had agreed to become his wife did things change. He persuaded her to come north to see his claim. Shortly after their arrival he discovered what other miners had known all along—Swenson had been cheating him of more than half the take for years by working through part of each winter, using fire to thaw holes slowly to bedrock. The rich muck and gravel dug out and customarily left to freeze until the spring cleanup had been thawed and secretly washed out long before Carmody arrived. Yet no one knew where Swenson had stashed the resulting gold.

At first Carmody was incredulous. But one night when Swenson was drunk, Carmody had overheard him bragging about it. He confronted the big Swede, who admitted nothing but, paradoxically, defied Carmody to do anything about it.

That had been only ten days ago, and Carmody felt foolish that his naïve faith in human nature had been so severely, and publicly, undercut. He knew he couldn't best the bigger man in a fight and hadn't the proof even to take it to a miners' court. So, with a pain in his heart, he swallowed his loss, which he estimated to be sixty to eighty thousand, and tried to decide the best way to end their partnership.

The final break had come when Swenson had made a play for Rachel. To Carmody's dismay, the demure young woman had responded to the Swede's advances. Carmody knew now what his limited experience with women had not accounted for—the fact that some are attracted to rough manners and ruder treatment, to men who are strong rather than handsome and spend gold dust with abandon. In short, she had fallen under the wild spell of life on the Yukon which made Carmody's tame proposal of marriage and a settled life in the States pale into nothing.

Even this loss might have been borne, and eventually proven a blessing, had he not let his pride get in the way. A few drinks, a loaded gun, the jibes of the other miners, had led to harsh words with Swenson and then "the last state of that man became worse than the first." The Biblical quotation rose up with a taste of bitterness.

"I've become a murderer!" he moaned, tears blurring his vision. His soul stood naked before a conscience that allowed for no excuses, no false justifications.

The sun was topping the eastern bank, and a flash of color jerked his attention away from his own misery. Blinking away the tears, he focused upstream and his heart began to beat faster. A speck of red in the middle of the river. It was too far away to see clearly, but he knew, without a particle of doubt, that it was the scarlet tunic of a Mountie. Constable Vernon Douglas was pursuing him in a canoe.

Regret vanished from his mind as he bent his back to the oars. The boat surged ahead, sliding over the glassy water faster than the current, while the forested banks unreeled steadily on either side.

Ten minutes later he paused to blow and look again. It was then he knew it was all over. The canoe was now close enough to distinguish, and was closing the gap even as he watched. A muscular Mountie in a light canoe was slicing down the river, overtaking the clumsy rowboat. They were probably little over halfway to Forty-Mile, and there was no hope of outrunning the lawman.

Carmody looked over his shoulder. A wide bend was coming up where the swift current swung to the outside. Maybe, if he could row across the flat water near the left-hand bank, he could cut off some distance, get around the bend and out of sight quicker, then take to the woods and let the boat drift on. By the time the Mountie figured out where they had gone, he and Charlie would have a head start into the forest.

He stroked hard to break the clutch of the current and drove the heavy boat to the inside of the bend. A hundred yards farther, he caught his breath as the keel grated on a submerged sand bar.

Damn! He rowed harder, and the boat spun off and floated free. His breath was coming in gasps. Again the wooden bottom scraped over gravel, and this time the boat slowly ground to a stop.

Desperately glancing at the canoe that was about two hundred yards away, he shipped the oars. Then, grabbing the remaining eight feet of rope that had been used to tie the bow of the boat, he vaulted over the side into the knee-deep water. The numbing cold stabbed at his legs.

"Charlie! Come help me!" he yelled as he looped the end of the rope over one shoulder and began to walk, dragging the boat behind him over the shoal. His feet sank into the soft sand, and the rope cut into his shoulder.

Suddenly the Indian was beside him and relieving him of the rope. The boat was jerked over the sand in the hands of the powerful packer, sliding over the soft sand bottom. As Carmody sloshed along, ankle deep, he remembered the Bisley in the pocket of his wool jacket. He drew it and checked the action and the loads. The Mountie's canoe was only a hundred yards away now and closing fast. Carmody looked for some cover besides their wooden boat. They were still too far from the shore. Piles of driftwood were imbedded in the shoals here and there, sticking up in spiky formations. He had already taken one life. He wouldn't hesitate to take another if necessary to avoid capture and the hangman.

It was clear they weren't going to make it. Carmody turned to face the oncoming canoe some thirty yards away, raised his pistol, and fired. The bullet threw up a jet of water ten feet short. He cocked and fired again, and struck the bow of the canoe.

The Mountie backed water with his paddle and turned the slim craft head on toward them. "Hold up there!" he yelled. "Stop firing!"

Carmody's answer was to drop to one knee in the shallow water, steady his gun arm, hold his heavy breathing, and fire again. But, at the last instant, the Mountie dropped into the bottom of the canoe, and the shot went high. Carmody had only one bullet left.

Charlie, dragging the boat, was several yards beyond him as Carmody sloshed awkwardly to catch up. Suddenly the bottom sloped off, and Carmody felt his feet sliding, then his calves being sucked down in the soft sand. Before he could react, the icy water was above his waist. He heard a warning yell bursting from his own lips as he instinctively lunged for the gunwale of the boat. He banged it with wrists and hands, still clutching the Bisley, and slowly dragged himself free of the clinging sand and water as Charlie was doing the same at the other side of the bow.

By the time he'd pulled himself up and tumbled, gasping, into the bottom of the boat, the Mountie's canoe was sliding to within twenty feet. One hand held the paddle while the other gripped his service revolver that was trained on them. "You men . . . push that boat toward the shore . . . now!"

Chilcoot Charlie pulled himself aboard, and he and Carmody each took an oar and poled the boat laboriously over the shoals the remaining thirty yards to the left bank of the river.

The Mountie had landed and was cautiously eyeing them as they drew near. One hand still rested on the butt of his weapon now back in his holster. Carmody and Charlie climbed out and tied the bow to a sapling.

The Mountie ordered Charlie to gather some driftwood. With the help of some dry pine needles, he soon had a fire going. Wet clothing didn't seem to affect the Indian, but Carmody was shivering uncontrollably. He stripped off his jacket and shirt and bent close to the fire, welcoming the heat of the leaping flames.

Charlie threw a last armful of driftwood on the ground and hunkered down, peeling off his soaked wool shirt and wringing it out.

The tall Mountie had seated himself a few feet away, his back against a tree. He had taken off his hat and laid it on the ground beside him. Carmody's Bisley and Charlie's knife were now thrust under the lawman's belt.

None of the three men spoke for a time. Carmody wasn't fooled by the outwardly relaxed posture of the lawman as he noted the Mountie's alert gray eyes following their every move.

"Charlie didn't . . . have anything . . . to do with this," Carmody said sullenly, trying to keep his teeth from chattering.

"He helped you get away," the red-coated Mountie replied evenly.

"Douglas, I knew you'd be the one . . . coming after me," Carmody said, his voice dull.

The fair-haired policeman regarded him with a steady gaze. "I didn't want to. Why'd you do it, Carmody?"

"I guess you and the whole territory knew he's been cheating me for years."

"You can't be your own law," Douglas replied, crossing one ankle over the other. "Even in this wilderness. You, at least, could have taken it to a miners' court. You didn't have to shoot him."

Carmody was silent, ashamed to admit that Swenson's play for Rachel had been the trigger for his actions. It didn't matter now, anyway. It was done, and he was going back to stand trial for murder. Maybe he'd wake up in the morning and realize this whole thing was a nightmare. None of it seemed real. Yet, as he sat down to unlace his wet boots, he knew the whole episode, terrible as it seemed, *was* real, and no amount of wishing could undo it.

Douglas stood up, picked up one of the larger pieces of dry driftwood from the pile, broke it across his knee, and added it to the fire. Then he reached into his side pocket, pulled out two sticks of what looked like black twist tobacco, and tossed each of them a piece. "Moose meat. I don't figure you brought anything to eat."

Carmody's mouth watered as he tried to gnaw off a hunk of the smoked jerky.

The sun rose higher, and shafts of light filtered down between the tall spruce trees, lighting part of the rocky clearing. The warmth of the fire and the weak sunshine on his bare skin were reducing the shivering, although Carmody was still chilled. He chewed on the dried meat, wondering if he would have a choice of a last meal just before he faced the executioner. Very likely he wouldn't have an appetite anyway. He wondered if Canadian law would allow him to make a will to leave his claim to someone. He could think of no one deserving, except perhaps the faithful Chilcoot Charlie, who might be spending some time in jail.

Douglas walked a few feet away and looked through the trees at the river. "Going to be some tough paddling against that current," he remarked. "Have to hug the bank."

Carmody silently resolved that he'd do everything in his power to make it even tougher for the young lawman. They would be crowded in the fourteen-foot canoe, and there would be ample time and opportunity for him and Charlie somehow to catch the Mountie off-guard and overpower him. It would be a tall order. Douglas was six feet of lean muscle and sinew with the caution and reflexes of a tawny mountain cat. And he was the only one with a sidearm.

"You aren't going to tie us up on the way back, are you?" Carmody asked, noting that Douglas was cutting the remaining eight feet of rope from the bow of their boat. "We could break off those two oars and help you paddle," he ventured.

"Tie that between two bushes and hang up your clothes to dry," Douglas said, tossing the rope to Carmody.

"Dammit, Douglas, you've got a reputation as a man who never shirks his duty. And you're long on honesty . . . as long as a July day in Dawson," Carmody said, thinking to penetrate the implacable demeanor. "But you're stiff as a poker. Did you know that men laugh at you behind your back because you see everything as black and white, right or wrong? You see no shades of gray, no . . . no half truths or partial guilt. To you, everything is either a hanging offense or no offense!" Carmody burst out in frustration at the icy manner of this blond representative of a far-off government.

Douglas's eyes flickered for an instant, and his stare went blank as if his gaze had suddenly turned inward.

Carmody moved to pick up his wet shirt and coat while Chilcoot Charlie flung his soggy shirt over a shoulder and began stringing the makeshift clothesline. The Indian's broad face was impassive, as if he had seen everything there was to see and life held no more surprises. Triumph and tragedy were treated alike. Carmody secretly wished he possessed some of that stoicism.

Douglas took the Bisley from his belt, thumbed open the loading gate and, one by one, ejected the empty shell casings, along with the one remaining cartridge, letting them fall to the ground. "Another thirty miles or so down this river is United States territory," the Mountie said. He tossed the empty Bisley and Charlie's knife onto the ground at his feet. "Wanted flyers will be circulated to all the posts of the Mounted Police," Douglas continued. "Don't be seen on this side of the line again, or you'll be arrested," he intoned in a voice as flat as if he were reading a warrant.

"What?" Carmody was nearly struck dumb by his sudden good fortune as relief flooded over him like a warm bath. Could he have heard wrong? What had triggered the unbending Mountie's change of mind or heart? "But . . .

but what about your oath to uphold the law?" Carmody burst out, in spite of his resolve to hold his tongue.

The Mountie's mouth compressed in a grim smile. "The law . . . like the Sabbath . . . is made for man, and not the other way around. My job is to keep order and dispense justice. And that's what I aim to do."

He walked down to his canoe and returned, carrying four small, rawhide pokes by their drawstrings. He dropped them on the ground at Carmody's feet. "There's roughly thirty thousand in dust," he said. "As often as Swenson was in Dawson, drinking and gambling, I figured he had it stashed for safekeeping with Tom McGrew at the saloon. Had to threaten Tom with arrest before he'd admit to having it and turn it over. That may not be all you were cheated out of, but it should pretty much square things."

Douglas retrieved his hat and took a few steps toward the canoe that was pulled up on the bank a dozen yards away. Then he paused and turned back to the stunned Carmody. "Oh, I'd watch my back trail if I were you, 'cause I'd wager Cache Swenson'll be after you like a wounded grizzly."

"*What?*" Things were unfolding too fast for Carmody to grasp.

"I can't know what was in your mind when you shot Swenson," Douglas went on. "So I don't know if you intended to kill him. But you're either a damned fine shot, or a damned poor one. In either case, I figure justice has been served, even if the letter of the law has not. And it will save the government considerable expense."

With that, Douglas shoved off the canoe and leapt in with the nimbleness of a cat. Settling himself with the paddle, he turned the craft and began stroking smoothly away.

Carmody heaved a long sigh and looked slowly around as if awakening from the terrors of a nightmare. Somehow he was no longer cold or tired, and the May sun shone on river and forest with a glow he'd never seen before.

He turned toward the Indian who squatted naked by the fire. His shirt and pants hung, steaming, from the line. "Charlie, you've just seen an unusual example of white man's justice," Carmody said, still feeling a little lightheaded.

"Huh! Damned funny. Mountie leave gold. Not like white man," Charlie grunted without changing expression.

"You damn' betcha he's not like other white men," Carmody marveled, looking upriver at the diminishing shape of the figure in the canoe. He wondered if Douglas would be held accountable by his superiors for confiscating the thirty thousand-dollar stash of gold that now lay on the ground at his feet. As a policeman, Douglas was not allowed to accept gifts, but Car-

mody suddenly determined to transfer ownership of his claim to the Mountie, anyway. "He can do with it as he pleases," he muttered. The idea somehow satisfied his sense of balance and fair play. "Then three weeks to Saint
Michael and out of the country," he breathed quietly, feeling a great weight
sliding from him.

"We go downriver with gold," Charlie said, holding his hands out to the
warmth of the fire.

"You betcha we go."

About the Editor

Jon Tuska is the author of numerous books about the American West as well as editor of several short story collections, *Billy the Kid: His Life and Legend* (University of New Mexico Press, 1996) and *The Western Story: A Chronological Treasury* (University of Nebraska Press, 1995) among them. Together with his wife, Vicki Piekarski, Tuska co-founded Golden West Literary Agency, which primarily represents authors of Western fiction and Western Americana. They edit and co-publish thirty titles a year in two prestigious series of new hardcover Western novels and story collections, the Five Star Westerns and the Circle v Westerns. They also edited *The Morrow Anthology of Great Western Short Stories* (Morrow, 1997) and are currently preparing the second edition of their *Encyclopedia of Frontier and Western Fiction* (McGraw-Hill, 1983).